"Where do you think you're going?"

He removed the mask. Allison gritted her teeth and looked up at him. She hated how he towered over her by a good five inches. His dark gaze raked over her, cold, intense, searching.

This was Rafael the FBI agent on assignment. Not the Rafe who'd charmed and coaxed her into spying on a dangerous biker gang months ago. Awareness shot through her. Try as she might, it was hard to ignore how powerful he looked. The faint spicy scent of his aftershave shot through the stench of ammonia and chemicals. Why did he have to be so sexy? She hated feeling like this. Attraction to a guy like Rafael was complicated, something best left for daydreams.

Not now, not when all her focus needed to remain on her little sister.

"I'm headed to work." She narrowed her eyes. "Unless you want to call the ER charge nurse and tell her why you've detained me, and you'd better have a damn good reason for doing so, I'm out of here."

Dear Reader,

When I created Rafe in *Escape from Devil's Den*, I knew this man deserved his own story.

Sometimes as an author, you create a character you cannot forget. Rafe is one of them. So I set about writing his story after *Escape from Devil's Den*. He's a Cuban American FBI agent with a lot of conflict. Rafe struggles with his identity. He doesn't want to forget his American father, a police officer who died in the line of duty, but he has strong ties as well to his Cuban roots and family.

Rafe is certain his family would never approve of Allison, the trauma nurse daredevil who loves motorcycles as much as he does. Neither wants to admit to the electrifying chemistry they share. Allison is under a veil of suspicion because her sister is marrying into the family of a well-known drug lord. When Allison, who would do anything to save her sister from this marriage, needs his help, Rafe joins forces with her to locate the missing bride-to-be.

I hope you enjoy Rafe and Allison's story. Happy reading!

Bonnie Vanak

DESPERATE JUSTICE

BONNIE VANAK

ROMANTIC SUSPENSE

Harlequin®
ROMANTIC
SUSPENSE™

ISBN-13: 978-1-335-47165-9

Desperate Justice

Copyright © 2025 by Bonnie Vanak

Harlequin Enterprises ULC
22 Adelaide St. West, 41st Floor
Toronto, Ontario M5H 4E3, Canada
www.Harlequin.com

Printed in Lithuania

MIX
Paper | Supporting responsible forestry
FSC® C021394

New York Times and *USA TODAY* bestselling author **Bonnie Vanak** is passionate about romance novels and telling stories. A former newspaper reporter, she worked as a journalist for a large international charity for several years, traveling to countries such as Haiti to report on poor living conditions. Bonnie lives in Florida with her husband, Frank, and is a member of Romance Writers of America. She loves to hear from readers. She can be reached through her website, bonnievanak.com.

Books by Bonnie Vanak

Harlequin Romantic Suspense

Rescue from Darkness
Reunion at Greystone Manor
Escape from Devil's Den
Desperate Justice

The Coltons of Red Ridge

His Forgotten Colton Fiancée

Colton 911: Chicago

Colton 911: Under Suspicion

SOS Agency

Navy SEAL Seduction
Shielded by the Cowboy SEAL
Navy SEAL Protector
Her Secret Protector

Visit the Author Profile page
at Harlequin.com for more titles.

For my friend Julie Ann, whose dedication to nursing
inspired me to write Allison's character.

Prologue

It had been a good day to be alive, until the moment a bullet zinged through the air and sliced his neck.

Another bullet pierced his abdomen. Blood, so much blood.

Rafael Jones Rodriguez struggled to hold a hand over the crimson seeping between his trembling fingers. Nearby, two FBI agents lay dead. They'd been caught in a nighttime ambush by local crime lord Hector Hernandez.

Sirens blared in the distance. *Have to live. So much to live for.* But he knew the odds. Knew he was bleeding out.

Rafe rolled over to his back, staring at the endless stars in the black night sky. He tried not to think of the dead agents and their families lost in grief. Or his family, and how they would weep and wail. Or Sofia. He promised to attend her quinceañera next year. His goddaughter would be crushed.

Cold, he was so damn cold. Pain faded as he shivered. Damn it, he was too young to die, but those sirens were far off. Each breath rasped out in short, jagged bursts as he thought of how precious and wonderful life was…and how he was going to lose it.

"Stay still. It's okay," a sweet voice murmured. "I'm going to take care of you. You have to stay still."

An angel hovered over him, her features blurred. *Guess this is it. At least I get an angel to escort me to Heaven, instead of a demonic chaperone to Hell.*

Rafe closed his eyes to surrender to the inevitable.

"Don't you dare die on me, you bastard. Not after everything I'm doing to save you. Damn it, stay awake!"

An angel with a foul mouth. Rafe's lips edged into a slight smile.

"Diablo," he murmured, fighting to stay awake.

As he felt himself slipping into the darkness, he heard more swear words, and the firm touch of an angel who knew what the hell she was doing.

Maybe, just for today, he would live after all…

Chapter 1

Today was a good day for a haircut, unless you happened to get your hair styled at the salon the FBI and DEA planned to raid.

A line of black SUVs were parked on the busy main street of Bistro Road. A tide of warm air and the brilliant yellow sunshine greeted him as FBI Supervisory Special Agent Rafael Jones Rodriguez opened the door of his vehicle. Miami in October was ripe with car exhaust, rapid Spanish in several dialects, people living their lives in a tropical paradise.

Movers and shakers, hot celebrities, bikini-clad models.

Drug dealers hiding their stash and laundering money through shell companies.

The Eleganza Salon was sandwiched between an insurance storefront (empty) and a small hardware store (closed). Glock in hand, Rafe opened the door. The pungent stench of ammonia, nail polish and hair products hit his nostrils, despite the N95 respirator mask he wore.

"FBI. Everyone remain where you are. No one move. We have a warrant to search the premises," he barked out in Spanish and English.

Five women, some under hair dryers, some seated in chairs before large mirrors, turned and stared at him, eyes wide like frightened deer. Rafe's expert gaze took in each one.

Agents in white biohazard suits streamed past him, several

heading to the back rooms before employees had a chance to dispose of incriminating evidence.

Rafe holstered his weapon. "Who's in charge?"

A thin middle-aged woman, graying hair cut short, expression sour, left her station. "I'm Catrina, the manager. Where's your warrant?"

He showed her the federal warrant obtained in court. The woman examined it, then glared at Rafe. She tossed the paper aside, but not before spitting at Rafe's feet and calling him foul names in Spanish.

Ignoring her, Rafe instructed the agents to search thoroughly. Bottles of shampoo, conditioner, everything. As lead on this joint task force between the DEA, FBI and local law enforcement, he wasn't letting anything slip by. This salon, owned by a dummy corporation Rafe suspected was connected to Hector Hernandez, had been under surveillance for a while.

Anything they could use to nail Hernandez, head of a Miami cartel, was useful.

For more than three years he'd hunted the man to put him away on federal RICO charges. Hernandez had shot him and killed two of his men last year. Nailing the bastard was his main focus.

And it was personal.

Taking scum like Hernandez off the streets would make the city he loved safer for law-abiding citizens.

"Yo, Mr. FBI man, can Yolanda rinse off her hair coloring before she turns from platinum to white?"

Rafe set down the shampoo bottle he'd examined and confronted the one woman he never thought he'd see again.

Dark brown hair spilled past her slender shoulders. She wore a black T-shirt, black jeans, yellow Dr. Marten boots and a scowl. More striking than beautiful, she didn't put up with any crap.

Allison Lexington. His confidential informant for the Devil's Patrol case a few months ago. Allison, the nurse and motorcyclist who made his blood heat and frustrated the hell out of him with never following directions. Endangering her life instead of obeying his orders.

He looked at the frightened hairstylist standing by a sink and nodded. The woman began washing her client's hair.

"What are you doing here?" he demanded.

"I didn't know it was a crime to get my hair styled." Allison made her way toward him. "You going to shoot me for having a blowout?"

"Rafe, you need to see this." Agent Juarez called out to him.

Bypassing Allison (why did she have to show up at this hair salon today of all days?) he headed toward the back. Tom had opened a case of shampoo still bearing the shipping label.

"I opened one bottle and got this."

Tom showed him the white test strip. Rafe's fury boiled up in a volcanic rush.

One pink line. Positive for fentanyl.

Rafe handed back the strip. Mere granules of dust could prove deadly. "Bag it for evidence and seal off the area."

In the back room, five cardboard containers were stacked against the wall by shelves of hair and nail products. Rafe squatted down to read the label.

"John Brown," he read aloud and photographed the label.

John Brown. Might as well call him John Doe.

An agent opened another box. Bags of rainbow-colored circles were inside. The bags were labeled Fun Times Candy. With extreme care, Rafe lifted one out of the box.

The test kit proved it was fentanyl, not candy. He heaved out a breath.

"There's enough of this here to kill dozens."

The team began the tedious process of logging everything

and carrying it out back to waiting vehicles for transport back to FBI headquarters. Rafe glanced at the clock on the wall and bit back a groan. He hadn't been able to get a judge to sign off on the warrant until after noon. This was going to be a long day, and an equally long night.

And he had no way to find out John Brown's identity. But he would. Soon.

So much for making his niece's quinceañera on time. He sighed. Sofia would understand. She always did. But his Cuban family? Nope.

Everyone in the hair salon had been detained by the local police, who stood guard over them. Absorbed in her phone, Allison hovered near a hair station. Another problem. What the hell was Allison doing here and why this particular hair salon??

Life wasn't fair, but she'd never whined about it. Wrong place, wrong time. But one of Diana's model friends had recommended this hair salon to try out styles before Di's wedding and Allison agreed to meet her here.

After texting her sis (stay away Diana, feds here) she pocketed her cell. Allison grabbed her motorcycle helmet, waved at the still-stunned women and headed for the exit.

She wasn't staying here for Rafael's shakedown.

Barely had she taken three steps when Rafe grabbed her arm. "Where do you think you're going?"

He removed the mask. Allison gritted her teeth and looked up at him. She hated how he towered over her by a good five inches. His dark gaze raked over her, cold, intense, searching.

This was Rafael the FBI agent on assignment. Not the Rafe who'd charmed and coaxed her into spying on a dangerous biker gang months ago. Awareness shot through her. Try as she might, it was hard to ignore how powerful he looked. The faint spicy scent of his aftershave shot through the stench of ammonia and chemicals. Why did he have to be so sexy? She hated feeling like this. Attraction to a guy like Rafael was complicated, something best left for daydreams.

Not now, not when all her focus needed to remain on her little sister.

"I'm headed to work." She narrowed her eyes. "Unless you want to call the ER charge nurse and tell her why you've detained me, and you'd better have a damn good reason for doing so, I'm out of here."

For a moment he studied her as if she were the suspect. Neither moved. Sweat trickled down Allison's back, plastering her black T-shirt to her back. This felt like a showdown, a power play.

She hated that. Hated not being in control.

"Let go of me," she muttered.

Knowing better than to touch him because he could arrest her for assault, she waited. Not caring if she made Rafael look bad in front of his team.

Her gaze flicked over the uniformed police, who seemed suddenly more interested in her and this standoff than gathering evidence. Suddenly she got it. It was all about who was in charge. Not showing weakness.

Yeah, she understood that.

Allison gave the men closest to her a pointed look.

"I'd hate for any of you to get injured or, God forbid, shot on the job, and I'm not there to treat you. I'm one of the best trauma nurses in Miami, and while you're staring at me, I could be saving lives."

Her gaze flicked back to Rafael. "We're on the same team."

Jaw tight beneath his well-trimmed black beard, he narrowed his eyes. "I'll be in touch about why the hell you happened to be here at this salon, this particular day. In the meantime, stay out of my investigation."

He released her and stepped aside. Made a mock sweeping gesture. But his dark gaze never left her, and she saw his pupils dilate.

Feeling as if the electricity between them could light up half of South Florida, she gripped her motorcycle helmet and slipped outside.

Allison grit her teeth. So what if he was cute and sexy and she couldn't forget him? Rafael Rodriguez was bad news. Her sister mattered more.

Her stomach trembled as she ran for her motorcycle. Allison bit her lip. Diana wasn't at the shop, thank the good Lord.

But having the hair salon raided gave her bad vibes. The kind of vibes she'd gotten while working as a confidential informant for Rafael when he gathered evidence of criminal activity in the biker gang he eventually took down.

Instincts always served her well in the past. She had to use them to investigate her sister's future family.

She'd do anything to keep her little sister safe.

Not even mighty FBI SSA Rafael Rodriguez would stand in her way.

Chapter 2

"I can't believe the FBI raided the shop, Allison! Catrina, Paul's aunt who manages the place, has been trying to get me in there for styling. Now where am I supposed to get my hair done?"

Allison studied her little sister. "Diana, the FBI raided it for a reason. They're looking for drugs. From what I saw this afternoon, they found them."

"The FBI has to be wrong." She waved a manicured hand. "They're always trying to frame people. Look at what they always do to Paul's uncle. Hector is a businessman and they're jealous."

Allison folded her arms and struggled for patience. Slow night in the ER and Diana had rushed in, needing to speak to "Ally, now!"

Diana paced before the nurses' station in the ER, her long brown curls bouncing with every move. With her big brown eyes, full mouth and perfect cheekbones, slim figure and long legs, no wonder her younger sister had been a model. No wonder Paul Davis had fallen in love with her.

If only Diana had fallen for a respectable guy, say, a financial investor. Or even a sanitation engineer. Anyone but the nephew of a suspected drug kingpin.

Allison bit back her frustration. "Diana, the feds have a good case. They found fentanyl. Do you know what that crap does to people? It kills. The feds probably raided it because they suspect Hector is involved. It doesn't exactly look good since Hector's sister is the manager."

Diana glanced at her cell phone. "They can't prove anything or Hector would be behind bars by now. Besides, Paul isn't like his uncle Hector. He barely knows him. He had little to do with him while growing up."

"Then why hold your wedding on Hector's estate?"

"Because Hector offered. He's trying to reconnect with his younger sister's only son after she cut off all communication with him. After she died, Hector reached out to Paul. He is Paul's godfather. It's his way of trying to make up for the past. Family means a lot to Paul. He has so little family left now. Why do you have a problem with that?"

I have a problem with his uncle, not Paul. Paul Davis owned a modest furniture store in Miami and was slowly expanding. Recently he bought a warehouse in North Carolina and hired artisans to make handcrafted furniture. Paul was head over heels in love with her sister.

Oh, she liked Paul. It was this shady side of his family she didn't like.

"Diana, I wish you'd consider postponing the wedding. You've only known him six months. It's one thing to have Hector Hernandez as a relative, I mean you can't choose your blood relations. It's another to have him pay for almost everything!"

Diana studied the modest diamond on her left hand. "Paul hadn't even seen him in years until Hector heard we were marrying, and offering to pay for the wedding and host it is a way of reconciling. And you still can't convince me Hector Hernandez is as much of a criminal as the press says he is."

"Diana…" She glanced up. Thank goodness it was a slow night tonight in the ER. "Honey, please think about this. Postpone the wedding."

Diana's eyes widened. "Four hundred guests, most of whom already responded, the flowers, cake... Paul's uncle footing the entire bill as a gift to him and you want me to postpone. He knows Paul and I don't have much money, and Mom and Dad..."

Mom and dad would do anything you ask. Anything for their darling little girl. Allison bit her lip. Forget about her parents, who adored Paul as much as Diana did. They didn't have much sense when it came to the real world and how tough life could be out there.

"Listen, I overheard one of the cops say the man who owns the salon is tied to Hernandez. The feds had a warrant. The agent in charge showed it to everyone there."

Diana's expression shifted to mischievous. "Was he cute? Some cops are... Oh! You're blushing!"

To her horror, heat crept up her cheeks. Allison scowled. "This is about you, not me."

She'd never told her family about being a confidential informant for Rafael and the FBI last year. One reason was because she didn't want them chastising her for going undercover for a dangerous biker gang. Now she was relieved Diana never found out about Rafe.

"It's about time someone caught your interest. Even a cop. I swear, Ally, you need to settle down more than I do. Mom and Dad think you only care about your motorcycle."

Mom and Dad wouldn't care, or notice, if I married my bike. Allison bit back a sigh. Diana mattered. Not their parents, who barely remembered Allison's existence.

Diana glanced at her phone again. "Wish I could chat more but I have tons to do before the wedding, Ally. Please don't worry about me."

This time, Allison sighed. She loved Diana, but some days her sister tried her patience. Even though she was thirty years old to Diana's twenty-five, times like this she felt as if she were eighty and Diana a teenager.

Diana glanced at a lower shelf where Allison stored her purse. "I left you a little gift to get you through the night. The sugar in the candy should help, Ally, but promise you'll find time to eat, too. I worry about you working these long shifts."

Allison laughed. "I'll be fine, jellybean."

"You always are, angel." Diana's dark eyes twinkled. "Though I think you are in love… I can see it on your face."

"With my motorcycle. And my profession, speaking of which…" She watched the ambulance lights flashing in the bay. "I've got work. I'll talk to you later."

Diana's smile dropped. "Ally, I didn't mean to tease. You know how I feel about you… You're my big sis."

She hooked her pinkie finger around Allison's. "Cradle to grave, and thanks to you, I got to postpone that grave for a few years."

"More than a few years." Allison's throat tightened. "Please, think about what I said."

"For you, I will consider it." Diana hugged her tightly. "Stay safe."

Allison headed for the double doors leading to the ambulance bay. Red lights, the screaming siren now silenced at the hospital, everything reminded her of that horrible day when Diana almost died.

She would do anything for her beloved, naive little sister.

Right now all she could do was hope Diana would change her mind about the wedding venue.

Maybe Rafael Rodriguez would find evidence to arrest Hector Hernandez and put him behind bars for good…before her sister's life was ruined.

Chapter 3

Screams and shouts alerted him to the dangers awaiting him. He, a seasoned FBI agent, shuddered in anticipation.

"Let's do this," he muttered.

Rafe took a bracing breath and opened the door to enter his niece's quinceañera party. The noise proved deafening. Salsa music, laughter, everything that was his big, noisy, loving Cuban family.

Purpose in his step, clutching the traditional doll he planned to give Sofia later, he headed to the reception room. The delicious smells of fried pork mingling with sweet pastries made his mouth water, reminding him he hadn't eaten since breakfast.

Double doors sailed open and his two sisters walked out.

Seeing him, Julia exclaimed and hugged him tight. He hugged her back. Veronica, his eldest sister, regarded him with a severe frown. She pointed to the gold watch her husband had given her upon the birth of Sofia, their first child.

"You're late."

Sorry, sis. I was looking for drugs. He offered a small apologetic smile. "My apologies. I tried."

No excuses with his family. Not for family events, or anything else. They simply didn't understand.

"You missed Sofia's entrance with her court. Her dance with them. Her *baile de sorpresa*. You almost missed the father and daughter dance." Ronnie heaved a dramatic breath. "Well, at least you made it. Unlike Julie's wedding."

Okay, he wasn't taking this lying down. Rafe heaved a breath. "You know I had to attend the funeral of one of my team…"

"And we nearly attended your funeral last year, Rafey! When are you going to quit that damn job and get a real life?"

Ronnie's verbal assault sent his blood pressure soaring and rocked him back on his Alden dress shoes. "Listen, Ronnie, if you're going to…"

Julie stepped between them, holding them at bay like a referee holding back two prizefighters. "Enough," she said in Spanish. "This is your daughter's day, Ronnie, and not a time for family arguments."

Rafe drew in a breath and smiled at his youngest sister. "Always, the peacemaker. Thank you, Julie."

He shot Ronnie a level look. "She's right. Let's leave this for another day. This is about your daughter's birthday, my niece and goddaughter. And right now, I need to see her."

Taking a deep breath to lower his blood pressure, he pulled open the door and strode inside. The hall was crowded, with lights sparkling from the disco ball shining above. His anger faded, replaced by pure amusement. Sofia loved glitz and glamour and had a thing for the 1970s. The DJ played "Disco Duck," which made him chuckle. Right now she was dancing with a skinny, shy kid named Mark, who struggled to keep up with the music and Sofia's expert moves.

So what if her mother could be a nag about his career and his life? Sofia could erase all his crabbiness and brighten his day.

You have to make the world safer for her, and all her generation.

Not tonight. Tonight wasn't about duty or worry about Hernandez and his gang getting fentanyl into the hands of innocents like his niece and her friends. Tonight was about fun, and celebrating Sofia turning into a woman.

She whirled, her pink taffeta gown swirling out around her, the rhinestone crown on her dark hair sparkling as much as the disco ball. Someone shone a spotlight on her. He clutched the Barbie doll he brought to symbolize the last childhood gift as she made her transition from girl to woman. A lump clogged his throat. Where the hell had the years gone?

Rafe slipped the doll into his jacket pocket. He headed to the buffet table, suddenly hungry. Hell, he hadn't eaten all day.

The usual array of food his family preferred sat in chafing dishes. A platter of raw vegetables and a dish of plain grilled chicken had been mainly ignored.

Croquetas de jamón and *mariquitas de plátano* for lighter appetites, along with *lechón asado, frijoles negros*, boiled yucca and more. His nose wrinkled. No good old American cheeseburgers here. Only Cuban food.

He selected a few carrot sticks from the vegetable platter and gnawed on them.

"Rafael, why are you hiding from me?"

He knew that deep, beloved voice anywhere. Rafe set down his plate, turned and hugged his eighty-two-year-old grandmother. "I'm not hiding. I just got here."

She'd find out soon enough.

"Did you eat?" she asked.

Elena glanced at the plate with the carrot sticks and shook her head. Suddenly he had no appetite. Rafe's stomach churned as he thought about the implications of the fentanyl they'd seized—drugs that could kill innocent, experimenting teenagers. His gaze shot over to Sofia.

Instead of answering, he asked, "Did you?"

Elena shrugged. "I'm not hungry."

He worried more about her lately. Looking more tired and worn-out. Yeah, she'd done a lot for this party, perhaps too much. An ever-present pang filled his chest. How much longer would his beloved grandmother be with them?

Those ancient eyes, filled with endless wisdom, searched his face. Elena reached up and touched his cheek with her paper-thin hand.

"You look tired, Rafey."

Emotion clogged his throat. He clasped her hand in his, feeling bones and sinew and love in her strong, capable hands. Hands that soothed night terrors, dealt equal parts of love and discipline, hands that worked endless hours at the family bake shop to support her family.

What would happen the day those hands no longer held life? The day they were folded over her chest as her family gathered around her coffin and wept for their nana?

Unable to think about it, he forced a smile. "Long day, Tita," he said, using the familiar nickname they called Elena. "I'm here now and I'm fine."

"Don't lie to your grandmother, Rafael. I know you. Your job is consuming your life," she said in Spanish.

"My job is my life," he shot back in Spanish. "I wish the family would understand that."

Rafe tensed, ready for another lecture about his job and his life. Instead, she patted his hand as he released hers.

"Your family is also your life, Rafey. Your heritage is part of you. You can't escape it." She shook her head in gentle chastisement. "Or me. Make us part of your life instead of trying to avoid us.'

He reached down and hugged her. "I'm not trying to avoid you, or the family, Tita. My job comes first."

When he released her, his grandmother gave him a sad look. "You need to settle down. Find a nice girl, marry her and have babies."

Rafe sighed. Same speech everyone always gave him. He understood, but sometimes it grew tiresome.

"The job keeps me too busy to date, Tita. Don't you have enough great-grandchildren?" he teased.

She didn't smile as usual, but rubbed her chest as if it pained her.

"Will your job be there for you when you're hungry? Lonely? When you're old and one foot in the grave like me, what will you have, Rafey? Job or a wife, children, grandchildren?"

Rafe couldn't answer, because as always, his *abulita* hit upon the heart of him and the questions he'd asked himself lately.

"I'll find someone."

"Don't wait too long. I may not be here much longer."

Alarm sped through him. She was looking tired and pale, and the fact she hadn't tasted any of the delicious food the caterer provided was distressing.

"Not you. You're strong. Go sit, Tita. You work too hard taking care of everyone." He kissed her paper-thin cheek again, feeling the rush of love and gratitude she always brought.

As he turned, his mama stood before him. "Rafey."

She kissed his cheek. His heart turned over. In her early sixties, Carmela was as lovely as he remembered from his childhood. With her long black hair (dyed now, though she'd never admit it), warm brown eyes and trim figure, despite the pastries she baked at the family business, his mother still commanded male attention.

Yet after his father was killed nearly twenty-three years ago, she never remarried.

Sometimes at big family gatherings like this, he wondered what his father would say or do. Jeff Jones adored his fiery Cuban wife and embraced her family. But his father was a typical American guy, dedicated to his wife and children, football season and beer with the guys and focused on his career as a dedicated police officer.

Until the day a drug dealer fired a bullet that claimed his life.

Her sharp gaze studied him. "This job is taxing you."

The job again, as if his family blamed the FBI for everything. He changed the subject.

"Mama, how come you never remarried after Dad died? Did the family pressure you to remain a widow?"

The question didn't seem to surprise her. Carmela looked around the room and gestured to everyone.

"Rafey, it was my decision, and my decision alone, to remain a widow. I loved your father. Jeff will always hold my heart. I could never love another man as much as I loved him, and the same for him. We shared a connection that goes deeper than marriage. One day, soon, I hope, you will meet a wonderful young lady and have that same kind of love and devotion."

My devotion is to my job.

He looked around the room. "Why did you stay in Miami instead of moving away and getting a fresh start in life? We could have lived near Dad's relatives in Ohio."

"I needed my family and their support. They were there for me in a way I hope you'll never have to experience. I was a policeman's widow with four children who relied on me to hold things together. And you, Rafey."

She stroked his hair back, her expression troubled. "You were so angry, so young. You needed your family as well."

Rafe picked up her hand and kissed it, rubbing it against his bristled cheek. "Mama, I do love my family. It's just…"

I need more. I need my career. I need to keep the bad guys off the streets so drug dealers don't create more widows like you.

He finally said what he'd been thinking and feared to admit. "I miss him. I always will. I don't want to ever forget him, and sometimes it feels like no one really remembers him."

"We remember, Rafey. But life goes on. Your father, more than anyone, would say that."

He shook his head. "It doesn't feel like anyone remembers him, Mama. Always at the family gatherings, there were things he liked, like domestic beer..."

"And hamburgers and American desserts that made his sugar rise." Carmela made a face and laughed.

"I like American desserts as well," he told her. "I'm American."

"You are American, but you are also Cuban, Rafey. Here." She touched his chest. "You were born in this country, you are a true American. But don't deny your heritage simply to honor your father. Honor him by living a good life. And be happy. That is all he would want for you."

She patted his hand again and went to join his sisters.

Rafe headed to the bar and had the bartender pour him a bourbon. Sometimes he didn't know who he was. White, like his father and American as apple pie and fast-food restaurants? Or Cuban, with big family dinners on Sunday and *pastelitos*?

The job made it easier. On the job, he didn't think about his culture or who he was. He was an FBI agent, dedicated to taking down the bad guys. Maybe that was why the job was his life. Maybe his grandmother was right. He avoided his family because they brought up an aspect of his life he couldn't face.

The job mattered most right now because, Cuban or American, he was the best person to take down Hector Hernandez. Rafe knew everything about the man, and putting him behind bars would make Miami safer for everyone. The beauty salon raid was only the tip of a dangerous iceberg.

His thoughts drifted to Allison Lexington. Why was she there at the beauty salon? Seemed awfully suspicious.

He hoped like hell she wasn't involved in something illegal. Because it would be a shame to put her pretty butt behind bars. To some, Allison being at the salon was only a matter of bad timing. But his gut told him otherwise.

Rafe had a bad feeling he was right.

Cousin Luis joined him at the bar, ordered a club soda. He grinned. "Why are you hiding? Did Ronnie threaten to fling a *chancla* at your head for being late?"

Rafe gave his cousin a pointed look. "Ronnie's wearing heels, not flip-flops."

"Ah, then you're running away again from the fam?"

The question stung because it rang of truth. Rafe shrugged, sipped the bourbon and watched Sofia dance with her father. He smiled at the love in his brother-in-law's eyes, the shining look on Sofia's. In a few years, she'd be off to college, maybe find love, marry and have a family. He wished only happiness for her.

"They're all worried about you," Luis said.

Rafe shot him a puzzled look. "I'm fine. Nothing to worry about."

Luis glanced at the bartender, gestured to the window. Apart from the crowd, his cousin spoke in rapid Spanish.

"Rafe, you could have died last year when you were shot. You don't know, no one wanted to tell you, but we were certain…we'd lost you. And Tita, it broke her heart. She was saying rosaries day and night. Never left the hospital. You were always her favorite."

Luis stated it as fact, without animosity. Guilt struck him as he studied his grandmother, chattering happily as she arranged pastries on a plate instead of sitting and resting. When he'd finally gained consciousness after the lengthy surgery, everyone had acted cheerful and happy. No one told him how worried they'd been about his odds of survival.

"Tita wants to know when I'm going to settle down." Rafe swirled the ice in his glass as if it held all the answers.

"You should. Or at least find a nice girl and date her."

"I date."

"No one you've ever introduced us to. Face it, Rafe, you adore women, but not to make a life with. I was like you, before I met my girl." Luis gave a merry wave to his wife, dancing with one of his brothers.

"Everyone loves your Ana. They approve."

"So find a nice girl to bring home to dinner."

Rafe wanted to laugh. A nice girl. A woman who was professional, like his brother's wife, who owned her own marketing firm. Or a doctor like his youngest sister, Julia. If the girl wasn't a professional then she'd better be a devoted wife and mother like Ronnie.

"There's got be to a woman out there for you," Luis insisted.

"No one holds my interest that long," he said.

Well, not true. One woman did—a Harley-riding, tough trauma nurse named Allison. Rafe's mouth quirked into a smile as he remembered her—all passion and fire and vitriol.

"Ah! I see that smirk. There is someone you like! Who is it?" Luis pointed to him.

"She's a biker and hung with an outlaw biker gang we eventually arrested for stealing jewels, running drugs and other assorted crimes. Should I invite her to Sunday dinner? Or would her boots clash with Ronnie's designer stilettos?"

Luis gave him a speculative look. "Is this the woman who had something to do with loaning you my car for that FBI case?"

"Yes and no. She was working on the case, but under my supervision."

"Ah. Hmm." His cousin looked curious. Luis flashed him a knowing smile. "Working under you, eh?"

Rafe bristled at the double entendre. "Watch it, Luis. She's not that kind of woman."

Luis raised his eyebrows and smirked. "Yeah, she's got you twisted in knots, coz. Good to see. You're far too serious. You need a woman to shake you up."

The bourbon he gulped left a trail of fire down his throat. Rafe took a deep breath to curb his temper. Luis was famous for teasing everyone. The bourbon took some of the edge off.

Family. He loved them, but damn, it was tough at times. Rafe set down his glass on the windowsill, then removed the doll from his jacket pocket and waved it.

"Excuse me. You accuse me of being too serious so I'm going to dance with my beautiful goddaughter. Or go play dolls if she's too busy."

Luis grinned as Rafe walked off, pocketing the doll.

Sofia had finished dancing with his brother-in-law and was taking a break to sip some sparkling cider. She spotted him and broke into a wide, welcoming smile. Much as she did when she was younger, she ran into his arms and hugged him tight.

"Uncle Rafey, I'm so glad you made it! I miss you."

"I miss you as well." He hugged her back.

"Let's do a selfie." She started to bring out her cell, then paused. "Or would that not be a good idea because you're an agent? I don't want to get you into trouble."

Touched at her thoughtfulness, he smiled. "A selfie for you is fine. Just don't post on social media because I don't want your followers to mock your old uncle."

They smiled into the camera together.

So tall. Beautiful. He thought of the bad things in the world and felt the familiar worry needle him.

"I'm sorry for missing your entrance and your *baile de sorpresa.*"

"Oh, it was so cool, Uncle Rafey! Everyone loved it. You should have seen the dance moves we did! But don't worry, it's on YouTube and TikTok."

A lump formed in his throat. *This is my life, watching my goddaughter grow up on a video instead of in real time.*

"*Princesa*, you look beautiful. You outshine everyone here."

She grinned at him.

"I want you to stay that way, hon. You know there's all sorts of things that an unsuspecting teenager can get into…"

His niece looked up with an eye roll. "Is this the lecture about dangerous guys, drinking or drugs?"

Rafe sighed. "Drugs."

"Bad bust today, huh?"

"We found some stuff," he said vaguely.

"I'm a big girl, Uncle Rafey. I know all the street drugs, and I'd never even take a whiff of pot. I'm the least of your worries."

She gestured to Elena on the sidelines. "Now, Tita, she's the one we need to worry about. She doesn't look well. I told Mama and Papi, but they said she's tired from all the party preparation."

Instead of dismissing her concerns as Julia and Ronnie were doing now, Rafe studied his grandmother. True, her color, even in the dim light, looked off.

But Elena sat down and seemed to regain her composure. Rafe made a decision.

"Let's dance near her so she doesn't suspect we're keeping an eye on her. You know Tita. She'll deny everything, but if we dance close by, we can monitor her."

"Yes!"

Sofia put her hand on his shoulder and another on his waist.

Emotion filled him. He remembered a family event, not too long ago, where she danced on his shoes because he towered over her. Now in stylish heels and with her mother's statuesque height, she barely had to crane her neck to look up at him.

They waltzed to a lively tune, sticking to the edge of the dance floor.

Elena rose, waved at them. "Eat something, Rafey, when you're finished."

Before he could answer, she took two steps forward and gasped.

He ran forward, his heart hammering in his chest.

"Tita!" Sofia screamed.

He caught his grandmother in his arms as she collapsed.

Chapter 4

Friday night in Miami's busiest trauma hospital usually meant anything from broken bones to upset stomachs to gunshot wounds. Tonight was unusually quiet, but Allison knew things changed in minutes.

Seconds.

Never say the Q word. Because after you did, all heck would break loose.

Any minute, an ambulance would screech into the bay carrying a moaning person extracted from a mangled car, or a mother with a screaming child who slammed his hand in a door. Never mind the times a guy brought in a girlfriend who had something inserted into a body cavity the good Lord never intended to house that object.

She'd treated nearly everything in her years as a trauma nurse.

But the last thing she expected to see tonight was Rafe, running into the ER through the ambulance bay, carrying an elderly woman in his arms.

His dark gaze met hers. "Help her. She collapsed. I think it's her heart. I did CPR and she's breathing, but barely."

Shock at seeing him again gave way to professionalism. Allison grabbed a gurney and wheeled it over. Rafe gently laid the woman onto it. After pushing it into a curtained room, she began taking the woman's vitals. Pulse thready and thin. Heartbeat with a sloshing sound. Murmur, probably.

"Is she on anything?"

He rattled off a well-known heart medication. Allison glanced at him as she slipped an oxygen cannula into the woman's nostrils.

"Did she complain of pain before she collapsed? Was it crushing chest pain, with shortness of breath?"

Chest pain meant bad things. If there was ST elevation on the EKG, Rafe's grandmother could have complete blockage of a coronary artery and that meant cardiac tissue dying.

Rafe shook his head. "She said she felt nauseated. Not crushing pain, but tightness in her chest. Got me worried."

"Women having heart attacks sometimes experience different symptoms, so it's good you kept an eye on her."

Another nurse brought over a portable EKG machine. Allison opened the woman's dress, thankful it buttoned from the front.

The woman moaned as Allison attached the sticky leads to her chest.

"Hey, gorgeous, what's your name?" she asked the elderly woman.

"Elena, her name's Elena," Rafe muttered, stroking the woman's white hair. "My grandmother."

"Tita, Tita, please be okay. Uncle Rafe, tell me she's going to be okay," a young girl sobbed.

"Rafey, why did you take her here? Miami Bayshore is closer."

"Rafe, shouldn't she be fully awake by now?"

"Rafe, you pushed awfully hard on her chest. Did you break her ribs?"

Allison glanced up. At least twenty frantic, upset people surrounded them, including a pretty teenage girl in a tiara and puffy pink dress. Her gaze shot over to Rafe's poker face.

Rafe looked up at the crowd.

"She's a good nurse. The best. Now, everyone, back off and let her do her job. Give Tita some room, please!"

"Do you happen to know all the medications she's on?" she asked Rafe.

He consulted his cell phone. "Everyone keeps a list on their phones in case of emergencies. I'll text them to you."

"I'm surprised you still have my number," she muttered.

"Kept it just in case."

In case of what? You wanted to ask me for a date? She shook her head, withdrew her cell and consulted the text. In addition to the heart medication she was on a well-known blood pressure medication.

"You have her number, Uncle Rafey?" The puffy dress teen looked interested more than scared. "Are you guys seeing each other?"

To her horror, Allison felt revealing heat suffuse her cheeks. She focused on Elena.

"We'll take good care of her," she assured Rafe and the others. "Stay in the waiting room, and as soon as we know something, I'll come out and bring you up to speed."

As she turned, Rafe caught her upper arm. His dark gaze burned with intensity. "Don't let her die."

A brief nod. She and the other nurse wheeled Elena away. Allison shifted to the job at hand, pushing back the thoughts of Rafe and his dark gaze, and how he changed from the intimidating FBI agent to a worried grandson.

His grandmother's life was in her hands now.

The doctor came over and began his examination. At least Dr. Charles, unlike some of the jerk ER residents working the weekend shift, was courteous to nurses and didn't act like God.

Elena began muttering in Spanish.

Her command of Spanish wasn't as great as her coworkers, but she was fluent enough. Allison soothed her patient, trying to reassure her.

Don't let her die.

What would Rafe do if that happened?

He hated waiting in a hospital emergency room. His family didn't like it, either, but other than the usual bumps, bruises or accidents with kids, none of them experienced what he had.

Waiting to hear bad news.

Sofia, sitting with her court, who looked as traumatized as she did, came over and joined him in pacing. "Uncle Rafey, Tita has to be okay. Right? We can't lose her."

"*Princesa*, the nurses and doctors are doing all they can."

"Like they did with you last year? We thought…" Tears glistened in her dark eyes. "We thought you were going to die in this hospital. Mama was even talking about funerals and burial plots."

Inwardly he cursed his thoughtlessness. Here he was, remembering the agents he'd lost and his family had been here, waiting to hear if he lived or died. Guilt filled him. Oh yeah, this was a well-known emotion. When he focused on the job, he neglected his family.

When he focused on his family's need, the job and his team took second place.

So where do I stand? I'll think about that later. They need me now.

Rafe hugged Sofia. "I'm here. I'm a tough guy. Elena is tough as well. You come from stock that's tempered as fine steel."

He glanced at his cell phone as Sofia brushed away her tears and walked off. Nearly two hours. Not a word. It could mean anything…

His family milled about the waiting room. Elena was the glue holding them all together.

Rafe knew his grandmother never fully approved of his dad. She always worried something would happen to him, leaving her beloved Carmela a widow. And then the worst happened.

Small wonder I have commitment issues.

He looked at his niece, who was doing her best to try to hold it together.

The double doors swung open, but instead of a young, tired resident doctor, Allison hurried out. She spotted him and started toward him, but his family beat him there.

They formed a circle, anxious looks on their faces. Rafe knew instantly it would be okay. Allison was smiling.

Through the relieved shouts and exclamations, he could barely hear her. Broken sentences reached him, including, "going to keep her overnight," "meds adjusted," "less stress" and "a couple of you can see her for a few minutes."

Relief made all his tensed muscles relax. He rubbed the back of his neck to ease the knot there. Allison looked at him.

"Headache?" she asked, amid the happy buzz of voices.

"Yeah. I'll live."

She looked him up and down. "Yeah, you will. Too bad."

He blinked as she flashed him her sassy grin. Rafe rolled his eyes.

Allison gestured to Sofia. "Let me guess. *Quinceañera* party interrupted?"

He nodded. "My niece Sofia's. No one will want to return to the hall. Most of the guests have left anyway."

Allison pursed her lips. She had a lovely mouth, soft lips in a Cupid's bow. A brief thought flashed across his mind—what would her mouth feel like beneath the subtle pressure of his?

You'll never find out, chump. She's not for you. Find a nice Cuban girl who prefers a Mercedes-Benz over a motorcycle.

"Your family is here, right? Most of them?"

Rafe glanced around the crowded waiting room. More of

the relatives had arrived to join the long wait. Except for two other strangers, his family took up all the space. "I'd say all of them, actually. And some of Sofia's friends."

Sofia joined them and slid an arm around Rafe's waist. "Thank you for saving my nana. My *quinz* doesn't matter as much as she does. That's the best birthday present anyone can give me."

Allison's smile softened. Never had she looked at him that way, but he felt a strange tug in his chest.

"I daresay all of you won't leave the hospital anyway, until you see Elena is okay," she said.

Vigorous nods all around.

She glanced at her phone. "It's late, but I hate to see a good party ruined. A *quinz* only happens once. Let me think."

As she glanced around, he recognized the spark in her eyes. Allison had a daring side, one he'd glimpsed when working with her when she'd accepted the assignment to be an informant.

"There's a new doctor's lounge on the second floor, away from the patient rooms. It hasn't been officially opened yet, but it's finished. We could set something up, if you rescue the cake and some drinks, no alcohol, and maybe someone can plug in their iPhone for music…"

Several voices began talking in excited tones. One of Sofia's friends who lived closest to the hospital offered to go home and get his portable speaker.

Sofia ran over and hugged her. "You're so nice!"

Rafe felt a tingle of gratitude toward her. "You sure this is okay? Don't you need approval?"

Allison grinned. "From whom? It's after midnight. Besides, I have a key."

There it was again, that spark of defiance and nonconformity. Troublemaker. He hesitated as Sofia gave him a pleading look. Hell, everyone was looking to him for the nod of approval.

"Uncle Rafey, please?"

Allison's grin turned crooked. "Please, Uncle Rafey? I promise it will be okay. I won't even be there long because I do have to work."

Instead of answering, he chucked Sofia under the chin. "You got it. Anything for you."

She clapped her hands, and the glum teens perked up.

Rafe turned to Allison. "Thank you for doing this for her."

Some unknown emotion crossed her face. "It's not a big deal. I hate seeing kids disappointed. Come on, I'll show you where the lounge is."

An hour later, the party was in full swing. Most of the adults sat on the sidelines drinking the sodas brought from the hall. The cake had been cut and Sofia presented with her doll that symbolized her last gift from childhood.

Never had he been more proud of his niece. Her selfless attitude toward the party and focus on her grandmother had both her parents beaming with pride.

The door opened and Allison walked in bearing a small bowl filled with colorful circles and some unopened bags. "It's my dinner break and I thought I'd contribute to the festivities with this candy. Not that any of you need more sugar."

She set the bowl down on one of the round dining tables. Rafe joined her.

Alison hummed along to the music and moved her body. "Good times."

Amused at her gyrations—yeah, she had rhythm—he waved at the speaker. "You like salsa?"

"Sometimes. No time for dancing, though. My schedule is usually demanding, and there's classes to keep up my license, things like that. I thought about taking lessons so I don't make a complete fool of myself at my little sister's wedding."

"How about a lesson now?" He inclined his head at the makeshift dance floor.

Allison blinked. "Ah, I don't know. I should return to the ER. I'm on duty... My break is nearly over..."

Not waiting for another excuse, Rafe put a hand on the small of her back and guided her to the dance floor.

"Okay, begin with your feet together, and then step forward with your left foot, and then move your weight to your right foot. Like this."

He demonstrated a few steps.

"Now, put your hand on my left shoulder," he advised as he slid an arm around her slender waist.

Rafe took her hand. "Salsa is all about surrendering to the music, to the beat, and letting go. It's about releasing emotions. Freedom to be yourself."

Stiff at first, Allison made a series of jerky moves. She gave a self-conscious laugh. "See? Two left feet."

"Relax. Listen to the music and go with it. No one here is watching."

"Except you."

Rafe twirled and moved his hips. "If it makes you feel better, I'm a lousy dancer compared to the rest of my family."

She followed his lead and then smiled. "I think you're great."

There it was again, that little skip hop in his chest, as if his heart gave an extra beat. The sweet floral scent of her perfume, or perhaps her shampoo, invaded his senses. As he instructed her in swirling her hips, his naughty imagination danced to his bed and a naked Allison swirling her hips in a different manner as they swayed to the rhythm of the desire between them...

Someone applauded. Glancing around, he saw his family

standing on the sidelines, watching them dance. A contemplative look on his mom's face. His sister Julia scrutinizing Allison in her scrubs. A knowing grin from a few, including cousin Luis and Sofia.

The music ended. Flushed, she shook her head and retreated to a table. "Thanks for the lesson. You're a great dancer."

Rafe gazed down at her, the feeling in his chest intensifying. Damn, why did he have to feel this way around her? Allison Lexington was all wrong for him. Yet he couldn't deny the attraction between them. Judging from her dilated pupils, rapid pulse and pink cheeks he knew were caused not by dancing, she felt it as well.

Intrigued, he leaned closer, captivated by her moist, red mouth. One kiss couldn't hurt. He had to know what she tasted like, felt like beneath his mouth…

"Hey, Uncle Rafey, want some candy?"

Jerked out of the enchantment, he looked over at Sofia. His niece held the bowl Allison had brought and was ready to tear into a packet of candy.

Fun Times Candy.

The packet was identical to ones they'd found at the beauty shop this afternoon. Alarm bells rang in his mind.

Damn, damn, damn!

Rafe pulled away from Allison and raced to Sofia, grabbing the packet before she could shake free the treats inside. Rainbow colored. Not candy.

Incredulous and infuriated, he whirled and growled at Allison. "Where the hell did you get this?"

Her mouth opened and closed. "It's candy."

Swearing, he removed his cell, made a quick call to one of his senior agents. He waved away the curious teens from the candy dish.

"No one touch this."

"It's just candy," Allison protested.

"Did you take any of this?" he demanded of Sofia.

Reddened, she shook her head. "N-no!"

"Did anyone eat this or even touch it? Damn it, answer me!"

Several teens shook their heads.

"What is wrong with you?" Allison asked. "It's candy."

"It's not candy. I don't know what your game is, but…"

Allison glared at him. "I don't have a game. I was trying to help add to the party. Now, if you'll excuse me, I have to get back to work."

She stormed out of the room.

Less than half an hour later, the agent he'd phoned had arrived with the test kit. Rafe fumed as he saw the results. Three agents bagged the evidence and removed it carefully.

He addressed his family. "Sorry, guys. Party's over."

Rafe headed downstairs to the emergency room. Allison was at the nurses' station, a half-eaten sandwich at her elbow as she worked on a computer. Blood stained her scrubs.

Rafe marched over to Allison and grabbed her wrist. "You're under arrest for the possession of fentanyl."

Chapter 5

Well, this truly sucked.

The night had started out as quiet, the dreaded *Q* word for first responders because saying it aloud meant you'd get slammed. Then Rafe's grandmother arrived with heart issues.

Then a GSW (gunshot wound) vic, to the chest, courtesy of the man's son, Ken, who swore it was an accident. The dad died, despite their best efforts.

Allison's repeated condolences and suggestions of getting help from a social worker had been met with an angry tirade of words until Ken peeled out of the parking lot, rubber tire marks on pavement.

His last threat to her was there would be hell to pay for letting his father die.

Guess this is my hell.

For an hour, Rafe had grilled her. Where did she get the candy? Why was it in the nurses' station? Who was her contact?

Sitting at a cold steel table, thankful only for not being handcuffed to the steel pipe running the length of the table, Allison kept her answers brief. She thought about demanding a lawyer but knew it would make her look guilty.

Besides, she was too damn worried about Diana. Where the hell had her baby sister gotten that candy?

"I know my rights, Rodriguez. And I know I'm not dealing drugs. The candy couldn't have been fentanyl."

He gave her a level look. "It tested positive. The lab is running results now to determine how much was in the pills."

The fentanyl had been in her space at the nurses' station, and worse, she'd brought it to the party for Rafael's niece and family to eat. She, who had dedicated her life to saving lives, could have killed innocents. This was the stuff of nightmares.

But she couldn't reveal the truth and put Diana in jeopardy. She needed to talk to her sister first.

But no way was she talking to her sister with the FBI listening to everything she said.

More than caring about her own hide, or the humiliation of being taken in handcuffs out of her job and hustled into a waiting black SUV, was her concern for Diana. Had her sister gotten into something she should have avoided? Or had she thought the candy, like Allison herself had thought, only candy?

"Allison, where did you get the candy?"

She stretched out her legs, still clad in nurse's scrubs, and studied a blotch of blood on her left thigh. The last patient she treated had bled out on the floor.

"I asked you a question. Stop ignoring me."

Allison glanced up at Rafe. "I'm not ignoring you. I was concentrating." She pointed to the blood spot. "Do you know how hard it is to remove old blood from cotton? All my scrubs are dirty. This was my last pair, and I had hoped to get home after my shift to do laundry."

He stared at her. "Laundry. That's all that you're thinking about?"

"Well, it's better than thinking that you're convinced I deliberately brought a bowl of fentanyl into your niece's makeshift party so I could overdose a group of innocent teens, Supervisory Special Agent Rafael."

Allison leaned forward as he placed two hands on the table and scowled at her.

"Convince me you're innocent, Ms. Lexington. Tell me who set you up if you didn't do this."

"I don't know."

Her gaze darted away. Too late she remembered that was a clear sign of avoiding the truth.

"You're sweating profusely, Ms. Lexington. Why?"

"It's hot in here."

"The thermostat is turned down to seventy."

More questions. More grilling. Allison's back began to ache, along with her head. She had been in the middle of gulping down a quick sandwich when Rafe arrested her.

At least he'd shown some concern, for he'd asked if she had touched the candy with her bare hands when she'd opened the packets to place it in the bowl. Allison had not.

Nor in her wildest nightmares could she ever envision it was fentanyl.

She rubbed her head. "Listen to me, I'm as concerned as you are about this. I'm a trauma nurse. I've seen what fentanyl does. Do you really think I'd want to deal in that crap? Just the dust alone is deadly! That's a clear contradiction."

"You're a trauma nurse who rides a motorcycle, and most trauma and emergency room nurses have seen what a bike crash can do to a body. That's a clear contradiction as well. Unless you have a death wish."

Allison sighed. Now he sounded like her coworkers. "You ride a motorcycle, too. Do you have a death wish?"

Rafe folded his arms across his chest as another agent cleared his throat. "Rafe," the agent began. "Maybe we should…"

"Leave us." Rafe didn't take his gaze off her. "Go find some paperwork to finish."

When the other agent left, Rafe pulled out a chair, the steel scraping against the linoleum floor in a protesting squeak.

"Level with me, Ms. Lexington. I know you. You're hiding something. Where did you get the damn pills? We're going to find out. Your hospital has surveillance cameras. It may take a little time. And in the time it takes us to find out who left you the pills, more innocents could get hurt."

His voice softened. "You're a nurse. Do you really want more of this crap on the streets for kids to eat and OD?"

Damn, he struck at the heart of her. Allison had treated more than a few overdoses of fentanyl, including a ten-year-old who'd been exposed to his older brother's stash. No amount of naloxone could have saved the kid, despite her best efforts. Remembering the child knotted her stomach.

"No."

His intense gaze met hers across the table. "Help me stop this crap before it's too late. Were the pills yours?"

"No. I thought they were candy."

"Who gave you the pills and said it was candy?"

Allison bit her lip. "I can't remember."

Her gaze darted away and she was sweating. Lying.

"Tell me or you're spending the night in jail."

Allison threw her head back. "Fine, put me in jail."

"I can't believe you'd go to such lengths to protect someone who distributes death in a pill."

"I saw you with your niece and your family. You'd do anything for your family as well!"

Oh damn. Allison slumped in her chair as a satisfied look came over him. "I see."

He consulted with an electronic pad. "You have a sister, Diana. She's marrying the nephew of Hector Hernandez in one month. Do you know who Hernandez is?"

"I know."

"I'm bringing in your sister for questioning."

Her mouth went dry as she tried to formulate a plan. She had to call her sister. Find out who gave her the pills. No way could she allow Rafe or any law enforcement agent to arrest Diana. Question her. Whatever.

She couldn't trust Rafe. Not with this.

Suddenly the bloodstain on the pantleg of her scrubs, and the matching one on her shirt, seemed much larger. Allison pointed to her clothing.

"I've been here for two hours. Mind if I go to the bathroom?" she asked.

His gaze narrowed. But he signaled to the window, rather, the one-way mirrored glass, and an agent came into the room.

"Escort her to the women's room and guard the door," Rafe instructed.

When she was in the bathroom, after making sure she was alone, Allison paced to the end of the room farthest from the door.

Like many of her coworkers, she kept the pockets of her scrubs filled with medical necessities. But her cell phone was close as well. Not in her pocket where it could fall out.

She shrugged out of the stained top of her scrubs, washed the blood off her stomach that had leaked through the scrubs and fished the cell phone out of her bra.

Allison shot off a quick text to her sister.

The candy you gave me is dangerous. Do not touch any more of it by any means.

She tapped the phone, waiting for a reply, hoping Diana wasn't with her fiancé.

A couple of minutes later, a response. Dangerous how? What's wrong?

The hell with texting. She called Diana. "Diana, where did you get that candy you gave me?"

A sleepy yawn. "Why? What's going on? Did it taste bad?"

A short laugh. Understatement of the year. "Who gave it to you?" she whispered.

"No one gave it to me. I saw it in a box marked Wedding Favors that Hector had brought into his house. There was a lot so I thought you'd want some to get through your shift. You've been working too hard, Ally."

Allison rubbed her tired eyes. "Diana, do not touch any more of that candy under any circumstances. Don't get near it. It isn't candy. It's fentanyl."

"It can't be."

"Di, listen to me. The candy you gave me tested positive for fentanyl."

"What?! It's impossible. My wedding favor candy? Did you open the bags?"

"Yes, but what does it matter?"

A long pause and then Di sighed. "There must be a mistake. Ally, you work in a hospital with fentanyl. Some of those pills must have gotten mixed up in the candy I gave you."

"No, listen to me, that's ridiculous…"

"You left it at the nurse's station, were you guarding it every single moment, Ally? It's candy, not drugs."

Major denial. Allison drew in a deep breath. How the hell could she get through to her sister. "No one is stupid enough to mix legal fentanyl pills in with that candy, Di. Listen to me, for God's sake, don't get near that box…"

"What box?" a deep male voice asked.

She quickly hung up. Damn.

The door to the women's room stood wide open. Rafael stood in the door frame. He strode inside, his gaze glittering with anger. Yet his grip was gentle as he took the cell from her shaking hand. He glanced at the screen and the last number dialed.

Allison suddenly became aware of the cool air brushing over her chest and bare torso and the fact she wore only a bra.

His gaze flicked downward and something else flared in his eyes. Pure male interest. But he looked away, still gripping her phone.

Rafe shrugged out of his jacket and handed it to her. "I'd advise wearing this."

Too tired to protest, she slipped it on, surrounded by warmth, his warmth, and the spicy scent of his cologne. Taking her upper arm, he marched her out of the restroom.

"I can't believe this," Allison muttered.

She'd wanted to crawl into a hole and disappear when Rafael caught her clad only in her bra, calling Diana to warn her.

No mercy. He marched her out of the women's bathroom into his large office with windows overlooking a bay of cubicles. Fortunately it was after hours and only a few agents were working.

And he'd had the courtesy to offer her his suit jacket.

Rafe had barked out orders to those who stared. He all but threw her into the chair in front of his desk.

"Your sister did this. She's in on it."

"No! She's innocent. I swear it."

"And why the hell should I believe you? Allison, you know how lethal this crap is and you're protecting a woman who is distributing it! I don't care if she's your sister, or even your damn fairy godmother. She's dealing drugs."

"She didn't know what it was! She thought it was candy for the wedding favors Hector Hernandez ordered."

Allison slumped in the chair, huddled into his suit jacket. It smelled like him, she thought vaguely. Spicy cologne, leather and a unique scent that was Rafael. Having his jacket envelop her should feel stifling and restrictive, but for some odd reason, she found it comforting.

Or maybe it's simply the fact you don't want to be nearly half-naked in front of the guy.

Rafe parked a hip on the corner of his desk. She didn't care for his accusatory look, laced with speculation about what she might be doing.

She saw that same look months ago when he'd coaxed her into spying on the Devil's Patrol.

Allison had a bad feeling about this.

"Your sister is innocent. So you say."

"Shish kebabs on a sidecar, Rafael. Leave her alone. You have no evidence she actually left the candy there or that she knew or didn't know it was a drug."

"Shish kebabs on a sidecar?" His mouth quirked upward.

"My new swear phrase. I'm trying to give up profanity. As I was saying, you need probable cause. You have nothing to go on."

"Probable cause? Been watching a lot of crime television?"

"One of my former patients was an assistant state attorney. Speaking of lawyers, I need one if you're going to hold me here."

His phone rang. Rafe picked up the receiver, listened, and hung up. He looked at her.

"Lab results are in. There were only trace amounts of fentanyl. The pills are mainly candy."

She let out a relieved sigh. "You can't hold me for trace amounts."

"I could keep you here, but I believe you're innocent."

Allison sighed with relief.

"But I'm going to bring your sister in for questioning."

Allison stared. "You can't do that."

He leaned back in his chair. "I can."

Questioning Di would agitate her sister, possibly worse. Allison knew this could go south fast.

"Please don't. Di is innocent."

He drummed his fingers on the desk. "Your sister…she's marrying Paul Davis, Hernandez's nephew. Wedding's at Hernandez's mansion on Starfish Island."

"How do you know…?"

"I imagine you'll be in the bridal party. And you've met the groom's uncle as well, maybe even have been there to the mansion a time or two to see the grounds and where the ceremony will take place."

Allison shot up in her chair so fast, the jacket tumbled off her shoulders. "Oh no, oh hell no. I know where you're going with this…"

Rafe stood and went behind her, placing the jacket back on her shoulders. "Then you know I won't take no for an answer."

"I am not getting you an invitation to that wedding!"

He stood in front of her once more, and his smile resembled that of a Cheshire cat. A lean-hipped, trim cat with intense dark eyes, and sexier than any man had the right to be when questioning, no, grilling, a suspect.

"A wedding invitation? No, my dear Ms. Lexington. Far from it. You and your lovely sister are going to get me onto Starfish Island and into that house where she got the 'candy' before the wedding. Tomorrow, in fact. Tomorrow will suit me fine."

Chapter 6

Taking risks came with the dangers of the job. But this kind of risk might get him killed.

Or worse—fired.

Rafe didn't care. When it came to Hernandez and how the bastard was no doubt distributing drugs that his own goddaughter had nearly eaten, well, he got a little mad.

Nothing else mattered but nailing the son of a bitch.

The task force had heard Hernandez expected a large shipment of fentanyl to his expensive mansion on Starfish Island. Rafe long suspected the drug dealer was smuggling in drugs from Mexico using sleek racing boats he owned. The boats docked at his private mansion, and Rafe suspected the drugs were unloaded under the cover of night. For the past six months, no activity was seen, but they'd received word things had picked up around the mansion. Boats were seen unloading crates of everything from silverware and glassware to linens.

Illicit drugs were nestled inside those crates. He'd bet his badge on it. Bastard was using his nephew's wedding as cover to smuggle drugs.

In all the instances law enforcement tried to catch him, Hernandez evaded them.

Couldn't even get enough probable cause for a search warrant. All Rafe needed was photographic evidence the drugs were on Hernandez's estate and they could obtain a search warrant and finally nail the dealer.

He pulled the ball cap low over his eyes against the noon-day sun. He wore loose khaki pants and a long-sleeved gray shirt over a plain white T-shirt. The pickup truck he drove had a sign that read Lopez Flowers and Landscaping.

To add to his disguise, he'd shaved off his short beard.

He had the worried sister in tow. He needed Allison there. Not so much to gain access, but because Diana was an unknown and he knew Allison.

Protest she might, but when it came to getting a job done, she was smooth professionalism.

The woman could lie with the best of them. Convincing enough to sell an air-conditioner to a scientist living in the Arctic Circle.

He didn't trust her fully, but he knew she would not jeopardize this opportunity.

Not because of her own pretty hide, but her sister's.

Like him, Allison would do anything for her family. Including sneak him onto the Hernandez compound on the pretext of hiring him as a florist and landscaper for the wedding.

He consulted his burner phone. No wire or button camera, either. Hernandez would surely have devices to scan for that. But he was ready.

A late model black sedan pulled up to the curb. Rafe watched as Allison got out of the passenger side and came over. They'd agreed to meet in the shopping plaza of a well-known Miami mall.

Her gaze raked over him once, twice.

"You look different."

Rafe rubbed his smooth cheeks. "I shaved."

"Hope you showered as well."

He gave a faint smile. "Yeah, I did."

Allison glanced at the truck.

"You can't take that onto Starfish Island. You're coming with us."

"I know. This is my cover. In case."

"In case what? You need to cut some grass along the way?"

Allison always had been cheeky. "In case anyone is watching you and your sister, and me by default."

She rolled her eyes. "Whatever. Let's go."

"Wait." He glanced at the waiting car, where her sister sat behind the wheel. "Same rules as your last assignment. If anything goes south, or sideways, you and your sister get the hell out of there. If you even get a whiff of danger, it's over. Get in the car and leave."

Allison didn't even blink. "What about you?"

Was that a flicker of concern in her eyes? "I'm a trained agent. I can take care of myself. I've done many undercover assignments."

"Oh? You won't fool anyone like that. I made it clear my sister agreed to this because she thinks you're a potential friend…with benefits. So act as if you like me and we aren't standing here having a convo about yard clippings. Diana's sure to be watching us."

Rafe hesitated only a minute and then briefly touched his mouth to hers. To his shock, Allison threw her arms around his neck and gave him a deep kiss. The kind of kiss a woman in love would give to her man, but whoa, he hadn't been expecting anything more than a peck on the mouth.

This was a full head-on collision with a soft, warm mouth that tasted like sin and sunshine with hints of peppermint and coffee. Rafe slid his arms around her slim waist and pulled her closer, wanting more. Forget looking good for her sister. He wanted this, from the moment she'd sat in his office months ago, scowling at him in pure defiance when he'd coerced her into becoming a confidential informant.

Allison made a little humming sound, and as his tongue was about to invade her mouth, a car horn honked.

They jumped back. Color suffused her cheeks. She licked her lips and looked as confused and stunned as he felt.

"Guess we'd better go." He jerked a thumb at the car. "Your sister's waiting."

He opened the passenger door for her and then climbed into the back. Diana, in the driver's seat, didn't turn to greet him.

"Hello, Ms. Lexington. I'm Rafael Lopez," he said, using a distant cousin's last name. "You can call me Rafe."

In the rearview mirror, he saw disapproval in her brown eyes. "I don't know why Ally thinks your flower shop can help with the wedding."

She turned to her sister and frowned. "You owe me for this."

Surprised to see Allison look meek, he watched her. "I know, sis."

Diana turned her attention to the back seat. "Rafe, what are your intentions toward my sister?"

Rafe almost choked. "Ah, pardon?"

"Dating. You're not using her for sex only, are you?"

Allison shot him a pleading look from the front seat.

He wanted to laugh. *Yeah, I'd love to use your sister for sex, after that kiss. More than sex. Felt like she wanted the same. But that's none of your damn business.*

He thought of several things to say in Spanish, none of them appropriate. "My intentions are honorable."

Honorable in using her as a CI to bring down a drug empire.

"I don't understand. This is the first time Ally's said anything about you and it seems like she is mad about you."

So Diana had watched. Silently he thanked Allison for putting on such a good show. Yet he wondered if it had been an act because, damn.

Rafe slid a hand between the seats and gripped Allison's cold, clammy palm. "I asked her to keep our relationship a secret. I wasn't sure if your family would approve of me because I'm Cuban American."

"Well, that's silly. None of my family is prejudiced against immigrants. Ally, didn't you tell Rafe anything?"

"I told him enough." Allison's voice remained tight.

"I don't even know where you met. Ally's been scarce on details. Rafe, how did you meet my sister?"

Rafael's gaze met Allison's as she turned her head. "Motorcycle rally."

True enough.

"Rafe likes to ride as well," Allison said a little too quickly.

"Ally said you're trustworthy." A haughty sniff. "And you're trying to help your cousin expand his business. You'd better be good at your job."

Oh, I'm really good at my job. Soon enough, you'll find out just how good. "Yes, miss," he murmured with as much meekness as possible.

Another glance in the mirror. "You understand the home where we are going is very exclusive? And I may hire you for the wedding only as a favor to my sister? There are rules at the house. You stick with us at all times. No wandering off. Hector has a large security team, and I'd hate to see you tossed out for prying."

"Yes, miss." *I know how exclusive this house is, and how the man who owns it should be sitting in a federal prison for the rest of his natural life.*

He began asking Diana questions about her preferences for the wedding. What kind of flowers, how many. Rafe jotted down notes in the electronic pad he carried. He'd spent more than a few hours last night, after releasing Allison from custody, prepping for this assignment.

Before today, he couldn't tell a peony from a petunia. Now?

He knew the best dealer for the potted palms Diana wanted, and how to get the dozens of lilies that were her favorite flowers.

He actually did have a cousin who owned a flower shop. Mike had prepped him on the landscaping and floral arrangements early this morning.

His cover established, he only had to play the part.

Falling silent, he let the two women talk about the upcoming wedding. While pretending to consult his notes, he listened to Allison argue with her sister that Hector's mansion was too extravagant and pretentious.

Diana seemed agitated as she navigated over the causeway to South Beach that led to the barrier island that accessed the elite community of Starfish Island.

"I know what I said, Ally. But Paul wants this. He…he feels like he owes it to his uncle. Hector is footing the entire bill because Paul is his godson and he wanted to do right by him."

"Diana, what about what you want? Capitulating to your groom's requests is no way to begin a marriage. Why can't you compromise and have the wedding at Mom and Dad's house? They have a large garden and…"

"Stop it, Ally. It's a done deal." He saw her gaze dart to the rearview mirror, and she lowered her voice. "I know you dislike Hector, but he's not the criminal everyone says he is. He has a legitimate business as an importer of racing boats. Nothing more. They're jealous of his wealth."

Legitimate business. Right. He'd heard that before. Legitimate business masking illegal activities.

Like physicians who wrote unnecessary prescriptions for opiates just for the kickback cash.

His thoughts drifted to when Florida operated pain clinics a few years ago, with doctors writing fake prescriptions to anyone who had an ache. Opiates and cash were passing through hands faster than spring breakers went through beer.

They'd shut down the pain clinics after a thorough investigation. Another score for the feds, the good guys who prevented more overdosing.

Now they had fentanyl to deal with, a deadlier drug marketed to young people in the form of candy. It made his blood boil. Filled him with disgust for greedy and uncaring jerks like Hector Hernandez. Tightened his resolve to shut him down.

The sparkling turquoise waters of Biscayne Bay stretched out before them as they drove over the causeway. Finally they came to the narrow bridge accessing the private island. Diana drove forward and gave her name to the guard at the gatehouse. Rafe handed over his fake driver's license.

The guard opened the gate and they drove down a street lined with sleek, tall royal palm trees. Well-manicured green lawns with trim, colorful landscaping hinted of the wealth behind the mansions.

Clusters of leafy trees peppered the island, sheltering the waterfront homes from view, but other houses stood proudly as sentinels of the island's famous historical past, with elegant colonial Spanish or Venetian styles. Courtyards, arches, clay barrel tile shingles—all of it looked elegant and wealthy.

Hernandez lived in one of the wealthier waterfront homes, shielded from view. The secluded fifty-four-million-dollar mansion gave the man plenty of privacy. The estate sat on a full acre of prime waterfront property. Not only waterfront, but deep waterfront, which allowed Hernandez to dock his yacht out back.

A little over twelve thousand square feet, it had six bedrooms, a chef's kitchen with a butler pantry for catering parties, a dining area to seat sixteen guests and, most impressive of all, a living room with floor-to-ceiling windows that overlooked the serene waters of Biscayne Bay.

He'd seen this house from the water while cruising in an

unmarked police boat. The thicket of coconut palms shielded most of it from curious spectators.

As Diana pulled up before a gate with the initials HH carved into the ornate ironwork, he saw two armed guards peer at the car. Majestic coconut palms in the front yard cloaked the mansion in a barrier of green.

Sunlight winked off the blue barrel of a long gun one guard carried. Yeah, they'd have no problem putting a bullet or two into your knee if you tried to muscle your way inside or even were caught sneaking over the ten-foot-tall white stucco wall.

Once inside, Diana parked in the circular driveway. As they got out, two more muscular guards approached the vehicle, swaggering as if they owned the place.

Diana smiled and they nodded at her. "I'm here to plan for the wedding. Is Hector here?"

First name basis. Interesting. *Is she that close to Paul's uncle and isn't only taking advantage of his hospitality for the wedding?*

"No, Miss Lexington."

She sighed. "Too bad. I wanted to talk to him about having the rehearsal dinner on the Old Glory."

Diana turned with a smug smile. "That's Hector's multimillion-dollar yacht. He usually keeps it docked here."

Rafe said nothing. Allison bit her lip as if biting back a reply. She handed over her cell phone to one guard. The man gave it to the other guard and began to frisk Rafe. They removed his cell phone from his belt and took the electronic tablet Rafe carried.

"Vendors who are not vetted previously are not permitted cell phones on property," one stated.

The other guard examined the electronic tablet Rafe carried.

"I need this for work." He showed them his notes on the tablet.

The guard grunted and palmed Rafe's phone and returned his tablet. The goon had the nerve to take his cell phone and was clueless about the tablet's video and phone abilities. Rafe simply watched the man tuck the phone into a bag, along with Allison's phone.

They did not confiscate Diana's.

No matter. He followed Diana and Allison on the stone path to the back of the estate, where a green lawn overlooked the sparkling turquoise bay waters. The palm trees flanked the pool, allowing a splendid view of the nearby Miami cityscape. Nearby, an infinity pool with a cascading waterfall and a hot tub had patio furniture arranged around it.

It was a clear, cool day in South Florida. With the stunning blue sky and the magnificent, sparkling waters of Biscayne Bay, you could stretch out by the pool and indulge in peaceful relaxation.

Except if you knew the real cost of buying this mansion—the lives taken by the owner's profession. Not that Hernandez gave a damn.

Diana stood near the pool, looking around uncertainly.

Rafe began typing on his tablet, pausing to take covert photos. Hernandez's guards failed to realize the tablet had an excellent camera. He swept the tablet around, getting several views, including the sleek black racing boat moored at the expansive dock.

Then he realized Diana hadn't said a word. Instead, she kept staring at the view with a perturbed expression on her face. She went over to the dock and kept looking at the boat.

"Diana, we're not holding the wedding on the dock. Can you join us?" Allison asked.

Diana held up a finger. "One minute."

An armed guard, pistol hanging from his belt, hovered nearby. Diana went over to him.

"Where is Old Glory? Paul told me his uncle would have the yacht here for the season."

The man shrugged. "Mr. Hector loaned it to a friend."

"For how long? I wanted the boat for the rehearsal dinner."

"Mr. Hector changed the plans. The rehearsal dinner won't be held here. Your parents know and are making alternate plans."

"Paul promised..." Diana turned away.

"Di, what's wrong?" Allison asked. "So what if you can't have the rehearsal dinner on the yacht? It's better to have it somewhere else, like a restaurant. Less fuss."

Busy taking photos of the water and the racing boat, Rafe almost missed the distress on Diana's face.

"Paul promised me the yacht," Diana said, biting her lower lip. "It would have looked so impressive with the wedding guests. He promised..."

As her voice trailed off, Rafe stepped up. He had to control the situation before he lost the opportunity. Clearly Diana was upset about the change in plans, but he sensed a larger issue here.

"Miss Lexington? Where is the wedding going to be held? Out here? Will there be a temporary deck for guests and dancing? Or do you plan to have chairs on the grass?" Rafe asked.

When she didn't answer, he repeated the question in Spanish. Finally she looked up at him. Rafe's pulse raced at the empty look in her eyes.

She had been bubbly and energetic driving through the gate. And now, on the grounds, Diana acted like a different woman.

Then she pushed back at her long hair and gestured to the pool. "Out here, on the grounds. I think there is a contingency plan if it rains because the house has a large living room where we can set up chairs. Um, I guess the flowers and trees, whatever you think is best, but something that can be moved indoors."

Perfect. Exactly what he'd wanted—access to the house's

interior. But he needed to know what else was bothering Diana.

His gaze flicked to the guard standing by the pool. "If you're worried the racing boat won't make a good backdrop for the wedding, I'm sure it can be moved."

Diana started to speak, then shook her head. She motioned to her sister. "Let's go inside the living area so you can see how much space there is and how we can arrange the furniture if we need to move the ceremony inside."

They entered the house through French doors leading directly to the living room. Though he was here to gather evidence, Rafe could not help but admire the Italian marble flooring, the stone fireplace, elegant silk furniture in subtle shades of ecru that did not contrast the splendid view from the windows, but enhanced it.

Then he remembered why he was there, and how many lives Hernandez and his drug operation had claimed, either through violence or overdoses.

Rafe asked questions about moving the furniture, how many guests and placement of floral arrangements and potted palms. While he talked, he moved around, taking photos with his electronic pad while writing on it.

"If it rains, we should decorate the entryway with flowers and potted trees, perhaps with fairy lights," he told Diana.

She led him down a long hallway to the front of the house. An attractive brunette, a housekeeper, judging by the gray uniform and apron, set a crystal vase of fresh lilies on a hallway table. She saw them and frowned. Diana swallowed hard.

"Hello, Lucy," Diana said.

The housekeeper glared and arranged the flowers.

"I love how you arranged the flowers," Diana told her.

"There's other things I'm better at arranging, *puta*."

Allison gasped at the swear term. The woman mumbled something and ran upstairs.

Rafe blinked. Something was off about that one. "What's her problem?" he asked.

"Nothing." But Diana stared after the housekeeper and muttered, "I can't believe Hector gave her a job here. She loves to make my life difficult."

As they went into the foyer, his gaze focused on the stacks of boxes near the sweeping marble staircase.

Allison gave him a questioning look. He saw it on her face. She suspected those weren't ordinary boxes.

Diana saw them looking at the boxes and shrugged. "Those will be gone soon. The wedding planner is picking them up. I don't know why they're still here."

Each box was marked in a black permanent marker— Wedding Favors.

"If these are for the wedding, I'd like to see the colors so I can match the lights on the trees," he said.

Rafe opened a box.

Damn. There inside were the same rainbow-colored candy Allison had had at the hospital. Though the candy at the hospital only had trace amounts of fentanyl, he suspected rainbow tablets containing pure fentanyl were mixed into the box.

Some wedding favors.

He'd barely had time to take one photo when Diana came toward him, scowling.

"Those are my favors for the wedding. Candy for all the guests. You're not supposed to touch them."

"Oh? Says who?"

"Hector bought them for us. It's part of his wedding gift to us."

Some gift. Drugs that could kill. Rafe knew these were not meant for the wedding, and he'd bet his salary they were destined for the speedboat outside.

Allison had seen inside the box and blood drained from her

face. She knew. These were the same type of pills she'd inadvertently offered to his niece and her guests at the hospital.

Damn.

He had to know, at least to clear Allison in this. "Miss Lexington, do you have any extras of those candies I can take back to the landscaping shop to match the colors?"

Thankfully, Allison spoke up. "Di, you should have extras. These look like the same ones you gave me at the hospital. Remember? You insisted they were just candy."

Blood drained from Diana's face. "It has to be candy, Ally, it must be… I had opened a box and took a few of bags for you, and when Hector found out what box I opened, he got mad."

How mad? He saw Diana touch her left cheek almost subconsciously. Did her heavy makeup hide a bruise? Hernandez was famous for his violent temper.

"Hector told me I can't have any. He's hiring someone to make the wedding favors with the candy, and he doesn't want me worrying about little details like this."

But she didn't sound convinced. More like she parroted words she was supposed to believe.

Through the double glass doors, he saw a car pulled up on the circular drive. Rafe's blood ran cold as he saw Hector Hernandez emerge from the black Mercedes-Benz.

This wasn't good. He hoped Hernandez wouldn't recognize him from the night the drug lord shot him and killed two of his men.

Because if Hernandez did…

Rafe was toast.

Chapter 7

Allison silently cursed, agreeing to this scheme as Diana's future relative strolled into the house. Dressed in khaki trousers, a blue silk shirt and with his graying hair slicked back, he looked like a professional businessman. But something about Hernandez, other than his questionable reputation, always creeped out Allison.

He saw Diana, stopped short. No welcoming smile or greeting. Only a frown, which deepened at the sight of Allison.

His olive complexion grew ruddy as he spotted Rafe. She had to stay calm and collected, play this out. Because her gut warned this was not a man who liked uninvited guests.

And he was smart enough to detect a fed from a mile away.

"Diana." Hernandez spoke with only the trace of an accent. His voice held no warmth. "I didn't realize you were coming over."

"Mr. Hernandez," she began.

"You should have told me, Diana."

Allison lifted her chin and forced a smile. She stuck out a hand.

"Mr. Hernandez, remember me? We met at the engagement party. I'm Allison Lexington, Diana's sister. A pleasure to meet you. I'm afraid this visit is all my doing. I promised to help Di with ideas for flowers for the wedding and some potted plants, and with my schedule this is the only time I could accommodate her. Not that your estate isn't gorgeous enough, but some of the colors Di has for the wedding…"

But he ignored her hand and stared at Rafe, who had pulled his hat low on his face.

"Who are you?" he demanded.

Rafe mumbled something about being the man helping with the design of floral and landscaping arrangements for the wedding.

"Who cleared this guy?" Hernandez demanded.

"He's my friend," Allison countered. "Rafe cultivates exotic flowers and also does landscaping, and I thought he could help with the flowers for the wedding."

"No one sets foot inside my house or on the estate without prior clearance." Hernandez turned to Diana. "You knew this, Diana. I don't care if it's your family or not. My guys need to check out everyone."

Hernandez turned to the man at his side. "Fire those two idiots at the gate who let them inside. Give them their checks and send them across the bay."

For a wild minute she wondered if the two men at the gate would only lose their jobs. Hernandez seemed like the type to clean house thoroughly.

To her alarm, the man turned to Rafe and his gaze narrowed. Rafe calmly lifted his gaze.

"Mr. Hernandez," he said. But his tone carried a slight note of contempt.

Oh dear. Allison knew she had to hustle everyone out of here. Now.

"I can smell a cop a mile away." Hernandez looked Rafe up and down. "Something around here stinks."

Rafe held the other man's gaze, but Allison could see the pulse beating at the base of his throat.

The FBI agent was either scared or furious.

Rafe gave a slow smile. "Maybe it's your cologne."

Big mistake. Her respect for the agent grew, but she saw the look on Hernandez's face.

The man punched him square in the jaw.

Reeling backward from the blow, he managed to hold his stance.

"Where I come from, we treat a man with respect in his home. I don't like your manners, you *cuca*."

Blood trickled from the corner of Rafe's mouth. A bruise was already starting to flower on his skin. But he lifted his head and stared at Hernandez as if the blow were nothing.

"Give me that thing," Hernandez demanded, pointing at the tablet.

A guard tore the electronic tablet from Rafe's hands and gave it to Hernandez. The man scrolled through the photos.

"Matching colors," Rafe said, not dropping his gaze. "Useful for the flower arrangements in coordinating the palette for the wedding. Muted hues will blend seamlessly with the brighter candy colors Diana mentioned for the bridal party."

"Toss this," Hernandez instructed to the guard. He glared at Rafe. "Muted colors my ass. I didn't hire you, and Diana is going to fire you right now."

Allison watched as the guard went outside and tossed the tablet into Biscayne Bay. There went evidence that Hector Hernandez was storing drugs.

"I'll expect compensation for my lost electronic device," Rafe said.

She had to hand it to the man, he had big cojones. Maybe even Hernandez thought so for a nanosecond, for his expression changed as if he were amused. Then his scowl deepened.

She went to Diana and put an arm around her for reassurance. Diana trembled visibly. Her sister always hated confrontations. She was a people pleaser. Naive and never wanted to believe the worst.

If this were my wedding, I'd tell this punk exactly what he

could do with his gift of the wedding ceremony and the cater-
ing. I'd rather get married in a garbage dump than set one
foot near this cretin. Or bring any of my family here.

Hernandez got in Rafe's face. "You have ten seconds to
get the hell out my home before you join your tablet. Only
I'm gonna chum the water with blood to get the sharks here
first so you can make a tasty snack for them."

In silence, they rode back to the parking lot to pick up
Rafe's truck. Diana drove again, but her hands visibly shook.

When they pulled into the parking lot, Allison glanced
back at Rafe. "I need a minute alone with my sister, please."

He nodded and got out. "I'll be over at my truck."

As soon as he left, Allison turned to Diana. "This is the
place where you really want to have your wedding? With a
man who threatens violence? Di, what gives?"

"Hector's not that bad." But Diana looked shaken.

"No, at least he didn't shoot Rafe. Di, please reconsider this
wedding. I'll help you find another venue. It's not too late."

"It is." Her gaze went downward. "I've invested too much
time in this and so has Paul."

"Well, it's your wedding, but damn, between Hector's temper and that nasty housekeeper who called you a...you know
what... Wasn't she the same woman who was at the dress
shop? The one who was nasty to you?"

"She's more than that. She's Paul's ex-girlfriend." Diana
bit her lip.

Allison groaned. "Di! This is bad news. Why the hell is
she working for his uncle?"

"Paul felt sorry for her. After Paul broke up with her and
she moved out of his condo, she was going to be homeless.
Miami is so expensive and she had no place to go. So he
asked his uncle to provide housing for her in exchange for
light housekeeping."

"Di, why would you have the wedding here if Paul's ex is going to be here as well? This is the last place I'd think you'd want to be married!"

"It's a perfect venue. Besides, Hector is giving Lucy the entire weekend off and money to go see her sister in Tampa. She won't be around."

Maybe Uncle Hector should join her. "You sure?"

Diana showed her a cell phone contact. "Positive. When Paul wasn't looking, I got her cell number from his phone. I was thinking of hiring a private detective to track her to make sure she won't interfere with the wedding. As for Hector, well, he cherishes his privacy. It's my fault for not notifying him."

No it's not. But she didn't argue. Allison took a picture of the phone number and name on Diana's cell. She tucked her own phone away.

An older model black sedan pulled into the parking lot. Diana's mood brightened.

"Paul!"

Her sister raced out of the car to greet her fiancé. He turned, then swept her into his arms for a long kiss.

She joined Rafe outside by his truck. "Do we wait here until they're finished or can I leave now?" he asked dryly.

"Come on. She tends to get scatterbrained around him."

Paul stopped kissing Diana as they went toward him. Arm firmly around her waist, he greeted Allison warmly and gave Rafe a curious look.

Rafe extended his hand, his expression neutral. "Rafael." The handshake was brief.

"Nice to meet you. Any friend of Allison's is a friend of mine. Especially since we'll be family soon."

"Rafe was thinking about helping with the wedding. His cousin is a florist." She pointed to the truck.

Paul kept his smile but shook his head. "Baby, I told you, Uncle Hector wants to handle everything, flowers, catering, everything. It's his gift to us. I'm his only godson. I told you this. Why can't you listen to me?"

At Diana's crestfallen expression, Allison wanted to kick Paul. "It's our way of helping, too. It is usually the responsibility of the bride's parents to pay for the wedding."

Diana's fiancé blinked. "Well, I suppose it wouldn't do any harm. I could talk to Uncle Hector. Anything to make you happy, sweetie."

Diana beamed. "I love you, bae."

"I can't wait until we're married. I'm going to spoil you with breakfast in bed and everything you ever wanted."

"All I ever wanted was you."

They cooed at each other like doves. Allison rolled her eyes at Rafe, who seemed to be suppressing a laugh. At least Paul seemed to truly love her sister.

But all this lovey-dovey stuff was driving up her glucose levels.

Rafe held up a hand. "It's all right. It's your day and I don't want to interfere. But if you need my help, be happy to offer it."

Paul grinned again.

Then Paul turned to Diana. "I got you a gift, baby. It's in the car. A little something to celebrate you quitting modeling."

Diana's expression went from sunny to cloudy in a minute. "Honeypie, I told you I want to keep working after we're married. My career is finally taking off and I have all the right contacts."

"My wife doesn't have to work. I make enough money to support you in style." He kept smiling, but Allison sensed an underlying tension.

"I'd best take off," Rafe said, nodding at them.

"Thanks again for offering your help," Paul said, but he was already opening the sedan's door for Diana.

Diana called out to her. "Ally, would you mind taking the Mercedes to my apartment? Thanks!"

Allison shook her head. Once more, Diana relied on her and didn't even ask how the hell Allison was supposed to get home. Or to work.

Uber, here we come.

Paul drove away, stopping beneath a shady tree. Through the passenger window, Allison saw Diana check her phone as she and Paul talked. Then Paul was on his phone.

At least he isn't texting and driving. How many car crash vics have I treated due to that?

Rafe watched them as well after he climbed into his truck. He rolled down the window. Allison touched the bruise on his jaw. "You should have that looked at."

He brushed away her hand. "I'm fine."

With the short beard, Rafe had been handsome and had an aura of a bad boy. This smooth, baby-faced look took years off his face. Not for the first time she wondered about the dangers of his job. Rafe was the type who sailed headfirst into danger.

Sometimes that danger came with the business end of a gun. She sucked down a breath, remembering the cops she'd treated for gunshot wounds in the ER. Allison glared at him, angry he'd endangered himself with his smart-aleck remark to Hernandez.

"You're lucky that pig didn't do worse after what you told him. He's got a lot of pull and no one talks back to him. Is there anything you got on him that you can use?"

"No." Rafe's hands tightened on the steering wheel until the knuckles whitened. The man had control, but barely.

"I can't even get a damn search warrant. My probable cause is now sinking into the water. Useless."

Allison leaned farther into the truck. She wasn't going to let this go. Not when Diana was endangered.

"Rafe, you and I know what was in those cartons. It has

to be the same candy, the wedding favors are drugs! You arrested me for possession of the same thing!"

"No charges were filed against you, Allison."

"I don't care about me, damn it!" Her fingers curled around his bicep, feeling thick muscle and sinew beneath the thin shirt. "It's Diana. I'm terrified of her marrying into this family. You saw how bad Hector's temper is. What if he unleashes it on her?"

"I know. But without any kind of evidence, my hands are tied." Rafe rubbed a hand over his face. "Listen, Ally, do whatever you can to get her to postpone the wedding. Encourage her to elope, far away from Miami. Something's going down the day of the wedding and it could get ugly, fast."

"She won't listen to me. Even my parents won't listen. They think I'm jealous. And you saw how Paul is. She'll do anything for him. It's more convincing him to elope than her." Allison dropped her hand. Never had she felt this defeated when it came to her sister.

Rafe squinted in the bright sunlight. "Jealous? Of what?"

A little tug of resentment pulled her, the same one that flared when she thought of how her parents adored Diana. "Of everything. Diana always was prettier and better than me."

His broad shoulders shrugged. "There's nothing to be jealous of, from what I can see. You have much more going for you."

Allison licked her lips, and there were flutters in her stomach from the unexpected compliment. "She's my little sister. I've tried to convince her to hold the wedding someplace else."

"Try harder." He started up the truck. "I'll do what I can from my end, but that's not much, until I can get some kind of evidence."

He gave a brittle laugh. "Unless I can fish my tablet out of the bay and restore it."

She couldn't help but touch his arm again, feeling the reassuring steel of his muscles beneath his skin. He was alive. They all were.

But it had been a scary close call with a man known for his violent temper.

He looked at her. "Do you need a ride once you drop off her car? I can take you wherever you need to go."

Touched at his consideration, she shook her head. "It's okay. I have the late shift today, and I'll just get an Uber back to my place. It isn't far. What about you? Are you going back to work now?"

Rafe nodded. "I'm going to have to update my director on what happened. Going in without backup, without protocol, well, I blew it."

Having been the subject of a director's wrath a few times for violating the rules, even though she'd saved patients' lives because of it, Allison knew what Rafe faced. Despite herself, she worried about him.

"Anything I can do to help?"

"I can handle it."

His dark gaze flicked to her and his expression softened. "I know you're worried about your sister. The wedding isn't for another month. Take her out of town on a vacation. I'd separate her from her beloved fiancé, and once you get her alone, talk some sense into her."

Rafe turned to look at the nearby car where Diane waited. "Guess we'd better continue with the show in case they're watching."

He framed her face with his hands, his fingers long and calloused. Rafe kissed her gently, barely a kiss, but it sent awareness zinging through her.

A five-second kiss from this man felt better than the tongue-dragging sessions she'd had with former lovers. It made all her nerve endings tingle and filled her with sensual longing.

"And Ally?"

Her heart fluttered faster, from the brief kiss combined with the nickname only a few close friends and family called her. "Yeah?"

His gaze narrowed. "You have a habit of making me lose all common sense and screwing things up. Do me a favor and stay far, far away from me."

Stunned and annoyed, she stepped back as he climbed into the truck and roared out of the parking lot.

Chapter 8

Ordered to take a leave of absence. Rafe blew out a breath as he checked over his motorcycle. He hated screwing up. Hated it even more because the agent in charge at the field office was right.

He'd gone undercover without backup or teamwork. And now he was certain Hernandez was checking him out. Rafe had destroyed the ID and everything associated with the fake identity. Still, he had to watch it.

He could have totally blown it. Or gotten killed. Hurt Allison and Diana.

"Stupid, stupid," he muttered in Spanish.

Letting Hernandez get the best of him wasn't his style. He'd always managed to be calm and cool under pressure.

But all he could see when looking into Hernandez's face was the laughing image of Sofia, ready to slip a deadly pill of fentanyl into her mouth.

A nightmare image of Sofia lying pale and still on the ground as EMTs tried to revive her and save her life.

Sofia, rushed to the hospital. Allison coming into the waiting area shaking her head, no they couldn't do anything more for his beloved goddaughter.

Sweat streamed down his back as he polished the chrome on the bike. Three weeks suspension with pay. The annual

Teddy Bear Run was in a few days, and he'd already arranged for vacation, but still…

This bit the big one.

When had he become reckless? Hernandez, yeah, he could blame it on the man, but deep down, Rafe knew there was more to it.

He examined his conscience and found a certain trauma nurse named Allison staring back at him. Allison, whose sister was marrying into that family. Allison, who loved her sister and would do anything for her.

Emotions had gotten the better of him.

His cell rang. Rafe smiled as he looked at the caller. Jason, one of his teammates, who'd risked his own life to take down a dangerous gang of jewel thieves.

"Hey, Jase."

"Heard what happened. Sorry, man." Jase sounded sympathetic. "Anything I can do while you're gone?"

"I'd tell you to keep an eye on Hernandez for me, but you have your own case files. How's Kara?"

"Terrific. She finally set a date for the wedding. Six months from now. You're coming of course."

"As long as it's not at a certain drug dealer's mansion on Starfish Island," he muttered.

"Far from it. Kara's parents have money, but not that much, and Kara wants something low-key. Intimate. A few family and friends."

"Congratulations. I'm happy for you."

"So when are you gonna find someone and settle down?"

"Who are you, my nana? I get enough nagging from them. Go focus on your own wedding."

"I will. But Rafe, life isn't only the job. One day you're gonna wake up and wonder what happened."

He rubbed the scar of the bullet wound. "Don't I know it. So you and Kara aren't coming on the ride?"

"Sorry, man. Too much wedding stuff. Maybe next year."

"If you both aren't expecting." He grinned, genuinely happy for his agent. "Keep in touch and let me know what's going on."

He hung up and pocketed his cell phone, feeling a ping of regret. Jase, married. One of his best agents now committed to someone other than the Bureau.

You need to do the same.

Maybe this ride would help clear the muck out of his head.

Sliding the black helmet over his head, he slipped onto the bike and roared out of his complex's parking lot. The hospital wasn't too far from his condominium, and traffic was fairly light this time of day.

One advantage of being suspended with pay—he had plenty of free time to visit his nana.

Inside the hospital he retrieved a visitor name tag, handed over his driver's license for them to copy and then, when they handed it back, went upstairs. Elena had been at the hospital since her collapse. The doctor said she suffered not a heart attack, but some technical term that meant she needed a cardiac catheterization. She'd had the procedure done yesterday and they kept her overnight, watching her.

The antiseptic smells triggered bad memories. Lying in a hospital bed, listening to the machines beep by his pillow, wondering how long he'd remain in bed.

Wondering who the angel was who'd saved his life. All he remembered was a quiet whisper, a firm, professional hand, and then he'd fallen unconscious. When he'd finally awakened, he was lying in ICU, a few of his family gathered around his bedside, crying with relief as he opened his eyes.

The door to Elena's room was open. He popped his head in, expecting to see one of his family members.

The family paid for Elena to have a private room. Dozing

off, his grandmother opened her eyes as he came inside. She brightened and struggled to sit up.

"No, no, stay still. I'll help you." Rafe rushed over and helped her sit, adjusting her pillows. He kissed her paper-thin cheek. "Tita, so good to see you. How are you feeling?"

"Bored. I want to go home."

"Where is everyone else?"

"Gone, I sent them away. They were nagging too much. Rafey, can I go home today?"

"Soon. I think you may go home by tomorrow. I have to check with Mama and your doctors."

The door to the bathroom opened. Rafe's mouth opened in shock as Allison strolled into the room. She saw him, narrowed her eyes.

Yeah, well, couldn't blame her for that. He had not been nice to her upon their parting.

But she plastered on a wide smile for his grandmother. "I thought I'd find these in the bathroom cabinet. Open wide," Allison instructed. "These mouthwash swabs are refreshing until you can brush your teeth."

Allison swathed his grandmother's mouth with something that looked like a giant cotton swab dipped in mouthwash.

She threw out the swab as Elena licked her lips. "That feels wonderful. Thank you, Allison."

"What are you doing here?" he asked her, frowning.

"The same as you. Visiting."

Rafe ignored her and squeezed his nana's fingers gently, relieved at the color on her face.

"Elena is a tough cookie." Allison smiled at the woman. "She comes from strong stock."

"Like my Rafey." Elena patted Rafe's hand. "He's a strong man. Handsome. And he's single. Very single."

Heat crept up his neck. "Stop playing matchmaker, Tita."

"She's a nice girl, this Allison. Smart and pretty. Nice fig- ure, too. Why don't you ask her out," Elena told him in Spanish.

He hoped Allison didn't understand that much Spanish. He glanced over, saw pink suffuse Allison's cheeks. Yeah, she did.

"Concentrate on resting and getting better, Tita." He ad- justed her pillow again. "Stop worrying about me."

"I always worry about you, Rafey. I will go to the grave worrying about you."

"No more talk of graves," he said lightly, continuing the conversation in Spanish. "Do you need anything?"

"I need you to stop running around, trying to save the world." Elena sighed. "Maybe if your papa hadn't died in the line of duty, you would have joined your mother in the family business instead of going into law enforcement."

Dumbstruck, he stared at his grandmother's knowing ex- pression. "What... Why..."

"I'm old, Rafey. Not stupid. I've been living long enough to recognize the symptoms of a son who struggles with a..." Elena's head turned toward Allison.

"What do you call it in English when a son worships his father?" she asked Allison in English.

"Hero complex?" Allison suggested.

Elena beamed. "I told you she was smart, Rafey. Yes, hero complex. You wanted nothing to do with the bakery business. You only wanted to follow in your father's footsteps and you ignored the family."

Truly red now, he sputtered, feeling the stinging truth of Elena's words. "I didn't ignore the family, Tita. And my brother also didn't choose to work in the bakery."

"Ah, but you were the youngest and missed him the most. You were only twelve when he died. I always worried about Carmela marrying a police officer, more than I worried about her marrying a non-Cuban. I feared the day he would never come home. You worshipped him more than anyone else."

This was unsettling. Did Elena have to share his whole damn childhood with Allison?

"I never ignored my family," he protested, drawing his hand away from his grandmother.

"You may not have ignored us, Rafey, but you chose the company of friends who were different. Look at that Jason, your friend. He became an FBI agent like you." Elena sighed. "I don't know who influenced whom."

"Long time ago, Tita. I always wanted to be an FBI agent. It had nothing to do with my father."

"Why did you become an agent?" Allison asked.

"It's personal," he grated out. Rafe glanced at his grandmother. Was today pick-on-Rafael day?

"You were there the day I graduated from the academy, Tita. You seemed proud. You never voiced an objection."

The woman sighed and plucked at the bedcover. "Because you were happy. That is all I ever wanted for my children and my grandchildren—their happiness. It's the same reason I did not forbid Carmela from marrying your father. Oh, Pedro, your grandfather, raged enough about her marrying an American and a police officer. But I knew my daughter. She was in love, and she has a stubborn streak same as you."

"I am not stubborn."

On the other side of the bed, he saw Allison raise her eyebrows and smirk.

"Well, maybe a little. But all for good reasons. You are so much like your father, Rafael. Everything is about the job and nothing left for family."

Ouch. That stung.

"And everyone else isn't focused on their careers?" he asked with a touch of bitterness.

"They have a good—what do you call it in English? Work-life balance. Their families come first."

Elena gave him a censuring look as if to state the obvious. *You don't have a wife or children.*

His grandmother turned to Allison.

"Rafey is dedicated to his job, the same as you are, Allison. Another thing you have in common. Except you save lives and he risks his. But I think you both would balance out your differences."

Oh hell no, his grandmother was setting him up? Rafe bit back a groan.

Maybe he should make a smart-ass remark about going on Tinder to find dates. But his grandmother had already suffered heart trouble.

Pink once more suffused her cheeks. Allison smiled at Elena. "I'll leave you now to get some rest. I have to go. If you need anything, press the nurse call button. I asked nursing administration to put you on the VIP list. They agreed and now they'll be sure to check in on you more often."

"Thank you." Elena's eyes closed. "I am rather tired. Rafey, would you mind walking Allison out?"

Cagey Tita. As his grandmother turned her head, he caught a slight smile.

Rafe kissed her forehead and bid her good-night. Outside her door, he gestured to the elevators.

They walked together. He became fully aware of the delicate floral scent emanating from Allison. Shampoo? Probably. Allison didn't seem the perfume type, unlike her sister. As a nurse, she'd also be cognizant of patients who were allergic to scents.

Her thick brown hair tumbled past her slender shoulders. Rafe's discomfort grew as he remembered busting into the women's room and catching her making a phone call, clad only in scrub bottoms and a bra.

Scalloped lace had edged the cups.

Enough of this. He scowled and punched the elevator button.

"Thank you for visiting my tita, but you don't have to look after her. You're a trauma nurse." He didn't want to feel obligated toward her. Hell, he didn't want to feel anything toward her.

Tell that to the part of you that keeps wanting to kiss her every time she draws near.

"It's no big deal. I like Elena. It's rare I get to save someone and see them after. Usually I'm bouncing from hospital to hospital."

"You're so dedicated to your profession." He punched the elevator button again.

"I was."

For the first time he realized she wasn't wearing scrubs, but jeans and a purple T-shirt. A visitor pass, same as his, was clipped to the shirt. Allison saw him stare and shrugged as the elevator doors opened.

A woman in pink scrubs stepped out, saw Allison and flinched. "Allison, what are you doing here?"

His companion turned as pink as the woman's uniform. "Visiting. I'm allowed to visit patients."

Compressing her lips, the other woman shook her head. "You should leave before the COO finds out. It's not good for our image."

Allison scowled. "What happened to presumed innocent until found guilty."

"You know what I mean. You're no longer on staff here."

Allison stepped into the elevator. Rafe joined her. The doors closed on the woman's grim face.

"You got fired?" he asked.

"Yes, Captain Obvious. Nursing admin said I violated the terms of my contract. The agency I work for is not happy with me, so I'm taking a break. I got yeeted out of here when admin found out you hauled me away in handcuffs for possession of fentanyl."

"You were released and no charges brought against you."

"Well, gee, Rafe, image is everything, isn't it?"

"I'm sorry."

She shrugged. "I can always find another job. I wanted to take time off for the wedding anyway, and to relax a little."

As the elevator doors opened to the lobby, he turned to her. "Good luck with your life," he said, meaning it.

He needed to stay far away from Allison Lexington and her troublemaking sister.

If he never saw either one of them again, it would be for the best.

Chapter 9

Every year for the past five years, Rafe had participated in the annual Teddy Bear Run to raise money for a well-known children's hospital. Riders throughout the South donated five hundred dollars for the event and received a plush teddy bear to give to the young patients. The event brought together bikers across the South.

His Harley growled into the parking lot of the Happy Times Diner. Rafe cut off the engine and waited. The owner of the diner was a big supporter of bikers and police. Rafe was first to arrive.

Rafe pulled off his helmet.

Samson Hendricks, Deputy United States Marshal, was next. Rafe raised a hand in greeting and adjusted his leather gloves.

"Hey." Sam switched off his bike and pulled off his helmet, his thick brown hair tumbling out. Rafe teased him about his girl curls. Soon, Sam would be back on duty and get a haircut.

"You back from your parents place?" he asked Sam.

Sam nodded. "Love it there, but not enough to transfer. Though the family keeps nagging me to turn in the badge and come home to the ranch."

Rafe understood that kind of pressure.

"How's it going, Rafe? Heard about the suspension from Jase."

"Been better. Looking forward to this, getting out on the

road." Rafe studied the way Sam used his left hand. "Finish with PT?"

Sam flexed his fingers in the leather glove. "Almost as good as new. New physical therapist in Miami is better than the one near my parents' ranch. Ready to roll."

Sam had a close encounter with a knife three months ago while serving a warrant. The suspect, wanted on an active felony warrant for a firearm, responded to the knock on his door with a twelve-inch butcher knife. Sam's fingers paid the price that day, but therapy helped.

The suspect was shot and, after being treated and well enough to be released, went to jail and is now awaiting trial.

Rafe rubbed his neck where the bullet nearly nicked his artery. As vice president of the Justice Riders Motorcycle Club, he recruited other law enforcement bikers needing an escape from the job. Every rider in the Justice Riders was law enforcement, active or otherwise. Most had survived violence on the job. Rafe needed a support system with other brothers in blue who rode and understood his love of bikes and the job, and the trauma that came from surviving extreme violence.

"How many are with us today?" Sam asked.

Rafe consulted his phone. "Nine in our group. You, me, Keith and Deb, Lou and Darla, Casey and two others joined at the last minute. Casey texted a couple of days ago she's bringing them in, said she would introduce them. Two women named Di and Al."

"Cops?"

"No, but Casey vouched for them. Plus, this is a different kind of run, every penny for charity, so I said yes."

Sam grunted, his green gaze alert. "Hope they know how to ride and won't slow us down. You make contingencies for the newbies?"

Giving a leisurely stretch, Rafe shook his head. "I'm not a

babysitter or a damn chaperone. If they can't keep up, they're on their own."

Rafe organized the ride for the Justice Riders and invited no more than ten riders in his group on the way to northern Georgia.

A couple pulled up on their bikes. Keith and Debbie Myers. Keith was a retired sheriff's deputy and Debbie still worked as an oncology nurse.

He wondered if Debbie knew Allison. Nurses had a tight-knit group much as cops did. Rafe tried not to think of Allison and the hurt look on her face as he'd driven away from her or the way she'd glared at him when he left his grand-mother's hospital room.

The woman was bad news for him. He tended to lose focus when she was near, and during this business with Hernandez, he shouldn't have lost focus.

Their dog, Comet, rode in a sidecar with Keith. The mongrel terrier had goggles on his face and was securely fastened into the seat by means of a harness. He grinned at Comet. Comet was a rescue the couple had adopted two years ago and en-joyed several adventures riding with them across the country.

Today the couple seemed quiet and even Comet subdued.

"What's wrong?" he asked, joining them as they parked their bikes. He bent down and scratched Comet's head. The dog's tongue lolled out.

"Darla and Lou won't be joining us." Keith's expression tightened. "Lou got hurt last night. Responded to a domestic violence call to save a victim."

Rafe went still. "How bad is it?"

"He's alive."

The terse answer told Rafe everything. He touched his neck again, anger and grief coursing through him. The risks of the job, but damn, it seemed they were losing the war to keep the public safe.

Was it worth it?

He watched Debbie slide off her bike and put her arms around her husband. After twenty-five years on the job, Keith had retired after being shot during a hostage situation. He'd spent four months in ICU and retired when he was released from the hospital.

This was one of the reasons Rafe hesitated in settling down. He had been to too many funerals, seen too many grieving widows.

"Casey canceled, too. She's not going when her partner is in ICU. " Debbie wiped at her eyes.

Rafe called Darla, but her phone went to voicemail. He left a message.

Whatever Darla needed, they would provide.

He hung up, wishing he could cancel everything and go to Lou's side. But Sam watched him, shook his head.

"You can't do anything, Rafe. Lou's solid. He'll pull through, and Darla has plenty of support."

"Yeah, she does. And we all need this ride." Keith hugged his wife back. "Let's do it. For Lou."

Rafe nodded. Their little group was down to four now. "We can hit the road now, make it to the first stop by noon for lunch. I've got reservations for all of us in the same motel in south Georgia where we stayed last year, off the interstate."

Comet barked. He petted him. "Yeah, it's pet friendly, bud. All the hotels on the way take dogs."

"What about the newbies?" Sam asked. "The ones Casey was bringing?"

"Casey gave them directions to the restaurant. They should be here soon," Debbie said.

Frowning, Rafe glanced at his cell. "If they're not here in ten minutes, we're leaving. No time for stragglers."

Though the day was warm and sunny, perfect for riding, the air carried a hint of a cool breeze. Rafe glanced to the west. Storm might be rolling in after noon. Best they hit the road now.

As he was about to give orders to roll out, two motorcycles pulled into the parking lot.

His heart skipped a beat or two as he recognized one of the women as she pulled up to a stop and pulled off her helmet.

Al was Allison.

This was not going well. Though she'd planned for a luke-warm welcome, this frosty silence from Rafe warned her they weren't welcome.

She threw Rafe a pleading look as he narrowed his eyes. His Harley was a big touring bike, dark blue and gleaming chrome with a sizeable wind screen, saddlebags and even a luggage rack, where he'd strapped down a large backpack. It looked perfect for long road trips.

A burst of jealousy shot through her as she imagined the road trips he took with girlfriends, long rides through the country, maybe making love under the stars…

Everyone kept staring at her. Embarrassed, she recovered. "Casey said we could ride with you." She lifted a hand to the other bikers. "I'm Allison Lexington and this is my sister, Diana."

They introduced themselves. Sam was a deputy US Marshal and Keith was a retired police officer. Only Debbie wasn't law enforcement. At least she had something in common with Debbie.

Diana looked wary. "You're all cops?"

She was quick to add, for Diana's sake, "Di, you remember Rafe? My friend who owns the landscape company?"

Diana frowned. "Of course I do. I thought you guys broke up."

Heat suffused her cheeks. Sam said nothing, to her relief. Surely the others knew Rafe did undercover work.

Rafe did not look overjoyed to see her.

Sam looked interested as he studied Allison. "How do you know Case?"

"We go back a couple of years. She got wounded on the job and I treated her."

"Wow," Sam murmured. "You're that nurse. The one who treated all those cops at the shoot-out on Bird Road."

Rafe scowled. "If you're done socializing, we need to get on the road before that storm rolls in." He gave Allison a level look. "First stop is Arbor Beach at the cultural center. They'll have snacks and a cash bar. But no drinking alcohol on this trip until we reach the hotel for the night."

Allison couldn't resist. "Yes, sir. I downloaded the map of all the planned stops on my cell."

"We'll take a break about three hours from here for lunch."

The guy named Sam with the gorgeous brown curls squinted. "Rafe, I thought you wanted to get to only the planned stops in order to make time."

"Well, I changed my mind," he snapped.

Glancing at Diana fiddling with her phone, Allison felt a surge of relief. Rafe did this for her sister. He probably suspected Diana wasn't going to last more than three hours without a break.

"Before we leave, here's the rules one more time. We ride in staggered formation, single file, on all roads except the interstate. Sam takes the lead in the left part of the road, Keith and Debbie behind Sam at the right, Diana behind them on the left and so on. Allison you ride in front of me. I'm in the rear."

"I've never ridden in staggered formation," Diana said. "Must we?"

Allison wanted to groan. She turned to her sister. "Staggered means every rider can see upcoming obstacles and maneuver if necessary."

"Or if a car decides to cut into your lane," Keith chimed in.

"Or if there is road debris," added Debbie.

Comet barked, as if even the dog understood.

Rafe nodded. "Use the usual hand signals to let us know if you need to stop, slow down, if you're running out of fuel. You know the drill."

To her relief, Diana smiled. "Paul taught them to me. Left hand tapping at your helmet means police ahead."

All the others stared at Diana. Allison cleared her throat. Couldn't her sister ever read the room?

"I'm not real fond of getting pulled over by cops," Diana said.

Leather creaked beneath his oh-so-fine butt as Rafe leaned back in his bike seat. "None of us are, which is why we don't speed."

This was going south, fast. "Di, you remember the other hand signals? The other ones you said Paul taught you? Like raising your left arm up and down to indicate you're speeding up, or left arm waving over your head that says you need to pull off," she said.

Diana nodded. "Those, too."

Mirrored sunglasses masking his eyes, Rafe looked neutral. He continued.

"Stay together. Have a problem with your bike, signal your partner, who will signal me."

Sam started to open his mouth, saw Rafe's slight head shake and shut it.

"No cell phones, texting. No calls on the road, only in an emergency. No speeding up unless you signal. No brake checks. We ride, rain or shine. Slow traffic or an accident— no breaking off from formation, unless Sam does, and deciding you want to ride in the breakdown lane or between cars to make time. If you have an emergency, call me or Sam. Our numbers should be in your cell phone."

"That's a lot of rules," Diana complained.

Allison glared at her. "Di," she muttered.

Rafe's gaze remained steady. "My group, my rules. Don't like it? You can go off on your own."

"We should get going," Allison said, desperate to bring peace between her sister and Rafe.

"Let me get the bears first. Lou picked them up for us. They're inside."

Rafe slid off his bike and went into the diner. He emerged with a bag. When he opened it he handed out the teddy bears, all wrapped in plastic.

"Lou had a hard time getting them because this year it seems a different guy is organizing the bear dropoffs, so please don't lose your bear."

All six bears were wrapped in plastic. All were dark brown.

Diana shook her head. "We already got our bears."

Plastic crinkled as Allison removed a bear from the pack tied to her bike with a bungee cord. Soft and tan, it was double-wrapped in cellophane and seemed to grin knowingly at her.

Rafe frowned. "Where the hell did you get those? That's not part of the plan."

"Well, we improvised because we were running late." Holding up the toy, Allison looked at Rafe. "We picked them up at a designated spot close to home to save time."

His mouth tightened. "Fine. Sam, can you return these two bears inside?"

As the other biker ran toward the diner, Rafe pointed to her seat. "You can't ride with the bear in the open like that, Allison. The bears are supposed to be hidden until we take them out for the photo op in town."

Terrific. She glanced at Diana, who shrugged. "I don't have room, Ally."

Everything was crammed in her saddlebags and her back-pack, including some of Diana's clothing. *Maybe if you hadn't taken so much makeup and outfits.*

Watching her, Rafe shook his head. "I have room. I'll take both."

"Thanks." She handed him both bears and watched him stuff them into a saddlebag.

He swept the others with a stern look as Sam climbed back on his bike. "Keep the bears hidden in your packs until we go to the rally. Then we tie them on the front of our bikes when we meet up with the others. It's a huge photo op for the charity and awareness."

They started up their bikes and roared out of the parking lot. Muscles tensed, she tried to relax. Usually she loved long rides like this, especially before the weather turned hot and the sun too intense.

Allison's thoughts tumbled like socks in a dryer as they rode north on I-95. She'd seen that scowl on Rafe's face. No time to talk in private and explain. Maybe later, at the hotel.

More than a year ago, when Diana pestered her to take her on one of her motorcycle trips, Allison agreed, only if Diana would learn to ride her own motorcycle.

Diana had taken classes with Paul's encouragement. Paul had a crotch rocket himself and often spent weekends riding. He even bought Diana a bike. The Honda Rebel he'd bought had a low seat and lower center of gravity, which made it easier for petite Diana to handle. The bike also allowed for saddlebags for Diana to store her clothing and cosmetics. It was smaller than Allison's big Harley. Money was no object. Allison swallowed her slight jealousy at the thought.

The important matter was separating Diana from her fiancé's family, especially dear Uncle Hector and his drugs.

Or his suspected drugs. But more and more Allison knew Rafe had just cause for his investigation.

She hoped Diana could keep up on this trip, for Rafe seemed impatient.

Chapter 10

Once on the interstate, she was glad Rafe made Diana ride in front of her. To her relief, her sister kept up, not deviating. Maybe the rides with Paul had paid off.

Aware of Rafe behind her on his big Harley, she began to take in the scenery. Soon they left behind the urban landscape and came to the wide, open green spaces north of West Palm Beach. Tree farms peppered the roadside. Cell towers stretched skyward. Some people thought Florida boring and dull apart from its pristine sandy beaches and turquoise waters, but Allison did not. She enjoyed the wind rushing past her, the variety of palm trees flanking the road like a phalanx of tropical soldiers, and smelling the fresh air and occasional earthy, clean smell of water from ponds. Yellow wildflowers peppered the swale separating north and south-bound lanes. Once in a while, she spotted a deer or rabbit in the fields off the interstate.

An electronic sign overhead warned motorists to look for motorcycles.

Passing motorists slowed down to look at Comet riding in Keith's sidecar. One car rolled down the window and a camera stuck out, snapping photos. Allison grinned.

As Rafe promised, they stopped at a fast-food restaurant off the interstate. Allison went into the women's room while Diana made a call, walking around the parking lot.

"Ten-minute break," Rafe warned.

When she emerged, he followed her to her bike. *Here it comes.*

She glanced at her sister, chattering away. Probably Paul. The diamond Diana sported on her ring finger winked in the sunlight.

She held up her hands. "Before you lay into me, this was the only way I could get Diana away from Miami. And Paul's family."

Rafe's expression remained neutral. "Why this ride?"

"I talked her into a last-time sisterly adventure before she settles down."

He looked different in the black leather jacket, black T-shirt, faded jeans, engineer boots and mirrored sunglasses. He'd grown back his short-trimmed beard as well. Stubble was a sexy look on him.

Bad boy Rafael. Well aware of her stirring female interest, she tried to focus on Diana.

She glanced at her sister talking on her cell phone. "Diana turned down all my other suggestions. She wasn't going to do this until I begged her to join me so we could spend time together."

Rafe bent down to examine her bike. "Nice job on lubricating the chain. Did this yourself?"

"Of course."

"Why not take her away on a weekend to Saint Kitts?"

"Who has money for that? If I had a choice, I would go somewhere else instead of doing this trip with you." Allison glared at him. "But this was the only option, the only way I could get her to come away with me. I'd already gotten the time off and signed up with another group, but yours had the only openings for two riders."

"Lucky me." Rafe stood up. "I'm not babysitting either of you."

"I don't need a damn babysitter. If she falls behind, I'll take care of her."

"I don't trust your sister."

Allison grit her teeth. "I'll take care of her."

"Who takes care of you? Seems you've always been taking care of her."

"I can take care of myself, and it's none of your damn business."

"It is my damn business if she's associated with Hernandez."

"Diana doesn't do drugs, either recreational or pushing them. I will vouch for her."

He pushed his aviator sunglasses up his nose. "She's marrying into a known family of a drug kingpin. You tell me, Allison. If she's so innocent, why did she get upset when I looked into those boxes?"

Allison started to answer, saw Diana approach and inclined her head. "We should get on the road."

When Diana got on her bike, Allison pointed at the phone. "Who were you talking with?"

Diana's eyes widened. "Just a friend."

When had her sister gotten so covert and sly? Allison felt a sting of hurt, shrugged and climbed back onto her bike.

Two hours later they arrived at the first official stop of the Teddy Bear Run. The town of Arbor Beach's cultural center had thrown out the welcome mat to all bikers on the run coming from South Florida. At least two hundred bikes parked in the driveway and on the grass before the building. A canopy tent shaded women standing behind a makeshift bar serving cold drinks. Chips, pretzels and cookies were arranged on platters on a long folding table beneath another canopy. Though it wasn't yet the heat of summer, Allison appreciated getting out of the sun. She felt slightly lightheaded.

Maybe the heat was getting to her. Or the stress of worrying about her sister.

After getting a chilled can of cola, she went to join Diane on one of the chairs set up beneath a sprawling banyan tree. While Debbie walked Comet and gave him a drink of water from the collapsible bowl she carried, Rafe and the guys in their group mingled with other bikers. Some of the bikers wore denim jackets bearing the names of biker gangs with members of law enforcement.

How long before Di realized Rafe wasn't really a landscaper, but a cop himself?

Hopefully she could get her sister to Georgia and eloping with her beloved long before Diana even suspected.

Not that Di disliked cops. But she didn't want Di blurting out to anyone in Paul's family that the man at his uncle's house had been a cop.

Diana excused herself to talk on the phone. She was lucky. She had Paul.

Sometimes Allison got so lonely the only cure was to slip onto her bike, ride off and feel the wind against her face. Feel alive again, feel some kind of belonging, even if it was only for a little while. On her bike, there was more than freedom and the feeling of flying.

There was escape from the dark thoughts tumbling through her mind. Surely there had to be more in life than traveling the country, working to save lives that often couldn't always be saved.

Lately she'd wondered what it would be like to settle down like Diana. Find a man who treated her like a queen, or at least didn't treat her like crap. Get married, have someone to belong to, who belonged exclusively to her.

"Too bad you have to marry the family as well," she muttered, fiddling with her long braid.

"Hey, stranger!"

Startled, she looked up and saw a biker dressed in denim, faded jeans and a white T-shirt. His face was ruddy from the sun and the smile he gave her was welcoming. Average face, brown hair a little too long, but not bad.

For a split second, confusion gripped her. Then he sat in the chair Di had vacated and sighed.

"Wow, Ally, you sure know how to hurt a guy's feelings. That night we spent wasn't that memorable?"

Heat suffused her face. She rolled the cold soda over her forehead and finally it clicked.

"Dan Johnson. How are you?"

"Doing mighty fine, now that you're here."

Dan. Nice guy, zealous about his bike and always on the make for women. They had gotten drunk together at last year's Teddy Bear Run and…

Well, she was usually careful about the guys she slept with, but he'd caught her during a vulnerable moment. She'd just come off an intense cell phone convo with her mother gushing over Di's latest success in modeling, and how she was dating a multi-zillionaire who recently bought a nineteen-million-dollar mansion on the Intracoastal, and Di's boyfriend invited them all to some fancy party for the Air & Sea Show at his condo on Miami Beach…

No amount of liquor could quell the hurt inside, or the slight resentment of her younger, more successful sister. But tumbling with Dan between the sheets had chased away the feelings that, despite her career, she was riding to nowhere, fast.

"We never did get that second date." He winked at her.

Allison sipped her soda. "You know that was over soon as it began, Dan. I told you last year, let's remain friends. Nothing more."

"I know. But you can't blame a guy for trying, not with a woman like you, Ally. You need a guy on the road to look after you." He patted her hand in a patronizing way that almost made her smack his fingers.

"Allison," she said curtly, pulling away her hand. "I need a man like my bike needs a flat tire."

He looked confused. "Why would your bike need a flat tire?"

Good gravy, this was pointless. Using metaphors to politely tell him to get lost was like explaining an aneurysm to a toddler. Well, not exactly. At least the toddler wouldn't be condescending.

"I can help you with your bike, check it over. You need to make sure you have enough coolant and transmission fluid before you get on the road," Dan told her.

"Really?"

Seeming to sense an opening, he began droning about the proper care of her motorcycle. Allison bit back a sigh. Last year she'd told Dan she did all her own maintenance. Seemed he'd forgotten about that, along with her insistence they could be only friends without benefits.

Rafe, in a group of other bikers examining a vintage Triumph motorcycle, glanced her way. His gaze lingered on her for a minute, then he pointed at Dan and gave a thumbs-up and a head shake.

You okay, he was asking.

Allison shot back a thumbs-up, nodded and smiled, not to reassure Rafe, but in remembrance of the special sign language they'd developed to communicate when she worked as his confidential informant last year. Sometimes Rafe would be at the biker bars where she hung out with the Devil's Patrol, just to check on her.

Suddenly she realized in all the times he'd checked on her, it wasn't because Rafe doubted she could get the job done.

Or that she needed rescuing.

It was simply to be there in case she needed him. Otherwise he'd back off.

His attitude was refreshing, especially compared to mansplaining guys like Dan who thought no meant yes.

Rafe was a rarity—a man who respected women enough to leave them alone when they wanted to be alone.

I don't want to be alone, though. Not when I'm around Rafe.

Was this sexy Cuban American sending her heart into overdrive? Jump-starting an engine that had gone cold?

Nope. Rafe and his hot guy vibe, charm and underlying tone of respectful concern had been making her heart race like a speed demon all along. This was only the first time she'd been fully aware of her feelings.

This can't happen to me. I can't fall for a guy like Rafe, who can easily break my heart. I'm a solo rider.

"Ally, did you hear me?" Dan waved a hand in front of her face.

She pushed off the chair and drained her soda. "I heard you. Now hear this, Dan. Thanks for the lecture on bike care. I'll keep it in mind when I lube the chain on my bike. Have a great ride and rally."

Chucking the soda can into a nearby recycle bin, she headed for her bike. Forget socializing. It was safer to avoid people and indulge in reading.

Fishing a book out of her pack, she brought the paperback over to a spot next to her sister, beneath a shady tree. Allison cracked open the spine and began to read.

A tap on her shoulder. "Ally, why are you shutting everyone out like this? There's plenty of men here to meet." Diana shook her head.

"Already met one and have no desire to meet others," she muttered, trying to focus on the page.

"Books can't help you with relationships."

She held up her tattered copy of *Animal Farm*. "Oh? They open your eyes to the world around you, Di. Give you a deeper perspective than the one you already have. You know, more than fashion magazines and wedding books."

"I have that book you gave me, Ally. *The Help*. I planned on reading it during this trip. I don't want to read children's books about goats and sheep."

Allison grit her teeth. "*Animal Farm* is far from a children's book. You can borrow it if you want. I've already read through it. Reading a book might take your mind off your wedding stress or your damn cell phone."

Diana scowled. "My 'damn cell phone' is my connection to Paul. He's worried about me on the road. He thinks I can't take care of myself and wants me to call him every time we stop."

"Guy thing." Allison set the book down. "Do you have to check in with him all the time? Doesn't he trust you?"

"He trusts me. He worries about me, Ally. And he thinks I should be home helping with wedding plans."

Something in her sister's voice told her there was more to the story.

"Di, you know, maybe a big wedding isn't a great idea. You've been to huge society events. They're impersonal. It's your day. Don't you want to be the star attraction at your own wedding?"

"Yes, but…" Diana rubbed a spot on her shiny blue helmet. "Paul says we owe it to Uncle Hector to have a lavish wedding. He doesn't want to hurt his feelings."

"What about your feelings? Your marriage?"

Diana started to open her mouth, then shook her head. "Topic closed, Ally. Why don't you focus on your own guy problems?"

"I don't have any."

"Oh?" Diana pointed to Rafe.

"Him?" She debated. Diana would find out soon enough.

"He's not a boyfriend, Diana. I only wanted you to think that so you'd take us to see Hector's mansion. I wanted to impress him. He's always been curious about the lifestyles of the rich and famous."

And drug dealers.

As Diana smirked, she added, "Besides, Rafe isn't interested in me."

"Oh, I knew you weren't dating and it was an excuse. You never mentioned him before. But if he's not interested, why does he keep checking you out?"

Her gaze flicked over to Rafe. Stunned, she realized Rafe was eyeballing her with much more interest than the sleek motorcycles at the center. Then she realized he was staring at her sister, and her heart gave a little pang of disappointment.

"It's not me, it's you he's checking out. You're the one all men stare at."

"Maybe." Diana shrugged. "You don't give yourself enough credit, Ally. You're smart, funny and attractive. You should go out on more dates. Find a nice guy."

"I don't need anyone." What was it about people thinking she needed someone?

"I know, I know. You're busy with your career. I get it. But Ally, you're my big sister. I worry about you. And next time you want a favor for a guy you're trying to impress, don't go to such extremes. I would have been happy to ask Uncle Hector for a tour of his house for you and Rafe."

Does that tour include where he stashes all his fentanyl?

Her little sister whipped out her cell phone. "And speaking of tours, it's time for me to post."

Allison rolled her eyes. "On your Insta?" She waved a hand at the phone. "Or your finsta, so Paul can see what you're up to?"

Di's finsta account was private, only for family and friends.

Like her parents, Allison had been added. Sometimes she even shared photos for Di to post.

"Paul isn't on my finsta. He doesn't know about it."

Allison tried to conceal her shock. "Why? Di, you're marrying the guy and you don't even let him know about your fake Instagram account for family and friends?"

Di shrugged. "I figure after we're married, I'll shut it down, make everything out in the open. That account is my way of keeping my private life private."

Private from the man she was supposed to trust and love? Allison started to ask, when Diana brought the cell phone closer.

"Hey, everyone! It's Di and I'm here with my big sister, Ally!"

Allison forced a smile and waved.

"We're on the road for my bachelorette party, heading out with a big gang of handsome and sexy bikers."

Diana did a quick sweep of her phone, showing the bikers. "I'll be posting more from the road. Remember to check my account for exclusive, behind-the-scenes content! Till later. Remember, you're the beauty inside and out!"

She signed off. Allison sighed. "You could have given me a warning and I'd have had my makeup done and my hair styled."

"Quit the sarcasm, Ally." Diana beamed as she pressed buttons on her phone. "Now it's posted to my Insta and my Jump ONit account. Do you know I have about ten thousand followers?"

I could care less. I care more about the fact you're hiding stuff from Paul. Why? Allison made a mental note to comb through Di's finsta account and see exactly what she'd been posting that she didn't want Paul to discover. Lately, she'd regarded Di's social media activity as amusing, a way for her sister to keep in touch with a small fan base who followed her fledgling modeling career.

"Are Paul and Uncle Hector two of them?" Allison asked.

Frowning, her sister finally set down the cell phone. "Stop making fun of them. Uncle Hector isn't the bad guy everyone thinks he is. He's maligned."

Maybe she could make Di see reason. "Di, Uncle Hector isn't a saint. Far from it. I've read the articles and heard the rumors about drug deals…"

"Nothing was ever proved. Stop it, Ally. He's Paul's god-father, and I won't have you talking crap about him. Or try-ing to convince me to call off the wedding simply because you're jealous."

"Diana, I'm…"

Too late. Her sister stormed off toward her bike. Allison hugged her knees. Less than five hours into this trip and al-ready it was turning into a disaster.

She had to find a way to drill sense into Diana and make her see reason.

Before it was too late.

Chapter 11

They rode for another few hours before stopping at a service plaza where Rafe had arranged a stop for gas and lunch. He gave them forty-five minutes, but said if they could cut it to thirty they'd make better time.

Allison had seen the ominous storm clouds to the west and agreed with him. Riding in the rain, even with proper gear, wasn't fun, and oil slicks made it hazardous, not to mention bad drivers prone to sudden swerving.

She volunteered to stay with Comet, who wasn't allowed inside the service plaza, while the others headed off.

Allison hooked up Comet's leash and walked him around the grass.

Diana pulled off her helmet and stretched, walking over to Allison. "Ally, do you have any money for lunch?"

Sighing, she pulled out forty dollars from the wallet in her waist pack. Another thing—her sister didn't like waist packs. Allison always had one to carry her valuables wherever she went riding. "Here. Get me a water and a sandwich. Anything but something hot. No hamburgers or meatballs."

Diana waved the money. "Be right back."

When she finished walking Comet, she handed the leash over to Debbie. The others had emerged with lunch and drinks. Rafe sat at a picnic table with Sam and Keith. Dressed in leather jacket, jeans and biker boots, Rafe looked sexy.

Hot. Allison felt herself staring. Rafe's gaze tracked her as she sipped her bottle of water. She ignored Rafe's scrutinizing look.

A twentysomething man ambled up to their table, hands stuffed into his pockets, looking around.

"Hey, you guys on those bikes?" The kid pointed to the motorcycles nearby.

Keith nodded.

"Cool. I thought so." The kid glanced around and lowered his voice. "Know where I can score some good weed?"

Allison nearly spit out her sip of water.

Sam and Rafe exchanged amused looks. Sam stood, hitching up his jeans.

"No, but if you do find some, let me know."

He pulled out his US Marshals badge.

The kid turned whiter than Diana's wedding gown. "Um, ah…"

"I'd like to know as well," Rafe said, showing his FBI identification.

"Sorry, I was joking man, just kidding."

They laughed as the teenager ran off as if the hounds of hell were pursuing him.

"If you'll excuse me, I think my outlaw wife and I will find some grass for Comet before we hit the road."

"Grass, not weed," Debbie chimed in. "Make sure he poops, too."

Keith winked. "The way she's demanding of me is criminal."

Rafe laughed and watched them head out. Sam stood up and nodded at Allison. "Think I'll stretch my legs as well."

Allison took the seat Sam vacated. The spicy scent of Rafe's cologne scented the air like an aphrodisiac. Why was she such a sucker for guys with a faint hint of cologne, scruffy day beard and tangled, dark hair that looked like he'd recently climbed out of a bed?

"That kid... Unreal." She shook her head.

"Biker stereotypes." Rafe rolled his eyes. "I can't tell you how many times on the road someone thinks I'm a bad boy because I ride a bike and wear leather, or how many drooling women cling to me like barnacles. And here I am, single, my only company a stuffed bear sitting on my lonely bed."

Allison had to laugh at the image. "Maybe you should have taken the teddy to breakfast and that kid wouldn't have asked you about drugs."

Rafe grinned. "Didn't want to ruin my image of the sexy, bad biker."

She gestured to his glass. "You already did, rough rider, with the chocolate milk. Milk isn't exactly sexy."

His grin widened. "That's what you think."

He sipped, leaving a slim milk mustache. About to point it out, Allison watched as he slowly licked the liquid off his upper lip. The deliberate gesture was teasing and provocative.

Still, she found herself more turned on than irritated.

Pretending otherwise, Allison took a big gulp of water. She glanced around, desperate for a diversion. Maybe the weather.

"Think we'll run into rain?"

Rafe wiped his mouth with a paper napkin. "I bother you, Allison. I can tell."

"Of course not," she lied.

"Liar," he said softly. "Your pulse kicked up, you're sweating a little and you keep avoiding my eyes."

She blushed. Lordy, she'd been chilled before but now her body felt like a furnace. At a loss for words, she shrugged. Suddenly her water bottle seemed fascinating. The way they'd stamped the logo on the label...

"The real question is how do I bother you? Annoying

bother? I think not. Bother in the way a woman is bothered by a man she's attracted to…"

"Attracted to you?" Her laugh sounded fake even to her ears. "I'm not going to sleep with you, Rafe."

"Did I suggest us sleeping together? I was thinking more along the lines of a first date, not in bed, but a restaurant." Rafe's gaze caressed her like a lingering stroke.

"Like this one? How romantic." She waved a hand at the service plaza.

Suddenly he frowned. "Speaking of food, where's your lunch?"

"Diana promised to get me something…"

Diana finally emerged from the building, carrying a sandwich. "Here."

Allison unwrapped the sandwich.

Meatball parm. Biting back her irritation, she debated. Eating this would give her indigestion all day.

She handed it back to Diana. "I'm not hungry. Where's my drink?"

"Forgot. Sorry."

Diana shrugged and ate Allison's sandwich, walking away to talk on her cell phone between bites.

The sisterly bonding this trip wasn't off to a great start.

Giving Diana a thoughtful look, Rafe went inside. He emerged from the service plaza, a paper bag and a bottle in hand. He handed it to her.

"Turkey on whole wheat, tomato, lettuce, light mayo. And a wild cherry sports drink." His mouth twitched. "I remember from that time when I took you to lunch."

She peered into the bag with delight. Her stomach rumbled.

How was it this man knew her preferences better than her own sister who she'd grown up with?

She gulped down a bite.

"Slow down or you'll get sick. And I'm not a nurse."

"You said we had to leave in forty-five minutes. Don't have much time."

"I'll make time for you," he said softly. "Eat."

Such consideration warmed her. "I remember that lunch. You gave me the ultimatum—work as a confidential informant for you or go to jail for aiding and abetting a criminal. Even though I didn't know he was a criminal and I was only treating a gunshot wound."

"You treated him."

"I'm a nurse. What do you expect?"

His mouth twitched again. "Take your time with your sandwich."

She drank some, polished off the sandwich in a few bites and balled up the wrapper.

"You eat faster than I do," he said.

"Like I said, I'm a nurse. I don't get much time to eat on the job. Sometimes I get so busy I can barely gulp down a meal, so when I do get a break, I take advantage of it."

"Unlike your sister." He inclined his head at Diana, still walking around the parking lot and talking on her cell, ignoring everyone else.

Allison drank her sports drink, eyeing him. He looked anything like a cop, which could be a good thing. Wind ruffled his hair. Her gaze traveled over the waistband of his jeans, caught a glimpse of a holster.

"Do you always carry?" she asked.

Rafe nodded. "Especially on the road."

"The others do the same? Concealed?" She gestured with the sandwich at Sam, scrolling through his phone, and Keith and Debbie, playing with Comet.

"Always."

Her gaze went to Sam's bike and the shotgun holster attached to it. The chrome holster gleamed in the sunlight.

Noticing her stare, Rafe pointed. "Sam's a deputy US Marshal. That's a legal Remington TAC-14. Department uses short barrel shotguns for witness protection and moving witnesses."

"Didn't know Sam was moving a witness on this trip."

"He's entitled to carry protection. Open roads can be dangerous. Cops know this more than anyone else, Allison."

A shudder raced through her. "Short barrel shotguns are easy to conceal. Guess that's why Sam likes his, but you can see he means business by carrying it on his bike."

"His weapon is part of him. Like mine." Rafe patted the hidden holster on his belt.

"I don't like guns."

"Probably because you've treated too many GSWs."

Surprised at his insight, she nodded. "Gunshot wounds are the worst, especially a high-powered gun like an AR-15. The damage is… "

Falling silent, she drank more sports drink, her appetite vanishing. Like all those other times in the emergency room after treating victims of gun violence, trying desperately to save them and failing.

"Devastating," he finished softly. "Vital organs shredded. Yeah, I've seen a few too many crime scenes. And no matter what weapons we carry, the bad guys always seem to be better armed."

He tilted his head. "You're an enigma, Allison Lexington. You're a trauma nurse. You don't like guns because you've seen the result of gunshot wounds, yet you ride a motorcycle."

"That's different. I love to ride, love the thrills and the freedom I have with being on the open road. I control the journey as best as I can and I never take risks on the road. Sometimes after my contract ends, or is terminated at a particular hospital—I work as a travel nurse—I'll take off for a few days to see the rest of the state."

"That can be risky for a single woman."

He sounded almost protective.

Allison shrugged again. "I always watch my back and I carry this."

His eyes widened as she removed the switchblade from her pocket and depressed the button. Sunlight dappling the trees winked on the six inches of steel.

Rafe laughed. "You would bring a knife to a gunfight. You think a knife is effective protection?"

"When you know what organs to hit to cause damage and then give you a chance to run, yeah." She folded back the blade. "I wanted to get a ballistic knife, but those are illegal."

Rafe's expression tightened. "They can pierce a cop's body armor. Drug dealers like them as much as guns because the blade is expelled with force up to sixteen feet away."

"I know." Allison swallowed hard, thinking of the case she'd treated. "Guy I had in the ER back in New York was a cop shot with one of those. A few inches lower and it would have hit his heart."

They both fell silent for a moment, as if digesting the wrath of violence they'd both witnessed in their respective jobs. Rafe gestured to her sister.

"Does your sister know anything about what you do?"

"Diana?" She couldn't help her slight laugh. "She's a model. Her world is about glam and social media and being an influencer and growing her fan base."

Rafe watched Diana, the sensuous way she flung her long hair, the sway of her hips as she walked. Her sister always commanded attention.

All those times in high school when she'd shown interest in a boy and then dared to bring him home, either to study or watch movies. Diana, her baby sister with the beautiful face and winsome ways, made the boys fall at her feet.

It was a fact of life. Allison was the smart and plain daughter and Diana the beauty. But damn, for once she'd like a guy to pay attention to her, really see her worth, not her sister's.

Rafe wasn't a guy Allison could date. He was too dangerous, too involved in a job that would always come first. Yet she couldn't help her attraction to him.

Then she realized Rafe wasn't watching Diana the way other men did, with an appreciative gaze roving over her lithe body and lovely face. His gaze was speculative.

Like a cop watching a suspect. It amused and alarmed her.

"No wonder Hernandez likes her. He always likes pretty women as decorations."

"She's not a decoration."

"But she is marrying into that family." Rafe narrowed his eyes. "Diana has to know what Hernandez is all about. No matter how clean her fiancé is."

"Paul's okay. He's head over heels in love with her. And she loves him, so I guess love is blind, for her, anyway."

"You don't want her marrying him."

"Yes and no." There it was, out in the open. "I think she's rushing into marriage, and I hate the fact Paul's uncle is Hernandez. Forget about the rep with the drugs and criminal activity. He's slimy. When I met him at Di's engagement party, he kissed me on both cheeks. I had the urge to sanitize my face."

Rafe's mouth quirked. "I can only imagine how distasteful that was to you."

He gestured to Diana walking away from Sam, who had joined Keith and Debbie. "Your sister has barely said two words to anyone other than you. For someone who's always on social media, she's being quite antisocial."

"She misses her fiancé." It sounded lame.

Rafe walked her over to the trash can. "You always make excuses for her?"

"It's not an excuse, it's the truth. I had to talk her into coming with me. Our family has a cabin near the bike rally, and

Diana wanted to see it one last time before she gets married. She needs the alone time."

"And what about your needs, Allison? When do you think of yourself?"

The question stung. It sounded almost like an accusation, but looking at him, his gaze was kind.

She shrugged. "Later. I'm trained to put the needs of others before myself."

"Work is one thing. What about your family?"

That hit too close to home. Allison drained her water. "What about you, Special Agent Rodriguez? Your job? Your family?"

"Supervisory Special Agent Rodriguez," he corrected, but with a smile. "We're talking about you, not me."

"You're Cuban, so I bet you have a family who is always in your business."

"Half Cuban."

"Aha. There you go."

"What?" He frowned.

"Most Cubans say they're Cuban. They're proud of their heritage. They don't say they are half Cuban, even if they are. At least the ones I've met. They may say they're Cuban American." Allison gave a long stretch. "Your nana said your dad was American. A cop who died on the job. That has to have an effect on you."

His entire demeanor went from friendly to ice-cold. "I don't want to talk about him. It's getting late. Let's roll."

As she barked at Diana to get on her bike, Allison donned her helmet and started up the Harley. She'd hit a nerve with him. So Mr. Supervisory Special Agent Rodriguez had a vulnerable spot when it came to his family.

Don't we all? Sighing, she followed Rafe out of the parking lot and back onto the highway.

Chapter 12

At the motel in North Florida, they checked in and were assigned their rooms. Allison arranged to share a room with Diana. Diana wanted her own room, but the motel was fully booked.

They'd barely spent a day together and all Diana had done was complain.

Dinner was on their own. Dead tired from the ride and worrying about Diana, who had barely kept up with the others, Allison opted for takeout at a chicken restaurant next door.

Her sister protested, again, wanting to try the Asian fusion restaurant down the road. Allison waved at her. "Go off on your own. I've got a headache."

Diana unpacked her belongings and arranged all her cosmetics on the bathroom counter. She began to brush out her hair.

"I'm so windblown, and I need to do another vid for my fans. I thought I'd do one on my bike," Diana called out.

Rolling her eyes, Allison touched her braid. "You need to tie back your hair, you ding-a-ling. You should know that from your rides with Paul."

"Paul doesn't go this far. He only takes me on back roads where we can go slow."

Allison stretched out on one of the beds and closed her eyes. Soon she heard the door slam behind her sister.

When Diana roared off on her bike, Allison walked over

to the fast-food restaurant. As she emerged, bag in hand, she saw Rafe and Sam eating at an outdoor table.

Sam waved her over. "Join us."

For a moment she hesitated. "I don't want to interrupt. Looks like guy time."

Sam laughed. "Cop talk. All gruesome. We could use an interruption."

Mindful of Rafe studying her, she swung a leg over the picnic table bench and sat far from him, but next to Sam. "Shop talk in my line of work is equally gruesome. I'm a traveling trauma nurse."

Sam whistled as Rafe kept eating. "I have healthy respect for trauma nurses. Especially after what happened to me."

He showed her his right hand and the two fingers with scars ringing them. "The nurse made sure one of the guys put my fingers on ice after they were severed. I went first, didn't wait for my team to back me up."

"You're such a cowboy," Rafe murmured, shaking his head.

"Yeah, tell that to my fam." Sam winked. "They're still waiting for me to return to the ranch."

"Let me see." She examined Sam's fingers. "Nice work. You had a good surgeon. And good PT."

He wriggled his fingers. "Guess what they used after he reattached my finger?"

"Leeches." Allison had seen this in her work. "They draw the blood from the hand to the reattached finger faster. It sounds and looks gross, but they're effective."

"Human leeches are worse," Rafe said, sipping his drink. "Like drug dealers."

Though she tended to agree, Allison remained silent, choosing to eat her food. She didn't know Sam, didn't know if the man had already formed opinions about her sister.

"Where's your sister?" Sam asked.

"She wanted a real dinner. I wanted some time away from

her." Allison sipped her drink. "I love her, but sisterly love only goes so far."

"Especially when the sister is in league with a drug kingpin," Rafe murmured.

She slammed down her drink. "Damn it, I didn't want to get into this with you, Rafe. Can't I even have dinner without you harping at me?"

"Simply stating a fact. You know I'm right."

"My sister is not a drug dealer."

"Never said she was. But she is marrying into that family." He leaned forward. "A family you'll become part of as well."

Anger and frustration boiled inside her as she stared at Rafe's calm expression, tempted to toss her drink into his face, except it was good lemonade and she didn't want to waste it.

"You're so arrogant."

"And you're acting foolish, Allison, and you're no fool."

Sam looked back and forth at them. He slid out from the picnic table. "This is where I'll say good-night and goodbye. I don't get involved in lovers' squabbles."

"We're not lovers," she protested.

"Could've fooled me." Sam winked and walked off.

She rubbed her temples, the headache growing worse. "Did you have to tear into me in front of him? I have enough on my hands."

His expression grew sympathetic. "Migraine?"

"No, just a tension headache. It's the riding."

To her shock, he left the table and came in back of her. Rafe lifted her braid and began massaging her neck. Strong fingers kneaded the tired muscles. She wanted to tell him to stop, she was fine, always she was fine, but damn it felt so good.

Felt good having someone else care for her needs for a change instead of her always seeing to everyone else's welfare.

"You're tense. Relax," he murmured. "It's not the riding. You're an experienced biker. It's all this worrying about your sister."

Moaning, she hung her head forward as he kept working her muscles. The man was a pain, but he knew how to massage away stress.

Bet he knows how to do something in bed equally as well.

Allison lifted her head and murmured thanks as he returned to his seat. She ate her dinner as he finished his drink.

"Ally, you can't deny Diana is in the middle of a dangerous situation."

"She's in love and I can't convince her otherwise. She's determined to marry Paul. It's a tough situation."

He leaned forward. "Then put the tough situation to good use. If she's truly innocent, convince her to get evidence on Hernandez to put him away for good."

Nearly choking on a sip of her lemonade, Allison sputtered. "Are you for real? You want my sister to rat out Paul's uncle? Not exactly a great way for her to start out her married life."

"She's our best shot at taking him down. No one can get close to him. You saw for yourself. All we need is evidence he's smuggling fentanyl and I can obtain a search warrant…"

She saw where this was headed and her temper rose. "You want to use my sister to get the glory of the arrest, the headlines. FBI man nabs known drug dealer. You'll do anything for your career."

His dark eyes flashed a rising fury as well. "I'll do anything to bring down that murdering asshole and make Miami safer for innocents. It's what I do, Ally."

Allison saluted him. "Yes, sir, Captain America."

"Call me whatever you want, but you know you'd do the same if you were in my shoes."

Wadding up her trash, she headed for the garbage can. "Not a chance. I don't use people to get what I want. Leave my sister alone."

She felt the weight of his gaze burn into her back as she headed back to the motel.

* * *

For all her agitation about the conversation with Rafe, Allison still managed to sleep. When she awoke, her headache had vanished. But Diana still slumbered. Allison almost regretted sharing a room with her sister.

Despite the animosity between them, she couldn't help her fascination and interest in Rafe. She daydreamed about inviting him to her room for more than a pajama party. Maybe a glass of wine or something more.

Much more. But not convos about her sister.

She showered, shivering in the cold water that awakened her faster than the hot coffee waiting in the lobby. In minutes she braided her hair, dressed and went to the buffet breakfast in the motel lobby.

Ignoring Rafe and the others, she chose a seat far from them.

Diana followed her a few minutes later, yawning. She frowned at the array of food set out for guests.

"Not much choice," she told Allison.

"Not all of us can afford a five-star breakfast at a waterfront restaurant," she muttered.

Heading into the restroom to splash cold water on her face, she left Diana to muse over the selections.

By the time she fetched a plate of food and balanced it with her coffee, Rafe and Sam were tossing out their garbage. Rafe nodded to her.

She watched him walk out the door, the way his jeans hugged his oh-so-fine butt. The man had killer looks.

Watching her from the table, Diana snickered. "I think I know what you really want for breakfast and it isn't eggs and sausage, but a different meal packaged in a nice pair of jeans."

Allison scowled. "Stop it. Eat your breakfast."

"Come on, Ally. Be human for a change and climb off that

pedestal and admit you want him. Or at least his bod. He's got a terrific bod and he's super cute."

Stung, she sipped her coffee. "Rafe and I are just friends, and I am not on a pedestal."

"Can't convince me of that. Everyone puts you on one, Ally. I've seen how they worship you."

"Our parents?" Allison ate some eggs. "You're the one who gets all their attention."

Diana's mouth turned down. "Right. They always worried I'm going to screw up again. Not you, the perfect daughter. And I've seen how your coworkers respect you, Ally. How they all look to you, even that ER doctor."

This was news to her. Allison drank more coffee and took a long look at her sister, seeing more than her perfect body, her astonishing good looks.

She set down the cup carefully and reached for Diana's hand. "Jellybean, are you okay? Do you love Paul?"

Moisture glistened in her sister's eyes. "Yes, I mean, of course I love him. I'm marrying him, right?"

Not a good answer. "Hon, if you want to back out, it's not too late. No one will think bad of you. It's your life."

Diana stared at her plate, her long hair curtaining her face. "It's not really my life, Ally. I can't screw up again. Not this time."

Now she felt truly confused. "Screw up? You, the perfect daughter?"

"Perfect?" Diana shoved at her plate. "You're the perfect one, the smart one with the 4.0 GPA who got a scholarship, and went on to get your master's as a trauma nurse practitioner. I'm the pretty, stupid daughter who Mom and Dad thought would never amount to anything much. Not like you."

Whoa. "You're not stupid, Diana."

What happened here? All this time she'd thought Diana

had everything, doted upon by their adoring parents. She'd been wrong, so wrong.

Misery etched her baby sister's face as she raised her head. "I can't afford to screw up again, Ally. I have to go through with Paul... He's good to me and loves me so much. He has business connections, he helped get me this new modeling contract in South Beach. I owe him."

"Owing someone is no reason to get married, jellybean. Love is."

Diana brushed at her face and waved a hand. "I love him, I really do love him. I just don't want to botch this marriage and look like a fool again."

Allison frowned. "You're not a fool, Di. And it's your life, not anyone else's. I want to see you happy."

Her sister squeezed her hand. "I know. I love you. You always have such good advice."

Troubled, she squeezed back. "Whatever you need, Di, I'm here for you."

"Anyway, can you give me a minute alone? I don't want those guys to see me unraveling. I have to keep up appearances."

"You can be yourself with me, hon."

A smile touched her wobbling lips. "I know. I love you, Ally. I do. But sometimes, I wonder...if it had been better you never reached me that day in the river."

Mouth dry, she stared at her sister. Diana had never talked of that day, and certainly not like this. *I saved your life and now you're wishing I didn't? What is going on with you, Di?*

"I... I... Jellybean, don't say such things!"

Her grip on Diana's hand tightened. "Your life is important, honey. You mean a lot to people. To me. I'd do it over and over again. You mean everything to me. Have you talked to anyone about this? You can talk to me. Say anything to me."

A slight laugh. "Oh, I don't really mean it. It's the wedding stress talking. I don't need therapy, Ally. Everything will be fine once Paul and I get married."

But she knew something more was going on. Allison rubbed her thumb over Diana's palm. "Big weddings are stressful, and this one seems over-the-top. Why not elope with Paul?"

"I don't know…"

Encouraged, she pressed on. "Call him. He loves you, Di, and wants to make you happy. Have him meet you at the cabin and ship your gown and everything up there. Mom and Dad will be thrilled."

Diana looked doubtful. "Mom was looking forward to a real wedding."

"It will be a real wedding, only this time Paul's uncle won't be in charge."

"Hector has been so wonderful and generous. He won't be happy."

"Forget him." Her voice carried an edge. "It's your life, Diana. Paul's family doesn't run your life or his."

"It isn't like that. Hector wanted to throw us a beautiful big wedding because Paul knew I wanted a dream wedding and our parents couldn't afford it. He'll feel terribly put out if I change things at the last minute."

"Paul?" At Diana's head shake she sighed. "Come on, jelly-bean. Who cares what Hector thinks? The only two people who really matter in this are you and the man you're marrying. If you're willing to give up a fancy big wedding that will cost thousands…"

"More than one hundred thousand, if you count my wedding gown."

Stunned, Allison blinked. "Okay, that is a lot of money. But the wedding is one day. Marriage is supposed to be for a lifetime. You have to assert your own needs if you want this relationship to last."

Diana looked troubled.

"Think about it, while you're taking your alone moments. Don't take too long." She gave her sister's hand one last squeeze.

Trudging back to the room, leaving Diana to have her alone time, Allison scuffed the heels of her Dr. Martens against the grass. Why did she even bother? Diana wasn't going to change her mind about marrying Paul.

As she started for the door, instinct kicked in.

Tired as she was, Allison knew she'd pulled the curtain shut across the door before leaving. Diana hadn't returned to the room and the privacy sign hung on the hallway door.

But the curtain was ajar. Allison swallowed hard.

The door was open. Certain she locked it, she pulled it open slowly and pushed back the curtain.

Everything was in disarray. Suitcases opened, contents strewn over the floor. No, only one backpack had been violated.

Hers.

Diana's pack lay untouched on the counter. Her makeup was strewn haphazardly over the desk as it had been last night and this morning.

Allison sucked in a breath as she searched the empty pack, saw her panties and spare bra scattered over the room. Shame and anger roiled in her stomach. Her pretty lace bra had been stepped on.

Her little electronic tablet that she carried to check email and enjoy movies was smashed to bits on the nightstand. Even her little travel pillow she always carried was ripped to shreds.

Her mouth wobbled with grief. This didn't look like burglary. Too much rage.

Diana's designer eye makeup and expensive cosmetics were untouched.

Allison rubbed her face, staring in disbelief. *I know I*

locked the door. I did. And Diana went out after me, did she forget to lock it?.

She checked her waist pack. As always, she'd taken her valuables with her to breakfast. Her clothing was scattered, but the sensor she used to detect cameras in a room was missing.

That and… She did a thorough investigation. The two teddy bears were missing, and then she remembered Rafe had offered to carry them since she was tight on space, having to cart some of Diana's belongings.

Allison walked outside, groaning. Last thing she needed was a break-in.

Rafe, who had the room next door, was walking out to his bike. He saw her distress, immediately ran over.

"What's wrong?"

"Someone broke into our room. Nothing's missing, far as I can tell, but it's a mess. None of Diana's things were touched, but my clothing…"

Her voice broke.

He placed his hands on her shoulders. "Stay out here."

Withdrawing his gun, he stepped into the room. Allison followed.

"Whoever did this is long gone, Rafe. They didn't take anything. But why do this?"

From the bathroom, he called out in a grim voice. "I know why."

Allison went into the tiny bathroom.

The small bottle of suntan lotion and pancake makeup she had on the counter crowded with Diana's things were smashed, the contents squeezed out.

But more disturbing was the message on the mirror written in Diana's expensive red lipstick.

TURN BACK ALLISON BEFORE IT'S TOO LATE.

Chapter 13

More than ever, Rafe wished Allison hadn't joined them on this trip. That message on the bathroom mirror was a grim warning, but for what, he didn't know.

Her sister's belongings hadn't been touched.

Allison insisted on cleaning up and not calling the police or telling her sister. She scrubbed the lipstick off the mirror as he silently helped pick up her clothing off the floor.

Rafe held up a pair of fire-engine red panties with lace. Nice. Under normal conditions, he'd tease her about them.

Instead he stuffed them into her backpack.

Much as he disagreed with her not calling the authorities, he understood. As he picked up shards of her shattered electronic tablet, he vowed to keep a closer eye on Allison.

Somehow he knew this vandalism was connected to her sister.

By the time they finished, he saw Diana approach on the sidewalk and he whistled to Allison.

She emerged from the bathroom and immediately embraced Rafe, looking up at him with a smile.

Again, the act. Pretending they were lovers. Too bad it wasn't real.

The door unlocked. Instead of releasing her—damn, she felt amazing in his arms—Rafe simply glanced at her sister.

"Pardon," he murmured. "Didn't realize you'd be back so soon."

Interest sparked on her face. Diana shrugged. "I can leave if you two need more time."

"We're fine." Allison wriggled out of Rafe's firm embrace. "We should get on the road anyway. Go get ready. I'm all packed."

She walked with him outside. He hated that this happened to her, and he worried about her. Allison was a gutsy woman, but a break-in like this, a targeted one, had to shake her.

"Why didn't you want to tell her?" he asked gently.

Allison sighed and pushed at her long braid. "Because my focus remains on getting her to elope with Paul, far from his family. How can I do that if she knows someone broke into our room?"

He gave her a level look. "Is someone after you, Allison? It's odd her things were not touched."

A deep sigh. "I'm not sure. There is a guy who I blew off at the first stop on this ride. His name is Dan Johnson, and we rode together last year."

"That guy you were talking with at the cultural center? Friends or lovers?"

The blunt question made her cheeks pink. "More than friends, but after one night, I told him it was over. I reminded him again yesterday I wasn't interested. He wasn't happy. I think he wanted to reignite our relationship. Not that we really had one."

Why did he feel relief Allison wasn't interested in that guy at the center? Rafe knew his feelings went beyond the job.

He needed to focus on the job, not his male interest in Allison Lexington.

"Who knew you were going on the Teddy Bear Run?"

She fingered the end of her braid. "Nearly everyone."

Rafe thought hard. Chances were it was this Dan Johnson,

but anyone could find out Allison's location with a few questions about the riders and their routes.

"But Dan Johnson thought you had a relationship, and he had a chance to score again, until you blew him off. And he knew you were riding with my group, so he knew you were staying here."

Most of the group leaders listed the itinerary of their rides and shared motel information in case someone got stranded.

Allison continued to play with her braid. "It was probably him. He must have seen us talking. He might be jealous of you."

"Because he thinks, like Diana does, that we're lovers?"

An inhalation of breath, dilated eyes and a galloping pulse suggested she liked the idea. Rafe's blood stirred at the thought. He couldn't deny the attraction between them.

Acting on it was another matter. Allison had been off-limits last year while working as a confidential informant. Now? He couldn't risk any personal feelings for her.

Then she shrugged again. "Maybe."

Giving her a searching look, he shook his head. "Regardless, I'm sticking close by you. This kind of personal attack could happen again."

"Are you saying we should share a room?" Her comment came with biting sarcasm.

"If we did, you know what would happen," he said softly.

Allison's breath hitched again. "Thanks for the offer, but I'll be fine."

"And I'm riding right behind you. Sam will take the lead and you'll be next to last, in front of me."

"Rafe…" She gave a little laugh. "You weren't so concerned last year when you made me a CI. You had faith I could handle those guys."

"That was different. This attack was personal, directed only at you. That message on the mirror had your name on it. I don't want you in the back of the group, just in case who-ever did this gets behind you."

He hoped she would follow reason. The thought of Alli-son alone on the road, with some jealous nutcase after her, perhaps finding her alone at a rest stop, made him worried.

More than other women he knew, Allison was so indepen-dent she'd refuse help for the sake of her pride.

Pride could easily get her hurt, or worse.

To his relief she nodded. "Okay. I get it. If Diana wasn't with me, I'd go off on my own. Get it? I'm not one for fol-lowing rules."

He rubbed his neck ruefully. "I know. Who is this Dan? What does he do?"

Never one to miss anything, Allison shook her head. "Why? So you can do a background check and start ques-tioning him? If it is him, I'll handle it. It's my business."

"And it's my group, and I make it my business to ensure everyone in the group is safe for the duration of this ride."

Maybe because she was tired, she finally capitulated and told him. "Last I heard, he worked as a welder for Markey Brothers Construction in Oviedo, Florida."

Rafe made a mental note to check into this Dan and ques-tion him about his whereabouts. If Dan was following Allison and did this, well, Dan would find himself on the receiving end of a little old-fashioned justice. If it involved Rafe's fists and Dan's mouth, well, so be it.

The thought made him nearly laugh. Rafael Rodriguez, straitlaced FBI man turned rogue biker.

"Good. Get your stuff and we'll leave in ten."

The weather held off for them through most of southern Georgia, but when they were south of Atlanta, Rafe radioed to Sam to take a break at the next rest stop.

Indigo storm clouds gathered north of them. As they pulled

off, Rafe squinted at the sky. Time for rain gear and getting the hell off the interstate. He'd changed their route, sticking to the busy highway instead of the smaller and prettier back roads because chances were this Dan Johnson would take the less traveled route.

But now the hazards outweighed everything else. Even if they rode in the slow lane, avoiding the middle of the lane to skirt oil slicks, the traffic would grow worse around Atlanta.

Traffic was always bad around Atlanta, and Rafe didn't want their little group breaking apart due to impatient drivers weaving in and out. With this threat to Allison, he'd make sure to check his mirrors to see if anyone followed them.

He made a quick call to Jase, asking him to find out everything and anything on Dan Johnson.

By the time everyone emerged from the restroom and they were donning their rain gear, Jase called back.

"Hey, Rafe. One Dan Johnson, background check. Guy is clean. No arrests, not even a traffic ticket. Pinged his cell phone and he's riding through Atlanta now."

Rafe's mouth curled into a smile as Jase gave him the number. He thanked him and hung up.

Next, he dialed Dan Johnson's number.

"Who is this?" Johnson demanded.

"Never mind who this is. I'm on the Teddy Bear Run and I have questions about Allison Lexington. I'm riding with her. What are your intentions toward her?"

A short laugh. "Intentions? None. Allison? Nice chick, but too independent for me. I like them needy."

"Where were you last night?" Rafe asked.

"What's it to you, dickwad?"

"Answer me or I have a few friends in law enforcement who will make certain you will stay stuck in Atlanta traffic, asswipe."

He could almost hear Dan swallow his own spit. "I was

staying at the Dollar Night motel in Lakeland City. Listen, buddy, I have no intentions toward Ally. She's a friend, nothing more, and she made it clear about that last year. Last night I picked up a chick in Gainesville and we spent the night together. I can give you her number…"

Rafe hung up, pondering.

Sam, sitting next to him on his bike, looked amused. "Girlfriend problems with Allison? Or potential girlfriend problems?"

He palmed his cell and scowled. "Allison's room got broken into this morning while she and her sister were at breakfast. Ally thought it was this Dan Johnson she had an affair with last year on the Teddy Bear Run, but the guy swears he was with another woman last night."

Sam dropped the smirk. "Damn, Rafe. You believe him?"

"I do. I don't know if I believe Allison, though. I think she used this Dan as an excuse to keep me from questioning her further about who could have trashed her things."

"Why?"

After listening to his quick summary of the problems with Diana and her impending marriage, and Allison's quest to push her sister into eloping, Sam scowled. "Let me know what you need from me, Rafe. You know I'm here for you."

Her sister was proving to be more high-maintenance than she'd ever anticipated.

Diana admitted she returned to the room while Allison was getting breakfast and "may have forgotten to lock the door."

Well, that explained how someone broke in. *They walked inside*. Allison grit her teeth as she followed Diana in single file as they rode north on the interstate. Checking her mirror, she saw Rafe directly behind her.

Usually she resented being shadowed, but his presence on

the bike felt reassuring. Diana may have been in blissful disregard for her sister's welfare. Not Rafe.

It felt good to have someone looking after her needs for a change.

The leather seat beneath her cushioned her bottom and the bike's throaty rumble reassured her. She focused on the road, trying not to think of who targeted her.

Dan Johnson wasn't the likely burglar. Dan was always on the prowl and probably found someone else to warm his bed. She'd only tossed that name at Rafe to get him off her case. Allison groaned as she realized her mistake. Rafe was thorough. He probably already used his FBI sources to track down Dan.

It might have been one of the other guys she'd ridden with last year. The possibilities were endless.

But why would someone trash all her belongings and then write a warning for her to turn back?

Chapter 14

Rafe made the executive decision to push farther ahead instead of stopping for the night. He told their group at the next rest stop. It wasn't as much to make up for lost time.

He wanted to put as much distance between Allison and the threat left on the bathroom mirror.

How many times had someone threatened her while at work? Someone who had lost a loved one, or helplessly watched a spouse in a coma, and blamed her because of the outcome?

Rafe began to understand why she chose to become a traveling nurse. No attachments, no bonds to either friends or a particular hospital.

Work at one place and move on.

Almost like running away from her problems.

When they finally stopped for the night, he asked Sam to watch over Allison as she sat in the bar, drinking a soda. Rafe checked into his room and made a few phone calls.

No progress yet on the Hernandez case. His director had assigned Jase to take over and Jase told him they had nothing yet. He looked at the teddy bears he'd brought into the motel room.

Rafe arranged them on the other double bed and studied them.

A short time later, he joined Allison and Sam at the bar

and ordered a bourbon on the rocks. Sam glanced at him and grinned.

"I'll leave you two alone. Gonna grab some z's. See y'all tomorrow," he said, sliding off the stool.

Rafe sipped his drink, enjoying the burn as it slid down his throat. He seldom drank on the road, but today rattled him.

"You are a bad ass, know that?" he asked her.

She stirred her drink. "I don't feel like one."

"You handled the trashing of your room as if it were nothing. If you'd have been any cooler, we'd be in the Arctic."

A brief smile. "Thanks."

More bourbon slid down his throat. Rafe began to finally relax. "You've always shown remarkable confidence and aplomb, Ally. Working as a confidential informant for me with the Devil's Patrol showed it."

"Not that you gave me much choice." Allison tossed her long hair. Suddenly he wanted to run his fingers through it. Maybe pull it back and stare into her eyes right before he kissed her, long and deep.

Rafe cleared his throat. "I know. I had you in a tight spot, but Ally, you must know if you didn't have what it takes, I'd never have put you in that position. My job isn't to endanger my CIs. You were different from the start."

Her hair curtained her face. Resisting the impulse to draw it back, see her expression and those soulful brown eyes, he waited for an answer.

"Different how?"

"Strong. Independent and confident. I never would have let you even set foot around those bikers in the DP if I didn't think you could handle them."

Now she did look up and smiled. "Are you flattering me?"

"I'm telling the truth, Ally. The biggest problem I had with you was you were too confident and courageous and I had to rein you in at times."

"I'm used to risks."

"Well, don't take any more."

His voice was sharper than he intended. Allison brought out feelings he hadn't had in a long time for a woman, feelings that had intensified since she'd become a CI. He wanted to throw a protective shield around her to keep anything bad from happening to her.

Expecting a sarcastic reply, he was surprised to see her nod. "I won't. I'm done with them. For now. You won't see me pulling any more risks on the road. This trip is all about my sister."

"I don't want to talk about your sister."

Allison gave a derisive snort. "Most men do."

"I'm not most men. She's nothing compared to you." Now he did reach out and tucked a strand of her amazing, silky hair behind her ear. "Not every man is attracted to only looks and body. Some of us, me in particular, are drawn to strong, independent women who can hold their own."

"Ah, the old brains over beauty noble speech." Allison blew bubbles into her soda. "Been there, heard that."

"Did I say you weren't beautiful? You are."

"Right."

At her derisive snort, he reached out and covered her hand. "I mean it, Ally. Don't sell yourself short simply because your sister is always hogging the spotlight. You are beautiful."

"Thanks."

Allison flushed and pushed back her soda. "I'm kinda tired, Rafe. Have a good night."

Gently gripping her wrist, he stayed her. "Ally, if you need anything, call me. Or knock on the wall. I'm right next door."

Her mouth quirked. "Why don't you just sleep in the same room as me?"

"Is that an invitation?"

He meant it as a tease, but not really.

"Maybe. If my sister wasn't sharing a room with me."

Rafe's heart skipped a beat at her sultry smile, and the way she trailed a finger down his bare arm. The promise and intent clear, he took a deep breath.

"I'll keep that in mind." He raised his glass. "When you are ready, I will be as well."

Ally flashed him another smile and walked off. He watched her, enjoying the gentle sway of her hips beneath her jeans. Denim never looked so good on a woman.

After paying for his drink he went to the lobby to arrange for a wake-up call. Diana was there in a chair, palming her cell phone.

Seeing him, she frowned.

Well, hello to you as well.

"I wish Ally never came on this trip. I don't think you're good for her."

Rafe arched his brows. "And you know best."

The sarcasm sailed over her brunette head. "I've been preoccupied with the wedding, but Ally's my sister. I don't want to see her hurt."

"Neither do I. I'm concerned about the break-in."

Diana looked bewildered. "What break-in?"

Sorry, Ally. Rafe told her what happened. Diana paled.

She set down her soda on the table and palmed her phone. "I need to make a call."

I bet you do.

A few minutes later, she returned. "He's agreed this is too dangerous. Paul is flying up to Atlanta, and he'll meet me at my parents' cabin. We're going to elope. He's already arranged to ship the veil and gown to the cabin. It won't make Uncle Hector happy, but Paul says it is for the best."

That will make your sister happy. While she's still sleeping…

"Speaking of your Uncle Hector, there's something I'd like to ask you, Diana," he began.

* * *

Allison slept deeply, immersed in a delicious dream about Rafael. Only wisps remained when she awoke, refreshed. Something about him being naked. Oh yeah, it was quite nice.

In a great mood, she quickly showered and took time selecting her outfit. For once she chose an impractical blouse, hand embroidered with black silk thread, and designer jeans. After brushing her hair, remembering Rafe's touch, she studied her appearance in the mirror. Maybe not beautiful in the classic sense, but not bad.

Certainly Rafe had thought so.

She downed coffee and a quick breakfast in the lobby. No one else was around. Through the lobby windows, she saw the others preparing their motorcycles.

Diana came inside, joining her. "Ally, I have some news. I've taken your advice to heart and called Paul. He's flying up to Atlanta, and Mom is shipping my gown and veil so it should be there when I arrive. He'll meet me at the cabin. We're going to elope."

Squealing, she hugged her sister. "I'm thrilled, hon. This is the best news you could have given me."

Diana smiled. "I'll meet you outside."

One thing about Rafe. He was organized and efficient and herded their little group together better than a kindergarten teacher nudging students into quiet time. She appreciated him letting her sleep late and cutting her some much-needed slack.

He greeted her as she walked outside with her belongings. She saw his hooded gaze before he hid it behind his aviator glasses.

They got on the road before nine o'clock. Skies were overcast, with thick clouds threatening to the east, but despite this and heavy traffic, Allison felt encouraged. With a little push, they could make their next stop for the night in seven hours.

More encouraging was Diana's news about eloping as soon as Paul arrived and he found a minister to marry them.

The Teddy Bear Run, which had started out as a disaster, was turning fun.

Humming, she relaxed and enjoyed the ride, the wind rushing past, the steady throb of the bike beneath her and its tremendous power. Rafe still rode in back of her, Diana in front and then Keith with Comet, Debbie and Sam leading their group.

Her burst of joy didn't last long. Taillights flashed and vehicles slowed. She geared down to a crawl, and then traffic came to a dead stop.

Idling, she pulled out her phone and called Sam.

"It's a bad wreck a few hundred yards ahead. We may be here for a while," he told her.

"EMTs there?"

"No. No cops, either. Must have happened recently. Traffic isn't backed up much."

Allison knew her duty. "Tell Rafe I'm headed there. They may need me."

"Allison, wait, it may not be safe…"

She hung up, pocketed her phone and roared on the breakdown lane ahead of everyone. The crash site was about four hundred yards ahead. Allison pulled to a stop and saw a small sedan, front end accordioned, and a bigger vehicle off to the side. She made sure she had her backpack and ran forward.

Good Samaritans had pulled out the passengers from the sedan. A woman, perhaps a middle-aged mother, lay on the swale, groaning.

Nearby people huddled over a child. An older boy, who looked about thirteen and wore a gray concert shirt, looked up helplessly. "She's my sister. I was riding in the car behind her. I don't know what to do."

Ignoring the roar of the bikes behind her, Allison raced forward.

Rafe joined her. He looked grim. "I told you, we stick together. When will you ever listen to me?"

"I'm a nurse. Let me do my job."

Squatting by the child, who looked about eleven, he joined her. Rafe smiled at the child, who struggled to breathe.

"Hey, sweetheart. What's your name?"

The girl coughed violently.

"Her name is Jenny," the middle schooler answered.

Then he looked at Allison. "How bad is she?"

Allison assessed the young girl. Her skin was pale and cool, clammy to the touch, and her heart rate showed clear signs of tachycardia. The chest wall sustained severe injuries and the girl was gasping.

She put her ear to the girl's chest.

"Poor breath sounds, asymmetric chest expansion and percussion. Her left lung's collapsed. I have to drain the fluid or she'll die before the paramedics get here."

The teen kneeling by the girl recoiled. "You can do that?"

"I'm a trauma nurse practitioner. You see anyone else around here who can do it, find them," she snapped.

She looked at Rafe. "Any cops here yet?"

As she asked, a highway patrol vehicle pulled up and a state trooper emerged.

"How far out are the EMTs?" she asked the officer.

"At least twelve minutes behind me."

The kid might not have that long. "I'll have to inflate the lung."

She glanced around. Diana was still on her bike, looking pale, but composed. "Di, give me the straw from your tumbler," she called out.

As her sister rushed over with the straw, Sam joined them. "What can I do?"

"What do you need?" Rafe asked.

"Get the kit from my pack and open it. There's a flask of alcohol in there."

When he did, she poured the alcohol over and through the straw.

Allison glanced at Rafe. "I have to drain the blood from the cavity around her left lung. Open her shirt. And try to keep her still. This isn't going to be fun."

As Rafe and Sam squatted by the girl, holding her, Allison disinfected her switchblade with the remaining alcohol. Doing a chest tube was dicey under normal circumstances, after an X-ray and official diagnosis, usually, and with a doctor's orders. Well, no doctor, and certainly no X-ray.

She pierced the skin between the ribs and the pleural sack. Thankfully, the girl was unconscious. But Jenny's brother turned a shade of green. Allison slid the straw into the wound.

Ignoring everything except her work and her patient, Allison focused with intense concentration. The world faded away. She could hear the sound of her own breathing, the rapid but steady beating of her heart.

Once she began suctioning, blood began pouring out of the straw onto the ground.

As the sounds of sirens echoed, she saw the girl begin to breathe easier. Her eyelids fluttered.

"Wow, you are so chill," the boy told her.

Saying a silent prayer of thanks, she looked up at the approaching EMTs.

The paramedics began treating Jenny as Allison rattled off the girl's injuries.

The middle schooler, who seemed ready to faint at the blood, gave her an admiring look. "Man, you have the rizz. You are the GOAT."

"Charisma. Greatest of all time," Rafe said, winking at her. "I tend to agree."

"I speak gen alpha slang," she muttered.

Rafe gently pulled her aside, leading her away as they loaded the girl into a waiting ambulance.

"I want to follow," she said, the numbness setting in. "I want to know what happens to her."

"I know," he said softly, sliding an arm around her waist. "Sam is finding out what hospital, and we can check in later from the road."

Diana came forward and gasped. "Ally, your shirt."

Glancing down she saw the pretty black-and-white embroidered blouse was drenched in crimson.

Jenny's blood.

Hiding her feelings, she shrugged. "Wouldn't be the first shirt I've ruined. Guess I'll have to go shopping. I wanted to get a cute dress for your wedding, Di. I'm still your maid of honor, if you wish."

Pale, but smiling, her sister nodded. "Of course you are. We can go shopping in town when we get to the cabin. But you should get changed before we leave."

Rafe followed her to the bike. Rummaging through her pack, she found a plain olive green T-shirt. So much for looking good for Rafe.

It was silly anyway, these girlish flirtations with Rafe. They would never go anywhere.

Folding his arms, he watched her. "Are you okay?"

Then he pointed to the green shirt. "You're going to change here, out in the open, in front of everyone?"

"I'm a nurse. Used to it."

He scowled. "I'm not."

Motioning to the others, he instructed them to block Allison from view of the lookie-loos stuck in traffic. With their backs to Allison, they stood guard.

Another shrug and Allison pulled off the ruined blouse.

The white lacy bra was also stained red. The sticky warmth nestled against her breasts.

Well, it wasn't the first time she'd worn a patient's blood like a shield. The bra could wait. As she unrolled her olive green T-shirt, Rafe spoke over his shoulder.

"Let me know when you're decent."

"I'm always decent." She studied the black leather covering his broad back. His cool, efficient manner proved soothing.

Chucking aside the stained, ruined blouse, she shrugged into the clean shirt. "You'd make a good nurse, you know. Good in an emergency. No panicking."

A slight chuckle. "I'll consider that if I ever quit my day job."

"All set."

Rafe turned. The others headed for their bikes, chugging water, eyeballing the traffic jam.

"You were great. As usual." Rafe's gaze was steady.

"We make a good team, Rodriguez."

He reached up, touched her cheek. "We do. Happy to be your sidekick anytime, Lexington."

Her breath hitched as his finger lingered on her cheek. Warmth filled her. She'd been cold, oh so cold, and focused on the girl, but aware of the man beside her, providing steady support.

Life had a habit of tossing the unexpected into her lane. She'd learn to deal, embraced the new and exciting, never been one to bond with anyone because loss hurt and she'd seen enough loss in her line of work.

So many jobs and shifts, burning through hours like a kid glutting himself on candy. Saving money, working until she was exhausted, all so she could keep herself from having time to reflect and think.

Because the more she thought about the pain of her life, of

shallow men who promised and loved and left, ghosting her without even a damn text…

Or worse, men who dumped her to pursue her beautiful and stylish sister…

Or parents who barely glanced at her accomplishments but gushed over Di… It felt better not to feel.

Not to care.

Cold and calculating was the best approach to her job and life. People lived, bled, lived again or died. They promised to care and abandoned.

But now, for once, she wanted to feel. Feel the hard embrace of a man drawn to women with smarts, a man who riled her, poked at her, made her feel awake and aware and, damn it…

Alive.

I've been like a walking zombie through life, and I no longer want this.

It felt daring, and scary, more scary than the first time she was faced with a crush injury in nursing school and not sure what to do. Then, her training kicked in.

Now? Unchartered territory.

But life was about risks and adventure.

Sex. Allison trembled as Rafe's simple stroke became a deeper caress. He cupped her cheek, his thumb lingering over her lip. Traffic sounds, impatient beeps, the screech of sirens, the cough of exhaust, all faded away.

Nothing mattered but Rafe, and his touch on her skin, bringing her back to life.

A gentle cough. Glancing away from the burning intensity of sheer want in Rafe's gaze, she saw Sam standing close. He shuffled his biker boots in the red clay of the swale.

"Uniforms said they'd let us ride in the breakdown lane to clear all this traffic as thanks for what you did, Allison. Best we get on the road before they change their mind."

Rafe still did not drop his hand. "Get the others ready, Sam. We'll take the rear. Be there in a minute. Make sure Diana rides directly behind you."

Sam's mouth quirked into a smile. "You got it. Don't take too long. If we're to make the border by night, we need to get cracking."

"Guess we'd better get cracking," she murmured.

Rafe finally dropped his hand. "Yeah. Can't wait to get to the hotel tonight and bed."

But as they headed for their bikes, she knew the look in his eyes didn't mean rest.

Chapter 15

When they stopped at a rest stop to eat lunch bought at a grocery store earlier, Allison changed her undergarments in the restroom. She couldn't help noticing her sister had gone quiet.

No complaints. Or gushing about how overjoyed she was to marry Paul. Or how she missed air conditioning in cars.

Too quiet.

They parked their bikes together, and as Keith and Debbie walked Comet, Diana, Allison, Sam and Rafe sat on the bench at a picnic table.

Rafe was quiet as he unwrapped his turkey sub sandwich. He took a long pull of water. Fascinated, she watched his strong throat muscles work. As he backhanded his mouth, his level gaze caught hers.

"We need to talk. About how you don't listen, Allison. You should have let Sam and me check things out back there before you took off without us."

Appetite gone, she set down her sandwich. "I saved that girl's life."

"You did, but you take too many chances. I told you the rules when we set out."

"Rafe's right. Tried to tell you to wait, but you hung up on me. You need to slow down, Allison," Sam added.

Terrific. She'd saved a life and they were criticizing her?

Then Diana started on her. "Ally, you should have done as Rafael and Sam said. They know what they are talking about."

All the patience she normally had for Di and all her composure suddenly flew out the window. Allison lost it.

"Shish kebabs on a sidecar, Di, leave me alone! Stop telling me what to do and how to do my job. I'm a trauma NP. You think they can do any better than me?

"You think these guys, just because they are men, know more about injuries and treatment? Maybe they should have saved you all those years ago. Maybe they could have done it faster and better!"

Damn. She didn't mean to bring that up, but Di pushed her to the limit. The light died in her sister's face, and Rafe drew in a breath while Sam studied his sub sandwich as if it were fascinating.

Tears glistened in Diana's eyes. She shook her head. "All I meant was, they're responsible for this group. They know the dangers of stopping like you did and trying to be a Good Samaritan. And yet you go riding off, without a care, without caring about what happens to us or the consequences."

A knot formed in her stomach. Di was right. She glanced at Rafe and his usual blank expression.

"You're right, Di. I'm sorry. I'm being a drip. I should…"

"You don't know what dangers are on the road, Ally. You always rush into everything without thinking. There are people out there who could kill you."

The last sentence Diana uttered in a ghostly whisper. For the first time she noted the paleness of her sister's face, the way her hands shook. This wasn't about her.

Any guilt vanished in a heartbeat. Something else was going on here. "Di, what is it? What's spooking you? Did you see something?"

A glance sideways at Rafe, who kept giving Diana a speculative look. A head shake.

"I'm tired. I want to get back on the road and to Mom and Dad's cabin," Diana mumbled.

She crumpled up her half-eaten sandwich and headed for the trash can. Allison looked at Rafe and Sam.

"Thanks a lot. Now look at what you've done."

As she scurried after her sister, she overheard Rafe say, "What we've done? How is this our fault?"

Rafe couldn't shake the feeling they were being followed. Maybe it was the usual paranoia he felt on a job, but this was vacation, or so he thought. Yet his instinct kept niggling him.

Allison wasn't the only one concerned about Diana's mysterious warning.

There are people out there who could kill you.

The convo with Diana hadn't gone well. He'd mentioned to her that he knew a federal agent, Jase, who could use her help in penetrating the thick security around Hector Hernandez. Diana could provide a valuable service the same way her sister had done last year.

She'd refused, so he'd backed off, but silently vowed to approach her later with the same request.

Right now his biggest concern was getting all of them there safely. No matter how illogical it seemed, he sensed someone following them. So he'd skipped the planned stops the others on the run would make and used his GPS to plan a new route.

Rafe used the facilities and washed his hands, studying the other faces in the men's room. Nothing unusual. No one paid him any attention.

Grabbing a cold soda from a vending machine, he sat at a picnic table watching people come and go. He'd given them thirty minutes here, knowing everyone needed a break after the traffic accident on the interstate.

The bright blue sky, with a few white clouds scudding by, and the warm sunshine made a near perfect day for riding.

More than a few motorcycles parked at the rest stop. Rafe took a long pull of his drink. A concrete walkway snaked around the pavilion to the tall oaks with Spanish moss dripping from the outstretched branches.

He wandered over to Allison, who was holding court with another group of bikers examining her wheels. They seemed more interested in the motorcycle than her, so he relaxed and hung back.

"Custom job." One man squatted down. "Where'd you get her?"

"Guy online wanted to sell because he was getting older and couldn't go on the road anymore. Bought her in North Carolina after I finished a job. Call her Phoenix." Allison patted her bike. "She rose out of the ashes of that North Carolina job."

Intrigued, he drew closer.

"What job? Why? You get fired?" he asked.

"Nah. They wanted me to stay, but the doctor I worked with in the ER was such a dickwad that I said the only way I'd stay was with a ten-thousand-dollar bonus. So I put up with him for another three months and got the rest of the money I'd been saving to buy her, and customize her.

"She's got T-Man heads and cams, chain drive conversion for better torque, Mustang seat..."

As she rattled off the specs for her customized bike, a few of the other men looked impressed. They began asking questions about her bike—where did she get it customized, how long did it take?

Rafe waited until the bikers left and Allison joined her sister at another pavilion. He watched them a few minutes. Allison and Diana seemed to have made up. Well, at least they were talking. Good to see Ally relaxed at last, the glow restored to her cheeks, the spark returned to her pretty brown eyes.

He didn't want to be smitten with her, but he acknowledged

his feelings. Ally made the other women drifting in and out of his life seem like paper lanterns. She was a bonfire, burning fiercely, unafraid to show the world what she was.

Though he knew she could hold her own, he harbored a deep need to protect her from harm. He didn't like the ominous warning on her bathroom mirror.

Two bags of pretzels in hand, Sam ambled over. Rafe nodded thanks and tore off the wrapping. He ate without really tasting it, his gaze roving around the rest stop.

"You're as nervous as a June bug ready to be jumped by a duck. What gives?" Sam asked.

"A feeling. Someone's following us. You get it?"

Sam paused in eating. "Other bikers here, maybe not as law abiding, but nothing sinister. The ones around Allison seemed legit."

Glad Sam was keeping an eye on Allison as well, Rafe took another bite of his pretzel and swallowed. "They were asking about her bike. It's not them. I don't know who, but my gut says someone is tailing us."

"Why do you think we're being followed?"

He told him about the warning on Ally's mirror at the hotel and how only Ally's possessions had been vandalized.

"You could be right. This run also brings together bikers from all walks of life, some of them not walking such a straight line. Could be someone in Allison's past with a jealous streak."

"Maybe." Rafe set down the bag. "But I get a feeling this is something more. Hope we don't get any more surprises on this trip."

Sam polished off his snack in a few bites. Like Rafe, he learned to eat quickly when given the chance for a break. "Supposed to be for charity. Always amazes me how something with good intentions can go south in zero to ninety."

Busy watching a group of bikers emerge from the wooded area behind the rest stop, Rafe didn't reply.

"Maybe we should get on the road," Sam mused.

The bikers who walked toward them all had a ragged air, but as one passed, he recognized the insignia on the back of the jeans jacket.

"Ex-military," he murmured, jumping up. "Keep an eye on Allison."

Rafe caught up to the bikers just as they climbed onto their motorcycles. He nodded to the eldest, who bore a Vietnam War vets patch on his worn denim jacket with an American flag patch.

"Thank you for your service," he said quietly.

The man's worn, grizzled face brightened. "You serve?"

"Not military. Government service, though." Rafe hesitated a moment and then told him, "FBI. My uncle Jose served, though. Desert Storm."

"War is hell, and some hells are worse than others. I'm Aldie Carlton, from Pensacola." The vet sat back on his leather seat.

"Rafe Rodriguez, Miami."

"You doing the Teddy Bear Run?"

"Yeah." Rafe scratched the stubble on his chin. "Need a favor from you, sir. See that pretty woman there at the picnic table? The one in leather? She came off a bad experience on the road."

The vet squinted. "Someone try to hurt her?"

Instantly Rafe liked the man's protective growl. "Not sure yet. An extra set of eyes on the road would come in handy."

"Want us to ride in front or back?"

Rafe thought quickly. "Front. You can take off now, and we'll follow soon. And let me know if you see anything suspicious, either biker or cages," he said, using the slang term for vehicles.

They exchanged cell phone numbers.

Aldie started his bike. "Be happy to protect your old lady."

"She's not…"

His words were drowned out in a choke of exhaust and noise as the bikers backed up and roared off. Amused, Rafe rubbed his neck again.

Allison, his old lady.

Not a chance.

Even if it were his little fantasy…

Without incident, much to Rafe's relief, they reached the small town of Stetson, Georgia, a couple of hours later, the town hosting the Teddy Bear Run. The hotel rooms Rafe had reserved wouldn't be ready until four, so they decided to have lunch at a sports bar overlooking the river.

Diana and Allison agreed to wait to go to their parents' cabin, where they were staying, and join them for lunch.

With a cool breeze wafting off the river, the brilliant blue sky and temperatures in the seventies, eating outside settled his nerves. Red umbrellas shaded wrought iron tables from the sun. Round containers of pink and purple flowers adorned the patio, and the servers were dressed in red-and-yellow costumes reminiscent of a Bavarian mountain town.

He ordered a lager, indulging for once, as they sat together. The soothing gurgle of the river, laughter of people floating downstream in tubes as they kicked and splashed, and the chatter of others on the patio made everything seem normal.

Still, he couldn't shake that feeling they were being watched.

Allison removed her denim jacket and hung it on the chair. With her wind-tossed braid, snapping brown eyes and cheeks pink from their ride, she looked vibrant. Such a far cry from the pristine, proper women in his family, who would no more think of climbing on a motorcycle than they would drink a beer in the middle of the day.

His cell pinged, reminding him to check in with his family. Excusing himself, Rafe walked away from the table.

After calling his mother and being reassured Elena was home and recovering fine, he checked in with Jase. Though Rafe's superior warned him to enjoy his time away and avoid work, he knew Jase would update him.

The news wasn't good.

"We put eyes on Hernandez and got nothing, Rafe, until yesterday. Get this—the DEA has an agent working under-cover at the estate next to Hernandez who saw he had a special guest. Guy had his head turned away, and the agent couldn't get facial recognition, but the visitor was riding a motorcycle with saddlebags. No helmet. Shoulder-length dark hair. We put better surveillance on him and finally got an ID. Guess where he ended up? With a group headed to the same place you're at."

Rafe glanced around the patio bar. "Who is he?"

"Name's Marty Kingman. Ex-military, dishonorably dis-charged two years ago, did time for possession and petty theft, released from prison about four months ago. We contacted local LEOs and got him pulled over for a traffic violation. He had four grams of marijuana on him and was carrying, so…"

"Having a firearm on him is violation of probation."

"That's not all. Confiscated his cell, and he had a photo of Allison with her name and the kind of bike she is riding. And there is a list of names as well."

Rafe's blood ran cold. He quietly swore in Spanish. "Where is this Marty now?"

"Jail. But these guys are like roaches."

"Where there's one, there's certain to be others. What was the list for and who else is on it?"

"He wouldn't say. There were initials by Allison's name.

CF. The others were Diana, her sister, photo of her and her bike, but the initials FF, and you with the name Rafael Lopez, a picture of you, looks like from a security camera, and a question mark by your name."

"What's Lincoln's take on this?" Lincoln was the FBI assistant special agent in charge, Rafe's boss. Jase reported to him when he was appointed as Rafe's temporary replacement on the task force investigation.

"You know him. He thinks Kingman is getting weed from Hernandez in exchange for security work and checking you and the women out since you're both on the same motorcycle run."

Rafe frowned. "Lincoln knows I'm with Allison and Diana?"

Jase sighed. "Rafe, it's not exactly top secret. We've been monitoring Diana's social media, and she posted a photo of all of you."

Damn social media. If Lincoln knew, others did as well. Others who didn't have good intentions.

Rafe snorted. Lincoln was excellent at managing groups of agents, but he'd been gone from the field a long time. "Right. Four grams of weed in exchange for favors from a guy like Hernandez who deals in millions of illegal drugs."

"I know. That's like going to the Miami ballet to see the shoes."

"Interesting analogy," he said dryly.

"Kara's got season tickets and she got me hooked."

Rafe studied Allison, so carefree and seemingly happy, unaware her and her sister's names were on a list. Ignorance could be bliss, but it was also dangerous.

"Find out what you can and report back to me."

"Copy that." Jase hung up.

When he returned, Allison and Sam were engaged in animated banter.

"This is my first run here. Seems like the town's been taken over by bikers," Sam said, digging into his lasagna.

Allison nodded. "It's a typical small town, but friendly to bikers, as long as they're law-abiding. Since this is a charity run, it's a smaller event, but they still have all the fun activities, and vendors hawking the latest bikes and accessories, motorcycle skills competition…"

"Competition?" Sam winked at Rafe. "You plan on entering, Allison?"

"Please call me Ally. I already registered in the offset cone race."

Rafe paused in picking up his beer. He set the frosty glass down and stared at her. "Since when?"

"Since a long time ago when I signed up for this rally."

"Not sure that's a good idea." He locked gazes with her. "You'll be out front with everyone watching."

"You think I can't do it?"

"I know you can, and that's what worries me. Anyone can be out there, watching you and waiting to attack."

There, it was out. His full-fledged worry, accelerated by the news Jase had delivered. He didn't know why Allison was on a list or what the initials next to her name were, or Diana's, but he was more concerned about them than himself.

Scowling, she braced her hands on the table. "Listen, Rodriguez, you can't tell me what to do."

"I can. I'm leading your group."

Here we go. Keith and Debbie paused in feeding bits of hamburger to Comet and looked on with interest.

"I've been riding in competitions in my oh-so-limited spare time for years. I've trained with motorcycle cops, for crying out loud. They're the best and I know some will be here at this rally, probably all armed, so who's going to attack me? Nothing to worry about."

Sam looked interested. "What kind of competitions do you prefer?"

"*¡Maldita sea*, Sam, *collate,*" he muttered under his breath. *Shut up now, Sam. She doesn't need encouragement.*

"I can do the speed run, you know, where you have to navigate your hog through the cones and you get timed on speed and accuracy. But since I have a big bike and I like to test my own abilities, I opted for the slow ride this time."

Sam looked surprised. "The one where you navigate through the cones at your own pace? Why that one?"

Fuming, Rafe wished Sam would stop acting so damn interested. His friend was making things worse.

"Because I like challenging myself with balance and control of Phoenix, without my boots touching the ground. That's the course I've been training on, when I can."

"That's a big bike you have for a little lady." Sam sipped his beer and grinned.

Allison's friendly smile slipped. Rafe almost laughed. Little lady?

"Your bagger weighs about eight hundred pounds. What happens if it falls?" Sam asked.

"I get back on, like you do with a horse. Except my Phoenix doesn't kick or demand a treat later."

"I'm signed up for that slow ride competition. First time." The look Sam gave her screamed *challenge.*

Allison's smile returned, with a hint of slyness. "Wanna take a bet on who has the better score?"

Sam stuck out a palm. "One hundred dollars."

She shook his hand. "You're on." Allison glanced at Rafe. "You in on this bet? You think Sam can beat me?"

Drawing in a deep sigh, he slid his plate aside, his appetite faded. "I know you can beat him, Ally. I've seen you ride. That's not my concern. My concern is putting you on display where you become a target."

Rafe looked at Diana. "That goes for you as well. I think both of you should lie low for a while."

Diana paled and set down her cheeseburger.

"Excuse me, I need to use the restroom."

Watching her leave for the restaurant, he knew Diana wasn't the problem. Diana would cooperate. But Allison on the other hand…

Expecting an argument, he was surprised to see her slowly nod. "I think you and I need to talk. Sam, can you keep an eye on Diana when she returns? We'll be right back."

Allison walked to the edge of the patio onto the parking lot. Gripping the railing preventing curious bystanders from slipping down the hill into the river, she spoke over her shoulder.

"What gives, Rafe? Why is Diana in trouble?"

Ah, so you don't care about your own welfare, just your sister's.

He hesitated in telling her. "That's classified."

"If it's classified, then I shouldn't worry about it and go about my business. Either level with me, Rafe, or zip it."

Saying nothing, he crossed his arms.

She fingered the edge of her braid. "Listen, Rafe, we need to trust each other. I'm not a drug dealer. You know me. You wouldn't have hired me as your CI last year if you didn't think I could handle the job or if you didn't trust me. So tell me why suddenly you're launching into overprotective he-male mode."

His mouth quirked. "He-male?"

"Yeah, the kind of guy who bangs his chest and insists that a woman can't defend herself, but she needs a big strong guy to do it. Like your friend Sam is."

"Sam's not a chauvinist. He's not accustomed to women like you who ride huge bikes and compete. He was trying to get under your skin."

"Well, he's nothing like you. You're far from the kind of

guy who would call a woman 'little lady' and insult her. You know I can handle myself. That's one thing I like about you."

This convo was going sideways. Before he could slip and start asking her other things she liked about him, he put the brakes on.

"Sam and I are exactly alike when it comes to some things—doing our jobs and protecting those under our care, especially when they receive valid threats."

Her eyes shadowed. "You got a threat against me, and Diana. That's why you're all he-male."

Sighing, he blew out a breath. "Yeah, you could say that."

"Exactly what kind of threat?"

Aw hell. He was already in deep, and knowing Allison, the more she knew the better precautions she'd take. He told her about Marty and Hernandez and the info found on Marty's phone.

"I don't know what the initials mean, or why you're both on the list. I'm on it as well, with no initials. Hernandez doesn't know who I am, but it's clear he wants me checked out," he said.

Allison looked confused. "Diana, I get it. I mean Hernandez has an interest in her because she's marrying his godson. But me? What do you think?"

"I believe it stems from our visit to his home. The man isn't stupid. He hasn't evaded arrest or the grave all these years for nothing."

"You want me, and my sister, to hide from this? Why, if you caught the guy?"

Rafe gave her a steady look. Her mouth opened. "You think there's more watching us."

"I kept getting the feeling someone was tailing our group. Nothing concrete, just a feeling."

"But you make your living from trusting your instincts, just like I do when I think a patient has something more wrong with him, or her, than the tests show. What do we do about this, Rafe? If I withdraw from this competition, isn't it going to raise more suspicions than if I proceed with my plans? Diana, I get it. She's not entered in any events anyway, and besides, Paul is flying up here so they can elope. She's got marriage on her mind, not motorcycles."

"When is Paul getting here?"

"He had to finish a project at work, so not until the weekend. Saturday."

"Two days away. Doesn't give me a lot of time."

"Time for what?"

He changed the subject. "Is the cone competition the only one you registered for at the rally?"

"So far."

"Stick to it. Sam and I will be out front. Keith and Debbie will hang out with your sister, just in case." Though he didn't want to display open affection to her, Rafe couldn't resist cupping her chin in a tender caress. Damn, he worried about this woman.

"Stay alert, Ally. I'm counting on you."

Allison couldn't wait to get to the cabin and finally relax. Nerves taut like coiled wire, she led the way on her bike down the gravel path into the woods off a side road.

Secluded from the road, built next to a winding creek with a clearing in the back with a fire pit, the log cabin was nestled against a thicket of trees. Built on ten acres, mostly forest, it was secluded and private and had provided them many happy hours exploring the grounds and playing when they were growing up.

Diana roared past the run-down barn that had been patched up over the years, set back a distance from the cabin. Allison stopped her bike and climbed off to check the barn. Locked still. She peered through the grimy window, glad the sedan her parents bought a few years ago remained inside. Though the area was patrolled by police and they had a good security system at the barn and cabin, she'd always worried someone might break into the fragile structure and steal the car.

She climbed back on her bike and headed for the cabin.

Sunshine dappled the tall pines, oaks and maples. She parked her bike next to the oak tree bearing the initials of every married couple in their family who had spent happy times in these woods, from their parents, right up to the great-grandparents who built it years ago. Cousins, uncles, aunts—the oak stood as a living family tree of life.

Ally traced her parents' initials. Soon the tree would boast another signature—Diana and Paul.

Long time before mine is on there. She sighed and glanced at the deck on the second story.

A long white box sat on the deck. Could only be one thing...

Squealing, her sister jumped off her bike, barely parking it, and dashed up the steps. Allison followed, jingling the front door keys.

They went inside with the box. The housekeeper, as promised, had not only cleaned, but switched on the air conditioning so the cabin smelled like lemons and clean air.

Not waiting, Diana placed the box on the dining table and opened it.

Her satin strapless gown lay inside. Atop it was the delicate lace veil that had belonged to their mother.

As Diana removed the veil, cooing over it, Allison's breath hitched involuntarily.

Their mom had promised it to Allison whenever "you decide to settle down."

It was their exclusive agreement, perhaps one of the few special considerations their mom had granted to Allison. But seeing that Diana was the first to marry, their mother asked Allison if Diana could wear it after Diana begged for the veil.

Though the lace was the original their mother had worn, Diana had embellished it with a sprig of silk orange blossoms and shortened it. Oh, she'd asked Allison first if she minded the alterations.

Still…

What was I supposed to say? Everyone knows I'll never get married at this point. Hell, I'm not even dating anyone.

Still, it did hurt a little, seeing Diana try on the lacy veil in front of the mirror hanging over the fireplace. Removing her cell phone from her jeans pocket, she took a selfie and then did a short video clip.

"Look, everyone! Isn't this a lovely antique veil? I'm wearing it for the wedding! It was my mom's. I adore old lace," Diana said, tilting her head for the video.

Feeling like an antique herself, Allison hung back, not wanting to get in the way. When Di finished the video, she smiled.

"You look divine." Allison pushed down the hurt and the snake of jealousy threatening to strike.

"Ally, you need to go into town and get a nice dress. You're still standing up for me, and I thought we could have the wedding here, at the cabin. Or maybe you can find us a place in town for a wedding and a reception, something that would accommodate about fifteen people."

Allison blinked. "I thought you were eloping?"

"We are, but there's us, Mom and Dad and your biker friends, and, oh, my friends may be flying up after to join us, and there's a couple of friends Paul has at his furniture warehouse in North Carolina. Better make it accommodations for twenty, and a hall with catering for twenty-five, just in case."

The little ceremony was suddenly turning into a production. Allison drew in a breath.

"How far is this furniture warehouse?"

"It's in Randall, north of here."

"Di, it's the weekend of the Teddy Bear Run. Everything in town is sure to be booked up. Maybe we should hold the wedding there. Has to be plenty of room in a warehouse."

"A wedding in a warehouse? No, use your charm, Ally. I know you can find something. Maybe Rafe can help you." Diana winked at her in the mirror.

"I have to practice for the competition tomorrow."

"You're good and you can do both."

As Diana preened, Allison went outside to haul her belongings into the cabin. Terrific. She'd have to return to town to scout out both hotels with available rooms and now a restaurant with a private room for the reception.

But she wouldn't lose her focus on the cone competition tomorrow. There was a practice lot near the hotel where Rafe and the others were staying. She could set up obstacles there and do a little run. She was good at it, really good, something that made her stand out amongst the competition.

Not so good at finding a guy to marry, like Diana had, and wear a beautiful white dress, floating down the aisle to her intended...

I don't look good in white. Okay, Miss Sour Grapes. Try to cater to your sister's joy. Besides, would you really want to marry a guy like Paul? I mean, the way he probably wants her to do dishes instead of modeling? Don't think so!

Amused, she trudged up the stairs with her backpack. Whatever Diana needed on this trip to reassure her and get her quickly married to Paul, she'd comply.

Her needs always came after her little sister's wants.

The following day, the Teddy Bear Run got off to a start at the county fairgrounds. Debbie and Keith had taken all the bears to photograph for Debbie's photo album and would return them for the big public relations photo shoot ride into town. Rafe had spent the previous afternoon in his hotel room, on the computer, accessing the FBI databases.

Jase informed him Marty was still tight-lipped, and in jail. Chances were he feared Hernandez's repercussions more than the FBI. Rafe had secured a list of bikers participating in the run and wanted to check all of them out. Most were law-abiding and there were several law enforcement bikers.

However, a few riders stood out, with criminal records. Yet none were felony convictions or anything violent. Mostly petty theft. None fit the profile Jase and his team created for thugs Hernandez would send after Allison.

It should have reassured him, but still, he couldn't shake off bad feelings.

So this morning after a hotel breakfast and plenty of coffee, he headed to the bike show. Several custom motorcycles were on display, including a cobalt blue custom bagger with thirty-inch blue wheels. As Rafe chatted with the proud owner, other bikers rode around the enclosed lot, showing off their bikes. He glanced around for Allison.

Not here.

He did spot Sam, dressed in blue jeans, a blue T-shirt, a denim jacket, a cowboy hat and boots, walking up and down the aisles. Sam saw him, headed over.

"This is better than a car show any day." Sam grinned.

"You see Allison?"

"Nope. Or her sister. Want me to keep an eye on them?"

"Just her sister. I can handle Allison."

Sam gave him a searching look. "Can you?"

"Ha." They walked outside the roped-off area displaying the custom bikes to the parking lot. He saw the women weaving through lanes, searching for spaces. "There they are."

He and Sam caught up with them as they parked. Diana beamed, the glow of a happy bride, he supposed. Allison seemed more subdued. Her long brown hair unbound, she looked mighty attractive today in a lemon yellow shirt, jeans that hugged her long legs and her usual Dr. Martens.

He barely glanced at Diana.

"Did you practice the slow cone drill?" he asked.

Allison made a face. "Only for an hour. I spent most of yesterday looking for venues for Di's reception. I couldn't find anything within forty miles except for a taco restaurant that has amazing fish tacos and terrific chili. They have a private room they can rent out for a small party. You think my sister would mind eating tacos, black beans and rice for her wedding dinner?"

Rafe grinned. "Tacos are good. I'd skip the beans, though. Might make for an awkward wedding night."

Allison pushed at the long curtain of her hair. "Now she's nagging me to go shopping and get a new dress."

"I thought they were eloping."

"Eloping her style means a smaller wedding, not Di, Paul and a judge willing to marry them at the last minute. I can't complain. At least I lured her away from Hernandez. I never want her near him again if I can help it."

A flicker of guilt went through him. He pushed it aside. All for the greater good, right? *You have an agenda, but it is for a higher purpose.*

You're using her sister for the greater good. Just like you used Allison last year to nail the Devil's Patrol gang.

He and Sam opted to avoid alcohol all day in order to stay sharp. They bought sodas at one of the vendors. Allison demurred, but Diana bought bottled water.

There were vendors showing off the latest motorcycle models, custom bike accessories and much more. Games and plenty of food and drink booths. They walked over to the Cornhole for Charity games. Rafe paid and asked Allison to be on his team.

He tossed the beanbag into the hole on the first try. Allison clapped.

As they played, Diana and Sam watched on the sidelines.

"You're not into cornhole?" Diana asked Sam.

"If I don't have to shoot it or catch it with a fly rod, my aim isn't that great." Sam winked and sipped his cola.

Diana rolled her eyes and checked her phone.

When Allison tossed in the winning beanbag and their team was declared the winner, Rafe let her select the prize. She chose a large pink stuffed teddy bear and handed it to Diana.

"Here. Maybe she can be in your bridal party," Allison teased.

Diana didn't smile as she took the bear. He wondered what happened to ruin her mood.

When Diana told them she was headed over to the booths selling everything from biker art to jewelry, Rafe signaled Sam to follow her.

Trailing Allison as she walked up and down the aisles of custom motorcycles on display, he was surprised to see an older model Harley at the end of one lane. A spry-looking senior stood by the bike, talking with another biker. Rafe recognized him as Aldie, the veteran from the rest stop who'd agreed to watch out for Allison.

When the bystander moved away, Rafe and Allison approached the older man, who greeted Rafe with a hearty handshake.

Aldie's admiring gaze swept over Allison. He stuck out a leathery hand. "Name's Aldie Carlton, from Florida."

"Allison Lexington." She studied the Harley. It was a classic and had seen better days. As opposed to the gleaming customized motorcycles on display, it looked a little battered and well-loved.

"Is this your custom bike?" Allison asked.

The older man snorted. "Right. Won't find me on any of them fancy-ass bikes with the specialized paint. I ride my Bessie, not stick her in a garage and take her out once in a while to show her off."

Allison grinned. "I like your Bessie."

"I'm holding a space for a young feller who had to run into town to pick up his girl."

Aldie had a shock of iron gray hair, a roadmap of wrinkles on his careworn face and sharp, intelligent blue eyes. He wore a ball cap proudly announcing he was a veteran.

Rafe nodded at him. "Thank you for your service to our country, sir."

Rafe bent down to examine the bike with interest. He ran a hand over the back shocks, the gleaming chrome.

"Nice restoration job, Aldie. I've never seen a vintage 1974 Harley."

The older man shrugged. "Did what I could. Guy who sold it to me way back told me these bikes have a rep for leaking oil. Told me if it don't leak at least a quart, leave it be."

Aldie patted the seat, covered with strips of duct tape. Well, not strips. The entire thing was held together with duct tape.

"She's gorgeous, Aldie. I bet if bikes could talk, she'd tell many stories about where she's been."

Cocking his head, Rafe smiled at her. He liked seeing this part of her. "Didn't know you were so imaginative, Ally."

She waggled her eyebrows. "Stick with me, Rodriguez. I'll show you how imaginative I can be."

I bet. He tried to keep from thinking of a slow ride with her in his bed, but his imagination won that battle.

Turning her attention back to Aldie, she gestured to the bike. "How long have you had her?"

"Since the early '80s, I think. Can't remember that far back." He guffawed.

"We've been on adventures, this baby and me. She used to

be a cop bike with a windshield, but the windshield was removed before I bought it. Wish it wasn't. Rode from Florida here with bugs in my face and one flew in my mouth. Had it open at the time. Ever taste a fly? Don't taste too good."

Allison laughed. Rafe grinned at the picture of Aldie riding with his mouth open, spitting out flies.

"When I go back to Florida, this will be our last ride." He gazed at the motorcycle as if fondly regarding a longtime partner. "I'm too old for this anymore. Reckon we're both destined for the junkyard soon. Told my kids I'd like to be buried with her."

Thinking of his beloved Tita, and how he'd nearly lost her, a lump formed in Rafe's throat. Allison shook her head with a fierceness he also felt. "You're not destined for the junkyard, and neither is this beauty."

His smile was sad. "Thanks, pretty lady, but I know when my time is up and it's soon. Wish I could ride back in style, but these old bones will need a few more rest stops. I'll make it."

"I have no doubt you'll do well," Rafe said, and his tone was firm with conviction.

A gleaming yellow motorcycle roared up to them, bearing a younger man and a woman. "Thanks for holding my spot, Aldie."

"Welcome."

Aldie nodded at them. "Gotta get back to my group. They're probably belting down beers at the bar. Baby of our gang is seventy-six. And they say you youngsters can party? We could teach you lessons."

They watched him mount his bike and ride off.

She pulled Rafe aside. "I have an idea. I have money. There's a bike repair vendor here at the show…"

"We could swap out the seat with a new leather one and put a windshield on," he finished. "Split the cost. Give him a gift certificate so he can select what he wants."

Rafe's grin equaled her own.

"But he has pride. What will we tell him?"

He considered. "How about we tell him it's our way of paying him back for his years of service to our country?"

Beaming at him, Allison nodded. "Can't go wrong with that."

She shocked him when her palm slid into his as she tugged him toward the vendor who could repair Aldie's bike.

But more than surprise, he felt a warm glow and a surge of unexpected joy mingling with desire.

Whoa, Rodriguez. Best to put the brakes on this right now.

And yet he didn't.

Chapter 16

That afternoon, after they presented a delighted and grateful Aldie with their gift certificate from the bike repair shop, Rafe watched Allison compete in the slow cone competition.

Impressed, he studied the way she maneuvered Phoenix around the cones. The big bike was awkward and heavy, and he knew from experience those twists and turns were a bitch, but Allison wove through the cones with skill. Mastering the course as easily as most riders drove on a straight line.

The orange cone formation became tighter, with little room for maneuvering, but Allison drove her bike on, not knocking over a single cone or falling off her bike.

Damn, she was good at this.

Was there anything she didn't excel at?

When she finished and pulled away from the cones, a cheer went up from the crowd. His worries about someone targeting her abated as he headed over. The judges announced the score.

Almost perfect tens.

"Looks like you're the winner," he told her, feeling oddly proud of her skillset.

Allison pulled off her helmet and finger combed her hair.

"Winning isn't as important as doing it right. I know that sounds hokey, but it's what I believe. I like seeing others compete as well because this kind of competition means safer biking."

"What's your secret?" he asked.

"You ride on the rear brake for control—" she displayed it by touching the brake with her foot "—and throttle at the same time. That's my trick."

"Nice." Rafe felt like a kid shown a new toy. "What about your line of sight?"

"Look at the horizon and don't look at the cones or you'll lose perspective and possibly balance."

He'd done a few slow cone drills with motorcycle cops before. Their skills were at par with Allison's, but she didn't ride for a living like they did. "Steering?"

"Counter steering." She demonstrated. "Push right, go right."

He nodded. "I've done the same, but as a drill to be a safer rider, not to compete."

"When you're going that slow, it's a good way to control the bike. I like the slow cone competition because it makes me more aware of hazards I could encounter. Like a dog rushing out in front of me, or a child."

"Or a car that decides to wander into your lane."

He wasn't surprised when the judges announced Allison had won. Everyone gathered around her, asking questions, congratulating her as she returned from the podium where the judges had given her a blue ribbon. Rafe gave her space, wanting her to enjoy the spotlight and the attention.

He felt tremendously proud of her accomplishment.

When the crowd thinned, Diana rushed up to her and threw her arms around Allison. "My big sister, the winner. Always."

He wondered at the slight bitterness in Diana's voice.

Allison touched the blue ribbon pinned to her denim jacket. "We should go celebrate."

Diana shook her head. "Ally, I'm a little tired. I'm going back to the cabin to take a nap."

Tired? Or bored? Rafe assessed her sister, who was looking a little pale. Wedding jitters?

Or jitters about what he had proposed to Diana?

"You sure you're okay? I thought we could eat dinner at that steak place on the river," Allison asked.

"I'm fine." Diana swatted the air. "I need AC and a good movie. All this fresh air is annoying."

Allison laughed. "Right. You would say that in the middle of all this lovely scenery."

'Don't worry about me, Ally. I need some alone time, 'kay?" She gave her a sly glance. "In fact, if you want to spend the night elsewhere, feel free. I could use a night alone."

She sputtered. "I have no intentions…"

"You should have intentions." Diana grinned at her and winked at Rafe. "Go for it, Ally. I'll be fine."

A blush tinted Allison's cheeks. "Diana Lexington, I have a good mind to yeet you into tomorrow."

Diana's smile seemed strained. "You mean throw me into tomorrow. That's what Mom and Dad would say. Not yeet."

With a wave, her sister headed away. As she rode off, Allison shuffled her feet. "I, um, apologize for her."

"Why?" He dug his hands into his jeans pockets.

"She comes up with the most absurd ideas."

"Is it so absurd?" He gave her a long, thoughtful look. "Spending the night with me?"

Her blush deepened. Allison looked past the rows of bikers, of men and women wandering up and down the aisles, admiring bikes. "No, it's not, but… I mean, you and me."

Damn, he liked seeing her blush like this, knowing the idea of them sleeping together did it.

Allison waved a hand. "For that, I'm not as inclined to shop for a dress for her wedding this weekend."

To his surprise, she winked at him. "In fact, I'm thinking of making a special appearance. She wants to have the wedding at our cabin in the woods in the yard by the creek. I'm considering running through the forest naked, screaming about Bigfoot. Care to join me?"

Rafe laughed. It felt good to laugh and release all the tension he'd been carrying on this trip. "Sounds like a plan. Do we run together or do you take the lead and I follow?"

"I should take the lead because, with that beard of yours, they might even believe I'm being chased by the mighty, mythical Sasquatch."

Pretending to be offended, he stroked a hand over the beard stubble. "Hey, I'm not that hairy."

Allison cocked her head to one side. "Dunno. Haven't seen the whole package yet."

And then, as if realizing what she'd said, she blushed again. He grinned, finding her reaction charming.

This kind of flirting was the type to lead to something… What, he wasn't certain, but he knew for a fact he was enchanted with Miss Allison Lexington, expert trauma nurse practitioner and motorcycle slow cone competition champion.

Sam wended through the crowd, joined by Keith and Debbie, walking Comet. "Congratulations, Ally! You're fantastic."

"We were thinking of celebrating your victory over steak and beer," Keith added. "Join us?"

"Maybe later," he said slowly, looking at Allison, who didn't seem enthusiastic about a group dinner.

Sam caught Rafe's look and grinned. "We'll be at the Pine Tree Pub on Main if you want to catch up with us. Or not." Sam waggled his brows.

Thankfully, Sam hustled the couple away before anyone started asking questions. Allison lifted her head and looked at him. She had the most amazing brown eyes. Up close, flecks of green sparkled in them like shining emeralds.

"Shall we go to dinner, Supervisory Special Agent Rodriguez?"

"After you, Allison Lexington, motorcycle winner extraordinaire," he murmured.

Tonight was going to be a special night, indeed.

Chapter 17

He chose the steak restaurant Allison had wanted to try out. During dinner, right in the middle of a delightful story Allison told about her favorite city to visit, Rafe's cell rang. He was ready to let it go to voicemail when he recognized the caller.

Greg Whitlock. He excused himself and asked Allison to order the cheesecake dessert.

Once more, the job came first. Rafe sighed.

It had to be important for Greg to call. The DEA agent was deep undercover in the same seamstress shop where Diana got her wedding gown altered. He'd found out the real owner was Hernandez, not the woman listed as the owner. The shop was yet another legitimate business laundering money for the drug lord.

"Rafe. Gotta make it quick."

He could barely hear Greg inside the restaurant.

Soon as he got outside, the reception was better. "What is it?"

"Bad news. Marty Kingman got released. Lawyer flown in from Miami to bail him out."

Hand tightening on his cell phone, Rafe tensed. "Has to be Hernandez's personal attorney."

"Our guys in Atlanta will put a tail on him, but it's not a priority. They're overwhelmed with a huge bust going down they've been working on for months. Field office can't assign an agent until next week."

"Any progress on deciphering the codes found in Kingman's phone?"

"No, but our coding experts think it has to do with Paul and Diana's wedding. Clearly Hernandez wanted you checked out. I did hear Hernandez say that Paul is wildly in love with Diana. He will go to extremes to get whatever she wants. This wedding at the mansion? It was Diana Lexington's idea after they attended a cocktail party there."

It made sense. Paul was a sensible, quiet businessman who was low-key and never had a good relationship with his notorious uncle. Not until Diana came into his life.

He heard noise in the background, and then Greg whispered, "Gotta run. Watch yourself and the women. They're still on Kingman's list."

"Thanks, man."

He hung up, frustrated and worried. No one in his office had yet deciphered the code Kingman had assigned to their names on his cell phone. Diana was probably not in danger. But he knew Allison could be a target.

All the more reason to keep her close, and safe.

When he returned to the table, she was digging in the cherry cheesecake. Extra cherries on top and plenty of whipped cream. Half was gone already. Rafe swallowed hard as she closed her eyes and licked whipped cream off the fork. Oh, to be that fork under her sweet tongue…

Suddenly he understood Paul's obsession with having Diana and granting her every wish. He felt the same way about Allison. Maybe it was like this, finally meeting a woman you'd risk everything for.

With her long brown hair loose, curled slightly at the ends, Allison looked fantastic tonight. She wore a pink denim jacket with flowers and a white sleeveless blouse and pink jeans.

The jacket was off, and the blouse showed firm breasts and toned arms. Utterly feminine, yet he kept thinking of her strength and courage.

Never had a woman's arms been a turn-on, but he stared at hers, thinking of her lifting patients, the tender way she'd stroked his sick grandmother's forehead, the selfless dedication to saving lives. The long hours on her feet, hustling here and there to care for patients.

Right now all he wanted was to feel those arms, and legs, wrapped around his naked body.

Rafe finally found his voice as he resumed his seat. "Hey, leave some for me."

Mirth sparkled in her brown eyes as she dug into the cake, leaned forward and lifted the fork to his mouth. Rafe's lips encircled the utensil. The sweet, creamy dessert's flavor burst with sweetness. He withdrew his mouth, chewed and swallowed.

He stared at her, the little pulse throbbing in her neck, the dilated pupils. Rafe slowly licked his lips.

"Delicious."

"It is a great cheesecake."

"I'm not talking about the dessert." Hell, he couldn't help staring at her lush mouth, his need to feel her soft lips growing stronger by the minute.

She vexed and intrigued him, and Rafe craved her like a drug. Forget any opioids trafficked by Hernandez and his cronies. Allison was more addictive and intoxicating. He felt alive and aware in her presence, all his pleasure receptors flaring to life.

It took all his carefully won control not to leap across the table and take her into his arms, kiss her senseless, then sweep her back to his room with the soft sheets and tip her back naked on the mattress and have his way with her.

He had no conceit, but he knew he was a good lover, always making sure his partner experienced plenty of pleasure before he finished. But damn, Allison brought forth all kinds of raging passion inside him. No more gentle lover. All his fiery need would release with her, the need to conquest and dominate and claim, like a caveman marking her as his own.

So much for civilized sex.

"You okay? You're flushed." Allison leaned forward, looking concerned.

Rafe swallowed hard, trying to chase away the image of a nude Allison writhing with pleasure beneath him.

"Fine." When did his voice grow so hoarse? "But I have to tell you, I'm sitting here having all kinds of fantasies about you right now."

Now or never. Allison's eyes widened. "What kind of fantasies?"

"You. Me. Naked. In bed all night." Had he added a deep grunt, like a caveman, he couldn't have made his intent clearer.

Her wild gaze whipped around, and for a heart-stopping moment, he feared he'd gone too far.

Spotting the waiter, she waved like a drowning woman flagging down a lifeboat. "Waiter! A box and the check please. We're in a hurry."

While the waiter scurried off, she pointed to her backpack. "I hope like hell you brought condoms, Rodriguez, because I didn't."

Rafe laughed. What a woman. "No worries. I came prepared."

Uncertainty flickered on her face. "So you planned to get lucky with some woman on this trip?"

Ally, don't do that to yourself. Rafe reached for her hand and caressed it. "Not some woman. You. You're the one I wanted, Allison. For a long time now."

Once inside his hotel room, she felt frantic to climb into bed with him. But Allison realized Rafe had different ideas.

She kicked off her shoes when he pulled her into his arms. Rafe leaned forward and cupped her face. Slowly, so slowly, his mouth descended upon hers. Firm and commanding, yet gentle and warm, oh, so warm and amazing.

Oh wow, the man knew how to kiss.

Crazy. She'd dreamed of kissing him. Such a kiss haunted her at night when she slipped into sleep and had the good sex dreams, the ones you never wanted to go away. The ones that left her aching and sweating and needy, but they were better than the awful emptiness of not having anyone or anything to look forward to.

Such a kiss would be life-changing. Her bar was set too high; her expectations too much.

This was what it was like to kiss someone you truly cared about, even if you only admitted it in your dreams. This was a kiss she never wanted to end, sensations she sank into deeper and deeper. It was hot and sweet and spicy all rolled together. Allison slid her arms around his neck, never wanting to surface for air, never wanting it to end like her dreams did. This was much better than any dream. This was real and she felt every nuance, every subtle slide of his lips over hers, sealing them together as if they drew breath from each other.

When they broke apart, they stared at each other. A pulse beat madly at the base of his throat. Rafe looked like he barely clung to control. This wasn't a guy who hesitated at going after what he wanted.

He went full steam ahead and right now, he wanted her.

The thought made her heady with power as they unzipped and unbuttoned and shed their clothing.

When she was fully naked, he pushed her gently back onto the bed. "I want you so much," he said in a thick voice. "I can barely wait. But damn, Ally, I've wanted this for so long, I want the night to last. I need to make it special."

Then he spread her legs open.

Rafe opened the take-out box he'd placed on the night-stand and dipped his fingers into the dessert. He held up the whipped cream and a bright, shiny cherry.

"Dessert. Never got mine."

Oh boy, this was going to be good. She shivered a little as he smeared the cream over her vagina, and then added the gooey cherry.

Then he put his mouth on her. Slow, even strokes, expert little flicks of his tongue.

"Mmm," he murmured.

Every movement of his mouth built the pleasure higher and higher. Suddenly he stopped and lifted his head.

"Shall I continue, *mi angel*?" he inquired.

"Oh, my sweet buttered biscuit, don't stop," she gasped, arching her back. "Please, Rafe, don't stop. I'm gonna die."

Licking whipped cream off his lips, he grinned the wicked grin of promise of a man who knew exactly what he was doing. "No, *mi angel*. Not until I send you over the edge."

His mouth descended on her soft flesh again. Allison moaned, grabbing fistfuls of sheet. Her hips automatically pumped in response to the motions of his mouth, readying her for the ultimate act of penetration. Sensing her frantic whimpers, he increased the pressure subtly, faster, harder, stroking her closer to the edge until sensations exploded between her legs.

With a sharp cry of his name, she came hard, seeing stars behind her closed eyelids. The sweet throbbing in her loins continued as he lazily finished with a slow kiss.

When she finally came back down to earth, Allison opened her eyes. He flicked out his tongue. On it was the cherry from the cheesecake. Rafe popped it back into his mouth, gave another teasing grin.

As he chewed and swallowed, he winked. "Got your cherry."

Laughter burst out of her. He was naughty and so much fun. Hell, she hadn't enjoyed an evening like this in ages.

It wasn't over yet, either. Rafe climbed onto the bed. Anticipation curled through her as she sat up, grabbed the dessert box.

"My turn." Allison licked whipped cream from the box and shoved him backward.

"Ally...be gentle with me," he mocked.

"Shut up, Rodriguez, while I have my wicked way with you."

Encasing his shaft with her mouth, she set to work on him, enjoying the way he moaned as he'd made her moan, watching him shudder, feeling a surge of her own power, having him under her and knowing she was the one in control of giving him mind-blowing pleasure.

He began muttering rapid Spanish, too fast for her to understand with her limited knowledge, but judging from his reaction, he sure was enjoying himself.

When he came with a shudder, exploding in her mouth, she lingered for a while, reluctant to stop sampling the last little bit of delicious dessert.

Allison sat back, licking her lips and giving him a smug smile. She plucked a cherry from the dessert box, placed it atop his still erect penis and carefully encased it with her teeth. She chewed and swallowed.

"I got your cherry as well."

A deep laugh rumbled from his throat. They were good together, she suddenly realized. Scary good.

The thought disconcerted her for a minute. What would happen when all this was over and he abandoned her, like the other guys had? Or she left him because she couldn't see herself in a relationship where he'd eventually hurt her because his career meant more than she did?

Think about it later. Enjoy the moments while they're here.

After a few minutes, Rafe sat up and reached into the nightstand for a condom. Allison helped him roll it on. She pretended shock while reading the label.

"Extra-large, huh? No modesty here, Rodriguez. You know a little humility…"

Her words were cut off as he kissed her roughly. Tangling together on the sheets, he finally rolled her over and entered her with a hard thrust that took her breath away.

Their gazes met, his dark and filled with desire. They began moving together again, her hips rising to meet the pounding thrusts.

She came again, hard, a few seconds before he threw back his head and shouted in Spanish, along with her name.

Heart pounding, she accepted his heavy weight, stroking his sweat-dampened back.

"Sure hope what you said was complimentary, Rodriguez," she teased. "My Spanish isn't that great."

Raising his head, he looked down at her solemnly. "Do you really want to know?"

Suddenly she did. Allison nodded.

"I said…a lot of things." He drew in a ragged breath. "But the most important was *mi corazón es tuyo*."

Now it was her turn to marvel. Allison touched his face. "My heart is yours as well, Rafael."

Rafe rolled off her and draped an arm over his head, closing his eyes. "Guess we're both screwed, huh?"

She playfully punched his arm. "Don't ruin a special moment."

"Moment? I'll have you know I last longer than a moment."

So that was what he was doing. Blurting out his emotions when he climaxed, admitting what he'd said and now trying to make light of it. She got it. Such intensity was tough for them both.

Usually they saved the intensity for the job, not moments like this. So she played along, rubbing her leg against his.

She tunneled her fingers through the black hairs on his chest. "You have a lot of hair, Special Agent Rodriguez."

"Supervisory Special Agent." He kissed her again. "It's a common trait of my people."

"Cubans? Or FBI agents? Or bikers?"

"Men who like dessert."

She laughed against his chest, enjoying the steady beat of his heart. Life, sweet and intoxicating, was filled with joyous surprises. Like discovering the guy you secretly crushed on for months also crushed on you.

And showed amazing moves in bed as well.

Allison snuggled closer to him, laying her leg over his. The crazy, ecstatic pleasure of sex slowed into a deep peace, the kind where she knew she'd sleep for hours.

His cell phone rang again. Rafe grunted, reached for it.

"Turn it off," she told him.

"Can't. Have to take this." Naked, he slipped out of bed and paced to the bathroom.

She snuggled under the covers, utterly content. The bed sank under his weight as he returned. Allison opened her eyes. Damn. He looked serious.

"Ally, I need to talk to you."

"What's wrong? You need a repeat performance? I'm game."

Rafe shoved a hand through his hair. "I'm serious, *mi angel*. We need to talk. It's about your sister."

All joking was set aside. Allison sat up, pulling the covers over her breasts. "I really do not want to discuss my sister right now, Rafe. Can we keep her out of bed?"

"This is the only time we can discuss her. When we're alone."

"I can't get a break from her. First I have to convince her to elope up here, and then when she finally agrees, I have to set up the wedding venue and do everything for her."

His gaze remained steady, not accusing but thoughtful. "Ally, when are you going to let go and let her make her own mistakes instead of covering for her? Seems like she's always handed everything, which means she probably doesn't appreciate them. You also have to consider that by bailing her out all the time, you're denying her the chance to become independent."

Deep inside, she knew he was right. And resented it. "Leave my sister to me, Rafe. I can handle her."

"There's something you should know about what is going on with her before you get too involved, Ally."

She had a bad feeling about this. "Di's fine. She's agreed to elope with Paul this weekend and everything will be fine. Paul's an upstanding guy. It's his family that is a little wonky."

Rafe tensed. She watched the taut line of his jaw. No more *mi angel* or passionate *mi amour*. Those moments were gone, perhaps forever. She wanted to make a memory, the smell of his spicy aftershave, the scent of clean sweat, sex and the feel of fresh, soft sheets.

"The phone call was from a member of my task force. Diana is under investigation, Ally. My team found a connection between the hair salon, where she was getting her hair done, to Hector and the so-called candy for the reception. And now, her wedding dress."

Allison sputtered. "You're accusing her wedding gown of smuggling fentanyl?"

"The seamstress who did the fitting was arrested for possession. We've had her under investigation for a few months now. She recently ordered a new commercial iron. The old one didn't work and was sent out for repairs. It had a false bottom, and we confiscated 125 fake oxycodone pills containing fentanyl."

All the joy evaporated out of her. Staring at him, she felt cold sweat trickle down her back. "This doesn't mean Di is guilty of anything. So she made a lousy selection of a seamstress for her fitting."

"Right. You don't think it's odd that your sister chose a seamstress who had few clients, operated out of a tiny storefront with bad lighting and looked more like a storage facility than a shop? When weddings in Miami are big business and most seamstresses operate shops that depend on elegant first impressions, with flowers and gilded mirrors and big windows and plenty of overhead lighting for the bride to see herself?"

She blinked. "You seem to know a lot about fittings."

"I have sisters. And cousins. I also know my city, Ally. And soon as I did a little checking on Diana and where she went, I got suspicious."

"Di is not a drug dealer! It's a coincidence. Nothing more." Allison's fingers curled tight around the sheet's edge. Talk about a mood spoiler.

"She's closely connected to one, one of the biggest in Florida, Ally." He brushed a strand of hair away from her face. "Open your eyes and stop denying the truth."

Swatting his hand away, she scowled. "My eyes are open, Rafe. You can't get Hernandez on your own, so you put my sister under surveillance, for what reason? So you can force her into becoming a CI like I did?"

A shadow crossed his face, confirming her suspicions. His mouth compressed.

"I told Diana it would be in her best interests to cooperate with the FBI."

Rage uncurled inside her. "Best interests? You mean your best interests. What's next, asking my parents to spy for you at the local grocery store? Checking the melons to see if they're stuffed with drugs? Is that what this is all about?"

She gestured to the bed. "You wanted me to sleep with you so you could get me to spill all the tea about my sister."

His dark brows drew together. "Of course not. I had no intentions of…"

"But your timing is awfully coincidental, Agent."

She felt like the biggest fool. And here she thought Rafe

had feelings for her. His lovemaking had been passionate, tender and exciting.

Even another one-night stand with chauvinistic Dan Johnson was better than this. She knew where she stood with Dan. He didn't coax her into bed and then try to get her to turn state's evidence.

He gently clasped her wrist. "Listen to me, Ally. What happened between us was a long time in coming. We both know it. We both wanted it and it has nothing to do with your sister being a suspect."

There was a softness in his deep voice that made her want to believe him. "I could no more resist making love with you than I could stop breathing, Ally. My feelings for you are separate from my actions toward your sister."

How could she believe him? "My feelings and yours don't matter. Family is family. I have to protect my sister. Her happiness and her future are at stake."

Rafe made an impatient sound. "Always Diana. Why do you sacrifice your needs for your sister? I get it about your dedication to the job. I'm the same. But every time your sister coughs, you panic. She's an adult, Allison."

"An adult you think is a drug dealer." Muttering a few choice curses in Spanish, she slid out of bed and grabbed for her clothing on the floor.

As she threw on her clothing, he left the bed. Naked, he padded across the carpet toward her. Allison tried to ignore how delicious he looked nude, the smooth muscles working under taut skin…

Remembering how he'd slid inside her and how amazing it felt.

"When are you going to stop protecting her and let her face consequences on her own? You can't defend her forever."

"She's my sister and I always stand with her."

"Even when you don't fit into her world?"

Ouch.

"Who are you to judge me? Or what I'm really like?" She picked up the pretty pink denim jacket with the flower print. So feminine and tailored. She paired it with a white silk sleeveless blouse and her hot pink jeans. Wearing it today, she'd felt pretty and desirable. Di had helped her pick out the outfit back in Miami.

Diana's voice still rang in her head.

"Layer, Ally. The secret of wearing a bold jacket like this is to wear it with confidence, let it shout out to the world you're a woman of worth, a hot babe! You need a white shirt underneath it, as to not diminish the jacket's flare. Or you. Stop hiding behind scrubs or T-shirts and baggy shorts. You've got a great figure and beautiful hair. You're a dynamo!"

A lump clogged her throat. For all the problems her sister could cause, Diana was the only one who truly believed in her potential. The only one who saw beneath the layers she'd built up to protect herself from those who could hurt her. The only one who thought she could be beautiful.

"I'm not judging you, Allison," he said slowly, pulling on his black boxers and a T-shirt. "I'm trying to make you see reason. Diana may be in trouble, deep trouble."

Allison crumpled the pretty jacket in one trembling hand. Now he was trying to placate her. Well, she wasn't going to be soothed with flattering words.

Better to be angry than clinging, pining away for a guy, waiting for him to call and finding out he'd ghosted her. Because he only wanted her for sex, not a relationship.

Or worse, to use her for information he needed.

Better to end this right now before Rafe broke her heart like the other men had.

"You don't fit into her world, Ally, because you're honest and dedicated and down to earth and real. Not shallow like the glam world of modeling."

Averting her eyes as he came closer, she snatched up her pack and stuffed the jacket inside. "You know, Rodriguez, maybe you should stop worrying about my sister and focus on your own damn family. Seems like you don't know where you fit in with their world as much as I don't fit into my sister's. Even with your own grandmother you seem out of place."

The words tumbled out before she could bite her tongue. Oh, how she wished she could snatch them back, but there they were, hovering in the air. She'd used his own words and confession about his family to hurt him.

A shadow passed over his face before his gaze went arctic cold. Well, if she'd wanted to put distance between them, it worked.

But this wasn't her. Nasty and sarcastic by using someone's vulnerability against them. Worse than pouring salt into an open wound, and damn it, she was a nurse. She healed people, not wounded them.

"I'm sorry, Rafe," she said and meant it.

"It's better if we avoid each other for a while. You're compromising my investigation."

Oh, she knew what he meant. There was no going back. It was over, before it even began.

"I am sorry," she mumbled.

"So am I."

Allison hugged her backpack tight to her chest as she ran out of the hotel room, slamming the door behind her.

Her motorcycle sat in the parking lot, all gleaming black steel and silver chrome, shiny in the moonlight. So shiny it was blurred.

Or maybe it was caused by the tears starting to trickle down her cheeks.

Chapter 18

Rather than return to the cabin, Allison paid for a night at a local campground. She stretched out on a picnic table, using her jacket as a blanket, and tried to sleep.

Too wounded to return to the cabin and face Di, she didn't want to be barraged with all those probing questions she didn't want to answer.

Finally she slept, nightmares chasing her of Rafe hunting her sister down to haul her to jail.

A recreational vehicle pulling into the campground woke her at dawn. Allison fumbled in her bike's saddlebags for a towel she always kept there and headed for the campground showers. After a quick hot shower, she steeled her spine.

Time to face the music.

Powering up her bike, she rode to the cabin.

Gravel crunched beneath her tires as Allison pulled into the drive, parked and shut off the engine. She yanked off her helmet.

Thick with pine, maple and oak trees, the woods surrounding their parents' cabin pulsed with bird song. A slim peace threaded through her as she took a deep breath, drinking in nature. Too long since she'd been here.

To her relief, Diana's bike was gone. Maybe Di went into town for shopping.

It was best anyway to forget Rafe, forget the amazing sex

they'd had, pretend it was as fleeting and memorable as her last one-night stand. Diana needed her for all the last-minute wedding crap over the next few days, to hold her hand through the jitters. They could open a bottle of cold wine, eat some cheese and share laughs as they watched a rom-com on Netflix.

Sister stuff.

Nothing compares to the night you spent in his arms.

A cool breeze ruffled stray hairs escaping her braid. Allison slid off the bike and rubbed her butt. All those hours of riding hadn't stretched muscles as much as riding last night in Rafe's bed...

Stop it.

You're the sacrificing type, Allison. When are you going to stop for a change and think of yourself and your life instead of your flighty sister?

When are you going to stop running away from everything?

"Get out of my head, Rafael Jones Rodriguez," she muttered, throwing her helmet onto the ground.

Tall fir trees sent the sweet scent of pine through the air. Allison headed for the steps leading to the second-story deck. The two-story wood cabin had been built on an acre of land, just outside the small town of Michaels. It had been built by her grandfather as a gift to her grandmother, back when the town had only 205 residents and a general store that served as a hardware, clothing and grocery store.

Now the town's population bloomed in the summer along with the flowers in the boxes the chamber of commerce planted for the enjoyment of tourists. They'd have no problem finding a pastor to perform a wedding. Maybe Paul and Diana could spend a few days at the cabin for their honeymoon and she'd grab a room at the hotel. The beds there were comfortable... Rafe's bed had cushioning, so soft beneath her as they tangled together, naked...

Halfway up the steps, she doubled over. Gasping, she put

a hand to her aching chest, dropping her pack. It tumbled, plop, plop, plop, downward to the soft pine needles peppering the ground.

Heart attack. No, it wasn't. But this pain, so visceral and sharp, felt like a heart attack.

Collapsing on the third step, she buried her head into her hands and tried to keep the tears at bay. Never had she cried in front of anyone, not even that terrible day when she'd done mouth-to-mouth on the cold blue lips of her sister after pulling her from the river.

Diana must not see her break down now, and she could be zooming into the drive any minute. Allison raised her head, gulped down a few deep breaths. *Hold it together, Ally. You've got this.*

No one had her back, so she had to do it.

I've got your back.

Yeah, right, Rafe. You lied like everyone else did.

She finally dried her eyes and trudged up the steps to the front door. Jiggling the knob, she was surprised to find it easily turn.

How many times had she warned Diana about locking the door when she was here?

The wedding dress was gone. But all her clothing remained hung neatly in the main bedroom closet.

Weird. But surely Diana had merely gone for a walk. Allison tried her sister's cell phone.

No answer. Allison hung up. Heart racing, she tried to hold it together.

Bounding down the steps outside, she went to the path in the woods by the creek, the one where they enjoyed hikes. Not that Diana was the hiking sort, but hey, maybe Di changed her mind. Maybe she decided she needed fresh air to clear her head.

Pine needles and fallen leaves littered the narrow trail. Birds called overhead, their cheerful song contrasting to her grim mood. In her mind's eye, she saw Diana out on a solo hike, her focus on her wedding and Paul and not mindful of surroundings. A black bear, and there were plenty in these woods, was on the path and Diana decided to do a selfie, though Allison and their parents had warned Diana many times about the wildlife…

She shook her head. Always the worst-case scenario with her little sister. Diana wasn't that thoughtless. Besides, she preferred selfies with celebrities and the beach, not these dark, thick woods.

Which made this even more worrisome because Diana wasn't fond of long hikes. She complained every time Allison dragged her along on one.

Allison began calling out her sister's name. If Diana was someplace on the path, maybe she had fallen and needed help…

No answer, except the birds chattering in the treetops. Sunlight dappled the trees. At least there was plenty of daylight and Diana wasn't out here when the temperatures dropped and it got inky black, so dark you couldn't even see…

Pressing on, she hummed a tune, remembering good times in these woods to offset her worry. That one time she and Di had gone hiking and found another pathway leading up the mountain and saw the most beautiful view…

Maybe Di headed there for a solitary reflection.

About half a mile from the cabin, the pathway became less littered with pine needles. Allison saw the indent of tire tracks.

Heart racing, she squatted down to examine them. Not a three-wheeler or an ATV they used to venture into the forest to chop firewood. Two tracks, front and back.

A motorcycle.

Intent on the tracks, she followed, and then they stopped at the fork in the path.

Allison glanced around and saw sunlight glint metal in the woods.

Sweat poured down her back, despite the day's relative coolness. Allison looked at the woods. There was a makeshift path cut through the brush. Diana, or someone, had pushed the bike through here.

Camouflaged by brush thrown over it, her sister's motorcycle was propped up by a tree. Allison felt the gas tank.

Cool to the touch.

Worry needled her. Where the hell was her sister and why had she hidden her bike? What was going on here?

"Diana! Where are you?" she screamed, on the edge of hysteria.

No answer. Allison began hunting through the brush. Maybe Diana was hurt, unable to cry out.

About thirty yards from the hidden bike, she saw a flash of white lifted by the wind. Her breath hitched.

"Diana?" she called out.

There, by the fallen half-rotted log. Allison's heart raced as she picked up the elegant headpiece, the silk orange blossoms crumpled, the veil's lace torn and dirty.

Panic raced through her as she examined the bridal veil.

Crimson droplets, the size of quarters, stained the lace.

"Diana!"

Oh dear heavens, please let her be okay, please let her be okay. Clutching the veil in her sweaty fist, she gazed around and saw something else glint in a thin shaft of sunlight. Allison bent down and picked it up.

The diamond gleamed, a promise of marriage and fidelity. The diamond Paul had given to her sister, the diamond Diana had squealed over and shown off to Allison and their parents.

"Diana!"

Only the mocking calls of birdsong answered.

Diana had vanished into thin air, leaving her engagement ring and bloody veil behind.

Chapter 19

He screwed up and Rafe knew it. As he dressed the following morning, he contemplated saying the hell with it and simply forgetting the investigation.

After all, he came here to relax, not to mention the fact he was suspended. Jase and his team could handle the Hernandez case. Besides, Diana probably wouldn't agree to accommodate his request to deliver information on Paul's uncle. Starry-eyed over her wedding, her loyalties remained with her fiancé and his family.

At least that's what he kept telling himself as he ate breakfast in the hotel lobby. He texted Sam that he had errands to run today and for his friend to keep company with Keith and Debbie and others.

'Cause he sure as hell wasn't terrific company right now.

Of all the regrets he'd had in life, what he'd said to Allison last night ranked up there with the worst of them. Even though what she'd said in return had hurt, she spoke only the truth.

He didn't fit in with his big, noisy, loving Cuban family.

Talk about bad timing. Lecturing her about her sister after the best sex he'd had in months, hell, ever?

Talk about a mood killer.

Rafe chased his eggs around the plate with a fork, wanting to hit his head against the table in frustration. How could he be so foolish?

Again, the job interfered with his personal life. Only this time, it wasn't because he'd dedicated himself to hunting down the bad guys.

It was sheer stupidity, all because he finally managed to pry Allison away from her clinging sister. Even if his intentions were honorable, they were horribly misconstrued.

Soy Idiota. You are an idiot.

He'd told Allison it was best to stay apart because she was ruining his investigation, but Rafe knew he was the one who was ruining it.

Maybe he should have tossed in the towel, enjoyed the motorcycle run for the sheer thrill of riding instead of constantly analyzing everything.

Looking for ways to get to Hernandez and get evidence. The crime lord was his albatross, his constant obsession, making him lose reason. Rafe closed his eyes a moment, seeing the dead faces of his agents. He owed it to their families to deliver justice. But was he fooling himself?

The man has evaded us for years. You think you can be the one to bring him down, after all this time?

Appetite gone, he pushed aside the Styrofoam plate and sipped coffee. Nagging instinct made him look up when someone entered the dining area of the hotel.

Or perhaps it was the subtle, enticing scent of a light floral perfume he instantly recognized. A fragrance that rubbed against him last night and burned into his brain as he'd made love to…

"Allison," he said aloud.

She stood a few feet away, and the first thing he noticed was her auburn brown hair, tangled and unkempt. Were those leaves in her hair?

Had she slept in the woods? Rafe glanced at the rumpled pink jeans, white silk blouse stained with dirt and the floral jacket with a slight tear. Same clothing she'd worn last night when she'd stormed out of his room.

And out of his life, or so he'd thought.

"Allison, why are you here?"

"I need your help." Allison didn't meet his gaze. "I wouldn't ask except… I'm desperate."

Rafe set down his coffee cup. "What's wrong?"

Biting her lip, she shook her head. Alarm raced through him. All these months he'd known Allison, even in the thick of being with the dangerous bikers, she'd never lost her composure.

Allison was calm and cool when everyone else got rattled and ran around shrieking like banshees.

Not now. He pushed out his chair, took her hand and led her over to a quiet corner by the elevators.

"Allison, what is it? Did someone hurt you?"

The old protective streak rose up in a fury. "Tell me and I'll find that son of a bitch and…"

"Diana's gone." She raised her gaze to him, and he saw, for the first time, the panic flaring there. "She's missing."

His mind raced. Rafe gripped her arms to steady her. Damn, she seemed ready to collapse. He'd never seen her this rattled.

"I need to call the police, but then I thought I'd call the FBI, and then I realized you're the FBI and I thought of you, but I can't risk calling the cops because they'd ask too many questions or not take me seriously or say it was a case of the wedding jitters and she ran away. But if it is, why is her veil splattered with blood? I didn't know what to do or where to turn so I came here!"

"*Dios Mio*, she's missing? Okay, take a deep breath. Let's sit down." He steered her over to one of the lobby chairs, now abandoned by hotel occupants who'd set out for the bike rally.

"Start at the beginning, from when you left my room. Tell me the last time you saw her. Leave nothing out."

In halting words, staring at the ground, Allison detailed what she'd found. Rafe listened intently.

When she finished, his heart sank to his stomach. Didn't look good, but he couldn't alarm Allison any more than she was already distressed.

"Diana's mood changed yesterday. Even I noticed it, and I barely know her. Did she get any phone calls, or texts, that upset her?"

Allison finally raised her head. "No. Paul is supposed to fly up later today. They were to marry Sunday. What am I going to tell him?"

"One thing at a time, Allison."

"Should I call the cops? I should. But I'm scared, Rafe. Can you help me?"

The pleading in her big brown eyes, the genuine terror—hell, they'd make the sturdiest man melt.

"No police for now. We need to check the hospitals first."

"You do it. I-I don't know where to start."

He nodded and began calling the nearest medical facility and a few clinics. Nothing.

Rafe thumbed off his phone. "Take me to the cabin. Did you leave everything the way you found it?"

She nodded.

Then blood drained from her already paling face. "Oh dear heavens, do you think she's still alive?"

Allison began to shake. "Oh no, if she's dead… She can't be dead! My poor sister, why didn't I stick to her side? Why did I leave her alone?"

Steeling himself against the need to take her into his arms, soothe her fears, he gave her a level look. "Get yourself together, Lexington. Stop getting hysterical. Do you want to find your sister or have a breakdown?"

Shocked, as he knew she would become, Allison gulped. She narrowed her eyes. "Find my sister. Are you going to help me?"

"Yes. Only if you do exactly as I say."

"I will." She parted her fingers in the middle and held up her hand. "Scout's honor."

He raised his brows. "Allison, that's the Vulcan sign for live long and prosper."

"Oh!" She gave a sheepish grin. "I never was a good Girl Scout. Too busy chasing the boys."

"I'll bet." But glad she'd finally regained her composure, he nodded toward the parking lot. "Go outside and wait for me. Let me get a few things and I'll be down."

When he arrived at the cabin and the trail where Allison had found her sister's bike, the ring and the bloodied veil, Rafe took over with smooth efficiency.

Using his bike gloves, he examined the veil. The blood splatters were even, almost too even. Squatting down, he examined the forest floor and decaying pine needles and oak leaves. No blood. No blood trail. Whatever happened to stain the veil hadn't happened here. The ring was also absent of blood.

He straightened, meeting Allison's worried gaze.

"Let's go to the cabin."

Not questioning him, she led the way. In the cabin, he examined everything, including Diana's bedroom.

Her clothing was still hung neatly in the closet. Rafe opened drawers, sifted through pairs of silk panties and lacy bras. He shut the drawer.

"Your sister sure did like clothing. I don't suppose you remember how much she packed?"

Allison bit her lip and shook her head.

"Did she have a purse?"

"No just her pack. And her cell phone, but I don't see it anywhere."

"Let's look around the cabin."

They searched inside and out on the deck.

As they returned inside, empty-handed, Rafe went into the bathroom to search it.

On the floor near the shower, he spotted a small crimson droplet. Still wearing his gloves, he opened drawers and saw a small pair of cuticle scissors.

The edges were red.

Dropping the scissors into the drawer, he looked at an anxious Allison standing in the doorway.

"No blood trail, no indication any harm was done to Diana. No, this is more like a statement, Allison. I think she did this to herself."

Relief mingled with bewilderment on her face. "Why would she cut herself? What kind of statement does that make?"

"Drama, maybe. Your sister does seem prone to it," he said dryly. "She craves attention and drama."

Allison blinked. "You think me forcing her into eloping had her creating drama to get attention? That's a stupid way of getting it. And as much as Di craves the spotlight and drama, this feels different."

"I can't argue that. The veil wasn't slashed by an angry bride. But the blood and the ring make no sense."

"Well, it's obvious she left. Or someone took her. Not through the woods, either. How did she get out? On foot?" Allison wondered.

"I doubt she'd call an Uber or Lyft and draw attention to herself."

Suddenly Allison remembered. "Damn. I totally forgot. Dad kept a car up here, on the property, for when he and mom would fly up here on weekends. It was easier than the long drive. The car is older, but he parked it in the old barn."

She hunted through the cabinet holding the DVR. "The keys are gone."

Rafe pointed at the DVR. "We'll go through this after we check on the car."

They went to the barn together. The padlock was gone. Even before Allison opened the door, she knew.

The car was gone. Rafe peered inside and then squatted on the ground to examine the tire tracks in the mud.

"I'll need a description of the vehicle to give to my team," he told her.

Back inside the cabin, Rafe opened the cabinet holding the DVR. Four cameras—three at the cabin's entrances and one on the tree by where cars parked. Two more at the barn. All wireless.

"Your security system still works?" he asked.

Allison rolled her eyes. "Duh. Why didn't I think of that?"

"Stress makes you forget." He thumbed backward through the footage and frowned.

Several minutes later, he blew out a frustrated breath. "All the footage since yesterday has been deleted."

"I don't even know if Di knows how to work the machine. Dad did show us long ago, but I never thought of her paying attention to something like that."

"Perhaps she did. You may have underestimated your sister, Allison."

Maybe Rafe was right, and Diana was involved in something shady. Allison shook free the thought.

"I know you two are close, but how close? Would Diana share deep secrets with you?"

"Why?"

"Mi familia." He shook his head. "My family. I have two sisters, and they loved to share secrets and swap notes. Julie

and Ronnie sometimes would leave notes for each other in their clothing hamper. I found one once and blackmailed Ronnie into giving me her week's allowance so I wouldn't tell our parents she skipped school to go to the movies.

Allison's mouth quirked. "You sneak."

"I prefer to think of it as being a good negotiator. Would Diana trust you with a secret?"

Her brow wrinkled. "Yeah, she would."

"If Diana were going to leave you a message for your eyes only, where would she put it? Not a text or an email, but something covert. Did you have a special way of communicating when you were younger, something to keep secrets from your parents?"

"Yeah." Allison frowned. "What are you thinking? Like spies do?"

"Something like that."

Allison exhaled. "I don't know. Maybe the blood on the veil is a message? But she hates pain."

Hates pain… That made Diana's actions even more puzzling. Why did she cut herself then?

"So, you think she'd leave me a secret message like the CIA spies do? Like a spy watch or a drop point?"

"It's possible. How would Diana leave you a message when you were younger? Think, Allison!"

She racked her brain. Then it clicked.

"Books. I was always nagging her to read more. Real books instead of fashion magazines. I would circle words in the book to help her when we were younger, and later, we'd highlight or circle words to leave secret messages."

She ran into her bedroom and rummaged around on the nightstand. "I brought two books."

In Diana's bedroom, *The Help* had been left on the nightstand. She handed *Animal Farm* to Rafe. "Here, you look through this one and I'll look through the other. Look for words circled in ink."

Allison handed him a tattered copy of George Orwell's *Animal Farm*. He found three words circled early in the tome: *before I die*.

This wasn't good.

As he showed it to her, she whispered, "Oh no."

Rafe took the book from her trembling hands.

At the book's beginning, the word *help* was circled.

The next word circled was *me*.

Diana's message was grimly clear. *Help me before I die.*

Chapter 20

Her sister was in deep trouble, and Allison had no idea how to help her. Or why Diana was in danger.

This was like a jigsaw puzzle with several pieces missing. She couldn't even determine what pieces were gone, or what the final puzzle revealed.

Rafe had insisted she step back and relax while he looked around the grounds thoroughly. She took advantage of this to shower and change into fresh clothing.

As she'd expected, he returned to the cabin without any other clues.

Now she sat on the sofa, gripping a steaming mug of coffee thanks to Rafe, who'd made a fresh pot.

She wasn't used to feeling helpless.

It reminded her of the terrible day when Diana slipped on the riverbank and fell into the water, nearly drowning.

She's not going to die. We'll find her.

"Where do we even start? Should we call the cops?" she asked him.

Glancing up from the kitchen table, where he was making notes on a pad, he shook his head.

"What about Paul? He needs to know."

"Hold off on calling him. I need to figure things out."

Calm and controlled, and utterly professional, Rafael proved a steady rock. Despite what happened between them, she could rely on him. *I trust him with this.* Rafe knew all about investigating missing persons. He was an FBI agent with skills and experience.

And I'm falling apart. Get a grip, Allison.

"What do we do?" She twisted her hands together. "I don't know what to do, what to think."

"We start at the beginning, with Diana's life." Rafe set down the pen. "Let's check her social media. Do you know anything about it?"

She told him about all of Di's social media accounts. Now she wished she'd paid closer attention to her sister's postings.

Allison scrolled through her phone, searching for Diana's accounts. But when she tried to pull up each one, she received a message saying the account didn't exist. Even her Jump ONit video account, so popular with twentysomethings who followed Di, had been deleted.

This was as troubling as the bloody veil. Diana thrived on social media attention and considered herself somewhat of an influencer. Social media helped her with exposure for her modeling career, and to get jobs.

She showed Rafe her phone and the message and told him about her sister thriving on attention. He frowned. "Does she have other accounts that you might not know of, a secret social media account?"

Allison felt a flare of hope. "Her finstagram! Fake Instagram she shares with family and close friends."

Allison checked the account and her heart sank. Only three photos remained on the account. One was a photo of a forest with Diana wearing jeans, a hoodie and a backpack, an older photo of Diana in a pink dress and another of their childhood home. She scrutinized the photos, looking for clues.

"It's still there, but she's deleted a lot of content. Including the vid of us at the first stop on the Teddy Bear Run, and the vid of her trying on the veil."

As Rafe took her phone and scrolled through the photos, she buried her head into her hands. "I don't understand. Why would she do this? Did someone threaten her?"

He kept looking at the photos. "How many photos did she have on this particular account and what kind?"

"Not sure." Allison searched her memory. Too often she'd dismissed her sister's fake Instagram account with the excuse she'd been busy with work. In truth, she thought the social media account frivolous and vain.

"I only checked it maybe a couple of times a month. Maybe she had about fifty photos? Most of them had to do with her moods."

"Like a journal?"

"Yeah." Allison rubbed her temple. "It was always about Di, and how happy she'd be if she got a good modeling job, or her complaining about her boyfriends, general stuff like that. Her relationships, or if she gained a pound or two. Honestly, I found it a little self-serving and whining, so I rarely went on there."

Rafe tapped the phone. "Any reason you can think why she'd delete all the photos except these three?"

More confused, she shook her head. "I mean, these aren't anything special. That's the house where we grew up in upstate New York before we moved to South Florida, the dress, that's an ordinary pink dress she always liked before she outgrew it, and the forest…"

"Anything special about the forest?"

"Not really, I mean, it was a modeling job for backpacks, one of her first magazine shoots. She wasn't even happy about it because Di wasn't into the outdoors. Is there a reason why she left these photos there? Maybe she was in a hurry to delete everything?"

He set down the phone. "Allison, people usually don't delete an extensive social media footprint unless they're trying to hide from the public. It's clear Diana is doing the same. Is there another reason why Diana didn't want to elope with Paul? A reason why she was adamant about having the wedding at his uncle's house, other than a huge society affair?"

"What are you getting at?"

His gaze remained calm and steady, but her heart began hammering hard. She knew what he thought, even before he told her.

"Diana could have been involved in smuggling drugs."

"She's innocent! Diana would never do that! She may be naive at times, but she's not a criminal."

"I told you before, she's under investigation because it's suspicious all the places she frequents were raided and fentanyl was found."

Her temper flared. "What are you thinking, Rafe? You never liked my sister from the moment you met her. You only wanted to use her in the same way you used me! You slapped a label on her she doesn't deserve."

"In investigations, these kind of questions are typical. You look for the victim's past and present, to see if they are involved in any kind of criminal activity."

To his credit, Rafe didn't rise to the bait and argue back. He remained calm and steady, a sharp contrast to the feelings raging inside her.

She glared at him. How could he be so calm when her entire world was shattering?

"There is a chance Diana may not be aware of what's going on, Allison. You said she's naive and trusting. Sometimes dealers use mules without them actually knowing what they are carrying."

He gave her a pointed look. "Diana does travel for her modeling work."

Oh dear. Allison rubbed her tired eyes. She hadn't thought of that, or even considered it. Diana was clean-cut, wholesome and always avoided the fast party life. Maybe it was one reason why she hadn't advanced as much as some models.

"I don't know. Maybe. I can't see her being fooled like that, though. She goes through everything in her suitcase. I taught her to be careful when she travels."

"Was Diana aware of anyone who bore a grudge against her? Someone, perhaps another model, who would gloat and feel smug if anything happened to her?"

"No. Di always said most of the people in the business liked her, at least from what I've seen. Can't you contact people in your office, have them do an official search?"

For the first time, Rafe looked frustrated. "I can't access my resources at the Bureau, Allison. I've been suspended. If you want to go through official channels, then call the police and I'll make the call to my team at the Bureau. Chances are they can't do much because the police here will investigate and, if needed, bring in the field office in Georgia to help."

"No." She thought of all the exposure, and the publicity. "I think… I think she's hiding because she's scared. That much is obvious from the secret message. Right?"

He nodded.

"Getting the cops involved risks getting the media involved, and if she's in danger…" Her throat closed tight. "It will increase the threat to her. I don't think she's being dramatic, Rafe. I'm sorry for snapping at you, but I'm really worried. My sister loves attention, but not like this. She deleted all her social media because she's hiding from everyone."

He came closer to her on the sofa and picked up her hand, gently pressing it. "I think you're right. But it's up to you what you want to do. I'm here to help out any way I can, as little as I can do."

Allison stared down at his hand. Long, elegant fingers and black hair dusting the knuckles. A capable man, and an excellent agent, he was more than his job. He was a rock she needed right now.

"Thank you." She slipped her hand away and stood, pacing. This closeness sent her feelings spiraling and she needed to focus on Diana.

Diana was hiding and wanted Allison to find her. The book and the deleted photos on her Instagram account indicated as much.

"Check her fake Instagram account and see if there's an update," Rafe advised. "I'll call Jase, see if he can pull some CCTV footage of the road outside your cabin."

"Can you do that or will it get you into trouble?"

He shrugged. "Jase will inform the local police there's a suspicious biker wanted for questioning. There are a few bikers at the rally we're keeping eyes on, so it's legit."

She checked the account. No updates. Minutes later, Rafe examined his phone to see the footage Jase had downloaded and sent to him.

Grainy and black-and-white, the security footage from the gas station on the corner of the main highway and the dirt road of the family cabin proved useless. There were a few bikes traveling back and forth during the suspected time when Diana vanished. Then she gasped, recognizing the family sedan.

"It must be her!" Allison's fingers trailed over the screen. "She's headed north."

"Any idea why? A hotel or a friend in the area she'd visit?"

Allison tried to think. "No. She hasn't been here in a few years. I doubt she knows anyone."

Rafe made an impatient sound. "I'm going to the barn again to look for other tire tracks. Stay here."

As the door slammed behind him, she tried to put herself in her sister's place. If Diana was terrified, where would she flee? Paul. Back to Paul, her refuge, her love. Every minute

Diana remained missing, it meant she could be in horrible danger.

She scrolled through her cell phone and pressed Paul's number.

He answered straight away. "Allison? What's going on? I've been trying to reach Diana and it goes straight to voicemail."

"I don't know." She swallowed hard. "I was hoping you had heard from her. She's gone."

Paul released a low curse. "What… Where do you think she's gone?"

"I don't know. I don't think this is wedding jitters. This feels more sinister."

She refrained from telling him about the bloodied veil and the engagement ring. "Paul, I can't help but wonder if your uncle had something to do with this."

There. It was out in the open.

A deep breath. "Hector? Why would he? But damn, you may be on to something, Maybe she got scared off because she was afraid of upsetting him after all the money he's spent on the wedding. It was a mistake to let him throw us a lavish wedding. I kept telling Diana it wasn't worth his involvement. I haven't been close to him, tried to keep him at a distance. It was all her idea to have the wedding at his estate. But she wanted a huge, beautiful wedding and knew your parents were strapped for cash."

Stunned, Allison gripped the phone so hard her hand hurt. "Paul, you should get up here and look for her. She loves and trusts you more than anyone. Even me."

"I already booked my flight for tomorrow. I'll see about changing it. Damn it, Allison, why did you have to take her with you? She was nervous enough as it is. She'd have been better off staying here with me in Miami."

At a loss for words, she could only mumble, "I only wanted a last nice sisterly trip with her, Paul."

His voice softened. "I get it. Di would do anything for her big sister. I know you love her. I'm just upset. Sorry. Let me know if you hear anything, anything, okay?"

"Yes, of course. You do the same."

She hung up, lifting her gaze to meet Rafe's angry expression. He'd returned to the cabin so quietly, she hadn't even heard the door close.

"I told you not to call him, Allison. If you're going to work with me, don't work against me."

"I had to tell him! What if Di returned to him and all this worry is for nothing? Why didn't you want me to tell him?"

"Because there's nothing to tell him yet, except the fact she's missing. And if she was with Paul, don't you think she'd have called you by now to let you know she was safe?"

He was right. She sighed.

"Where would Diana go if she didn't leave the area? Sleep overnight in the forest near here? There's miles of forest for hiding."

Allison shook her head. "I can't see Diana camping in the woods. She fretted every time she broke a nail. My sister's idea of roughing it is a motel without room service."

"Then we'll start at the hotels. Text me her photo."

After doing so, she mustered her strength. "You mean I'll start at the hotels searching. Not you."

"I'll go with you." The determination on his face she knew well. This was Rafe with laser-focused attention on catching the bad guys.

"You're suspended."

"Tough." He muttered something in Spanish and then gestured to his bike. "Grab your helmet and get on."

Allison felt a tug of gratitude mingled with alarm. Rafe still thought Diana was in cahoots with Hernandez and smuggling drugs. If they found her sister, would he call the police and arrest her?

Rafe's bike was bigger than hers, but he handled the machine with expertise.

The engine rumbled beneath her, the seat vibrating as she wrapped her arms around his lean waist. Her fingers gripped his leather jacket for reassurance more than balance—she trusted him with this at least.

Rafe was a good biker. She turned her head, studying the landscape as they headed into town and the hotels. Allison pulled the helmet's visor up to study the pedestrians ambling on the sidewalks, browsing the shops, talking and laughing and shopping. No one looked familiar.

Her breath came in short, stabbing pants as anxiety built. Allison focused on the steady thrum of the motorcycle and moved her hand upward to rest on Rafe's chest. The rhythmic beat of his heart calmed her. He was a rock in a turbulent sea, and even though she knew their differences were too vast to overcome, she needed him now.

Wind rushed past her, tugging at the edges of her jacket and swirling around her legs. Cool air caressed her face as she snuggled closer to Rafe. The fresh and clean scent of the open road filled her senses, grounding her in the present.

He pulled into the parking lot of the first hotel Allison knew Diana liked.

After he parked out front, they went into the lobby. Double glass doors with brass knobs gave the hotel an air of elegance, much like the marbled lobby did.

A bored clerk glanced up from a computer screen at the front desk. "We're full," he said.

"We're searching for a young lady," Allison began.

The clerk rolled his eyes. "Isn't everyone this week? Go take your funny business elsewhere."

Rafe approached the clerk. "We're looking for this woman. Diana Lexington." He held up his cell phone photo of Diana Allison had texted.

The clerk barely glanced at the photo before shaking his head. "Haven't seen her."

"You didn't even look." Allison's temper shot up. "Look again, chump."

Ignoring her, his attention dropped back to his phone. Sounds of a video game ensued.

Enough of this crap. Allison hoisted herself up and vaulted over the counter. She grabbed the startled clerk by his starched lapels. "Listen, you asshole. It's my sister. She's missing and I'm losing patience. Take another look before I break your cell phone in half and maybe your fingers in the process."

Squeaking, the clerk looked at the photo she had on her phone.

"N-no. S-sorry. Haven't seen her. There's been…a lot of people coming and going! I got on shift a short while ago. I can't be expected to memorize their faces."

Allison grabbed the man's cell phone and tossed it onto the counter. Her fingers wrapped around his. "Look at your register. She's from Florida. Her name is Diana. Did she check in last night?"

"I can't do that."

Allison tightened the pressure on the man's hand. "Oh?"

He squealed and threw Rafe a helpless glance. "Please, I didn't do anything. Get her off me."

Rafe looked amused. "Sorry, buddy. Once she gets started, it's hard to stop her. I suggest you cooperate."

With his free left hand, the clerk accessed the computer registry and scrolled through it. "No Dianas here. Most of our guests are men."

"Ally," Rafe said softly. "Let him go."

With some disgust, mainly for herself for losing it, she released his hand and returned his phone. "Here. Sorry."

The mumbled apology didn't wipe the scared look off the

clerk's face as they walked out. She gazed up and down the street.

"Di, where are you?"

Rafe looked into her eyes, his resolve unwavering. "We'll do everything we can to find her, Allison. I promise."

But hours later, the search proved fruitless. At the last bar past the edge of town and down a side road, Allison knew Diana wouldn't have been here. The Dive Bar was run-down, with a neon sign with the *r* blinking. Grime coated the windows. They trudged inside. Her nose wrinkled at the smell of cigar smoke, beer and something unpleasant.

Rafe slid onto an empty bar stool and beckoned her to join him.

"I'll be right back," he murmured and headed to the restrooms.

It was barely past eleven. By the time Rafe emerged from the bathroom, a man with a crew cut and a friendly smile came out of the kitchen and stood behind the bar.

"Can I help you? Lunch isn't served until twelve thirty, but the beer is always on tap and icy cold."

Though he appeared relaxed, Allison sensed a different vibe coming off Rafe. She decided to let him do all the talking.

"Two cold beers," Rafe told him and pointed to a popular domestic brand on tap. "What's your name, friend?"

"Andy. I own the place. Reason why lunch isn't served for a while. Most of my staff got trashed last night. I'm the only one who made it to work."

When the beer was served, Rafe raised his glass. "To your sister and her intended. May they have a happy life together."

Dutifully she clinked glasses, wondering what the hell he planned.

"A wedding, huh?" The bartender wiped down the counter in front of them with a rag that seemed dirtier than the counter. "So you're not here for the Teddy Bear Run?"

"It's serving double duty," Rafe said. "Though I suspect the bride may be upset at the motorcycle rally getting all the attention. She's a bit of a drama queen. She got a little drunk last night and didn't make it home yet. Any chance she was here last night?"

Rafe showed the cell phone photo of Diana. Andy nodded and grinned. "Yeah, she was a little trashed. I offered to let her crash at my place, but I got busy and when I turned around, she was gone."

Allison's heart raced. "What else do you remember?"

"I remember her because she was a real looker and she was the only person here driving a car. Everyone else was a biker."

Allison sat up straight, trying to mask her hopes. "Oh? Did she say anything? She's my sister. Please. I need to find her."

The bartender's grin dropped. "Not much."

"What did she say?" Rafe asked, setting down his beer.

The bartender averted his gaze. "She said she wished you had let go of her hand that day in the river."

Allison's heart raced. Damn it.

Rafe, bless him, didn't let up. "What else? Where was she headed? And why?"

But the man shook his head. "Sorry, buddy. It was busy."

Rafe gave a chilling smile. "Busy enough for you not to remember anything other than she was driving a car and wished she'd died in a river? Or how pretty she is and how much you wanted to let her stay at your place? Or what? So you could take advantage of her?"

The man's mouth opened. "Listen, I would never…"

"Oh yeah?" Rafe slid off the bar stool and leaned on the counter. "Tell me exactly what she said. It's either here or at the police station."

Blanching, the bartender gulped. "Um, you a cop? But I can see your bike outside."

"There's several of my friends in town who are cops and

bikers. I know your business, Andrew Raine. I checked with a few people I know. Your liquor license on this dump expired two months ago and you're known for hiring illegals to work under the counter and work cheap. You skirt the law, but know this. Unless you start talking, I'll have all my cop friends storm in here and shut you down faster than you can pour another beer."

Impressed, Allison wanted to applaud.

"Okay! I'll talk, just don't shut down the place."

The man held up his hands. "There were a few guys bothering her at the bar while she was trying to eat. I told them to get lost, and she thanked me and said she only wanted beer and a club sandwich. She barely ate, was crying too much. When I asked her what was wrong, she said her life was in ruins and she didn't know what to do next. I was trying to help!"

"By offering to let her stay at your place," Rafe said flatly.

Andrew grew even paler. "I was only trying to help her."

"Did she say where she was headed?"

"No. She only said she wished she could return to a happier time in her childhood when the only secret she had was in the tree house where she used to hide to eavesdrop on her sister. I guess that's you."

Allison narrowed her gaze. "You'd better be telling the truth, and if my friend here obtains a search warrant, you had better not have Diana bound and gagged in your bedroom."

"No, no, never! I'm not like that. Sure, I like to hit on a pretty woman, but that's not my scene."

"What exactly is your scene?" Rafe asked.

"I'm just a businessman…"

His voice trailed off as Allison walked to a security camera on the wall above a tall cardboard box near the entrance.

"Mind if I check your cameras to see if she left with anyone?" she asked sweetly.

"The cameras don't work. They're a decoy. I fell behind in the rent and couldn't pay for the upkeep."

She peered inside the box. At least ten tan teddy bears stared back at her. She wrinkled her nose. The bears smelled like stale beer and cigar smoke.

The kids would love those. Not.

"Hey, get away from those. They're a donation," Andrew protested.

"A donation for who?"

But the man's face grew pale. "Someone's picking them up later. Donating them to the local hospital I think. I just offered to be the pick-up place. Look, you'd better leave. I don't want trouble."

Rafe looked Andrew up and down. He plucked a twenty-dollar bill from his wallet and tossed it on the counter.

Outside, Allison felt her first surge of hope. "We know she was alive last night, at least when she left here. But where did she go?"

Rafe picked up his black helmet. "What did Diana mean by wishing you had let go of her hand? What gives?"

Allison's throat tightened. He might as well know now, because sooner or later, she'd have to tell him about that horrible day. If it provided even a slim clue to finding her sister, she'd take it.

"When I was twelve and Di was eight, I saved her from drowning during a family vacation up here. We were in a kayak, took it out against our parents' wishes. I was paddling downstream, but the current was ripping. It tipped and Di was swept downstream. I grabbed her hand and got us to the shore. I told her if she was going down, so was I. I wouldn't let go for anything."

Tears clogged her throat. "She was my sister, Rafe. My baby sister. And now she's talking like that? Wishing she would have died instead?"

He put his hands on her trembling shoulders. Even through

the material of her denim jacket, she felt the warmth of his caring touch.

"Hold on," he soothed. "People say all kinds of things they don't mean when they're upset. Sometimes it's the only way they can cope with terrible news. They exaggerate. And create drama."

Allison shrugged off his hands and wiped her eyes with an angry fist. "Didn't sound like drama to me. Sounded like she's giving up."

"If so, why would she leave you those clues?"

She scowled. "I don't know. Everything is so complicated, and every minute we don't find her means she's slipping away from me."

"We have a lead," he pointed out. "She did say she wanted to return to her childhood and her secret tree house where she spied on you. Where is this tree house?"

Pressing a finger against her temple, she tried to think. "It was by the barn on land my father bought years ago. But Dad tore it down years ago because the wood was rotting and he didn't want Di to get hurt falling through the floorboards."

"What about the barn? Still here?"

"I think so."

"Let's go, then."

A short while later, they parked their motorcycles along the gravel road leading to the barn. A barbed wire fence separated the roadway from a pasture. Sunshine warmed them as they walked up the road. As their boots crunched the stones under their feet, Allison lifted her face to the clear blue sky. Green fields, rolling mountains in the distance and a thick forest made for a bucolic scene. Ordinarily she'd enjoy a stroll in the country. Not today.

The stone barn had been rebuilt after her father purchased the land twenty years ago with the intention of building a home and moving. The move never happened. He rented the barn to a local farmer who also rented the pasture, but the lease expired last year.

Rafe stopped. His harsh intake of breath followed. "Look. Is that your parents' old sedan?"

Her heart dropped to her stomach. Parked near the driveway leading from the road to the stone barn was an older model sedan. Rafe jotted down the license plate.

"I don't know. Could be."

But she knew it wasn't necessary. Her sister was hiding inside.

They waded through the knee-high grasses to the double doors. One was wide open. Smells of animal scat and hay filtered through the musty air. Dust motes danced in sunbeams streaming through the single grimy window. In the southern end of the barn, a hay pile nearly reached the loft.

It didn't feel right. Something was off about this place.

Chills raced down her spine as they entered the darkness. "That door should have been closed," she murmured. "Di would never leave it open. Our dad drilled it into us that we always left the door closed so stray animals can't get inside."

Rafe gently pushed her in back of him. "I'll check things out. Stay back, just in case."

"It's my sister." Allison pointed to the eastern corner of the barn. "If she sees you, she may not come out. Dad used to store water there and horse blankets. See if anything's been touched."

She climbed the rickety wooden ladder to the barn loft, the creak echoing through the abandoned building. The sweet smell of a hay pile below the loft mingled with the musky scent of abandonment and animal scat. Dust motes floated in stray beams of sunshine coming through the grimy window. Anticipation and worry raced through her. Di surely had to be here. As a child, her sister adored playing hide-and-seek in the barn.

As she climbed high enough to see into the shadowy loft, she spied farming equipment and old furniture. Something moved in the shadows.

"Di? Please don't be scared. It's me, Ally, jellybean. I've been so worried about you."

Allison climbed a little higher, her eyes adjusting to the dim light.

Suddenly, a figure lunged from the shadows, and something kicked her in the head. Yelping with pain, she managed to hold on to the ladder, but the dim figure pushed the ladder over. Falling, she managed to aim her trajectory at the hay bale, where she landed with a poof.

Vision blurred, she heard boots on the wooden floorboards of the barn, and Rafe's deep voice yell out.

As she struggled in the musty hay, Rafe freed her. He brushed hay from her hair and face.

"Ally, you okay? Did you get hurt?" he asked, voice thick with concern.

"I'm okay. My pride is hurt more than anything." Wincing, she touched her head where the attacker kicked her. "Good thing I have a hard head."

He gently touched her head. "You may have a concussion."

"Doubt it." She started to stand, but he put his hands on her shoulders. "Easy. Sit for a few minutes."

"You should have run after the guy," she told him. "He got away."

"I'm more concerned about you."

The proclamation made her heart beat faster, even as she winced from the pain. "Get a look at that son of a biscuit?"

"Medium height, build. Dressed in black. Stay here. I'm checking the outside."

He returned shortly. "Found a ladder under the loft window. He must have used that to get away."

"That car we saw was probably his, not Di's."

Rafe examined her head. "You're not bleeding, but that was a nasty fall. You sure you're okay?"

"I'm fine." Allison swallowed her distress as she touched her head again. "Help me up, please."

At his frown, she sighed. "Look, I'm a nurse. I know I'm okay."

Rafe helped her to stand and put his hands on her shoulders. His touch warmed her and felt reassuring. Calm and collected, he was good in an emergency.

Good in everything, actually. The feel of his strong hands on her trembling shoulders reminded her of exactly how good he'd been when they'd made love.

Here she was, thinking of sex when Di was still missing. In danger. Allison trembled inside.

Rafe backed up. "I'll have Jase run the plate on that sedan, see if it belongs to your family or someone else."

As he called Jase, she leaned against a pillar. That was a sliver of hope at least. She glanced around the gloomy barn and shivered, thinking of her delicate sister sleeping in the loft, fearful and apprehensive. Maybe the person who attacked her had taken Di as well.

Rafe hung up and shook his head. "Plate belongs to a car reported stolen a few months ago. If that was your family's car, someone put the stolen plate on it. I'm taking a look at that loft."

As he investigated, she sat, holding her head. Soon he returned.

"I found this by a few horse blankets." Rafe held up a tube of cosmetics.

Allison took the lip gloss and examined it. "This is Di's favorite shade. I'm sure it's hers. Maybe she left it for us to find?"

"Another damn clue." He examined her head. "I'm taking you back to the cabin. This needs medical attention."

"I'm fine."

But as she stood, she staggered, stricken by a sudden bout of dizziness. "Give me a minute."

He didn't. Rafe lifted her into his arms and carried her over to his motorcycle and set her upon it. "Can you hold on, or should I call for an Uber?"

"I'll be fine. Where are we going?"

"Hospital. You need to have that looked at."

Allison blew out a breath. "Listen, Rodriguez, I know my body. I just need to rest a bit. Take me back to the cabin. No hospitals, no doctors."

She appreciated this side of him, in control and concerned for her welfare. Everyone else in her life always took it for granted that she was the person who cared for others.

No one ever cared much for her, until Rafe came along.

"Ally, I need to call this into the local authorities. Stolen license plate on that car makes it a crime, and if you want to find your sister…"

"No!" She thought of how Rafe thought Diana was involved with drugs, but he was willing to set aside his suspicions for the search. Locals would be less charitable.

"Please, I need more time."

They returned to the cabin. No sign of the car Diana had taken. Against more protests, Rafe carried her into the cabin and set her on the sofa.

She heard him call from the bathroom. "Where's your first aid kit?"

"Don't have one."

He popped his head out the door. "You're a nurse and you don't have a first aid kit?"

"Don't need one. I carry one in my pack, and you don't need to play nurse with me." She gave a light laugh. "I mean, play me with me. Damn, am I making sense?"

"No. And yes."

She went to the bathroom to inspect the lump on her forehead as Rafe fetched her pack and handed over her kit. Not too bad. Whoever attacked her hadn't much strength, and the move served only to knock her off the ladder. She swallowed a couple of anti-inflammatory pills and got a frozen bag of peas for the lump.

They went into the living room and sat on the sofa. Rafe pulled off her Dr. Martens and placed her feet on his lap, massaging them as she put the frozen peas against her head

"Damn, that feels so good. Maybe I should get hit on the head more often," she told him.

He frowned. "Don't even joke about it. Tell me about the lip gloss I found. Any idea why she'd leave it behind?"

"None, except she probably wanted us to find it, let us know she was there."

"Allison, you keep saying your sister is innocent. Why wouldn't she call you to tell you she's safe?"

The delicious massaging of her feet ceased. Allison swung her legs over to rest them on the coffee table. Rafe turned into a serious FBI agent. Direct. Questioning. Impartial.

"She's scared. Something must have scared her off and she can't call me directly. She's on the run."

"Can you think of anyone in Diana's life who would want to hurt her?"

Allison's head throbbed, but she realized the importance of his question. "You believe me, finally. You think someone is after her and she's not into smuggling drugs and has nothing to do with drugs."

Expression guarded, he shook his head. "I'm eliminating all possible reasons why she ran away, especially now that we know she was here and the person who attacked you may have chased her."

"I didn't get a good look at the person."

"Think, Allison. Perhaps someone in her past, or her fiancé's past?"

His next question gave her pause. "Could it be a woman?"

Allison pressed a hand to her throbbing head. "I don't know."

"What about a former girlfriend?"

Not that Paul had many of those. "Paul was always quiet and devoted to his business. He had dated, but nothing serious. Paul's low-key and average, and he's never had a lot of money. All his income and time went back into his business."

She thought hard. "There's always women who get jealous in the modeling world, but I can't think of one in particular who would target Diana."

Then she remembered. "Paul's ex was hung up on him."

Rafe made notes on his phone. "Who?"

"Lucy. Late thirties, dark hair and eyes. She works as a housekeeper in his uncle's house."

He glanced at her. "The brunette who was nasty?"

"Yeah, I forgot you met her. Briefly. Miserable woman. She works for Hernandez part-time in exchange for living in the guesthouse. I saw Di have a run-in with her."

"At the house?"

"No. She worked at the dress shop where Diana had her wedding gown altered. Lucy had started working there, and when Diana saw her she wanted to change seamstresses, but it was too late. Not enough time before the wedding. I went with Di for her second fitting, and Lucy looked at Diana and sniffed and told her, 'You think you have it so good, *puta*, just wait and see. You'll get yours."

"You can't recall her full name? Saw it on a name tag, perhaps?"

Allison shook her head. "Maybe. I don't know! Why can't I remember?"

"Stress affects memory. Close your eyes. Think of sounds, smells. The sewing machines running, the women talking, fans stirring the air and the rustle of fabric."

Closing her eyes, she envisioned the small, dark shop and

the rows of industrial sewing machines, the glaring fluorescent lights overhead and the women bent over the machines. The place reminded her of a sweat shop, but not wanting to ruin Diana's excitement, she'd kept her suspicions to herself.

"Maybe her last name reminded you of something. A celebrity, a town, a favorite drink."

The spicy fragrance of his cologne enveloped her in a warm blanket of scent. The shop smelled of machine oil, the sharp smell of fabric, the heavy and cloying scent of inexpensive perfume. Lucy had kept watching them as she and Di made their way past the rows of machines to the back where fittings took place. The harsh overhead fluorescents, Lucy's pretty face sallow, the dinky plastic name tag reflecting the light...

Allison's eyes flew open. "Martin. Lucy Martin. I remember now because I had made a stupid joke at the dress shop, asking if she were related to Ricki Martin, the singer, to break up the tension."

Rafe smiled. "Good job. Do you recall anything else?"

"Lucy said Di would come to no good end because men only wanted her for one thing. Di was snarky and said with her looks, she was surprised Paul ever slept with her."

He winced. "Ouch."

"I thought I might have to break up a catfight, so I hustled Di to the back room. When we left, Lucy was gone for the day."

"Anything else you remember?"

"Diana did tell me it bothered her Lucy worked at the same shop where she was getting her fitting. She was going to change shops, but it was getting too late." Allison studied her hands.

"Why was Lucy working at the Hernandez house?" Rafe narrowed his gaze. "It seems awfully suspicious."

"Paul asked his uncle to hire Lucy because she was living in her car. He felt bad for her because she couldn't afford a place in Miami and he'd kicked her out of his condo when they broke up. He told Di it was only temporary."

But Rafe narrowed his eyes. "Allison, I would never do favors like that for an ex. Those kind of mixed messages give the wrong impression to a woman."

She had thought so as well. "I got the feeling from what Di said that Lucy found a lover with deeper pockets, like Paul's uncle. She may be more than Hector's housekeeper. But she's still a likely suspect. Lucy was upset at the breakup, from what Di said."

Rafe texted on his phone. "I'll have Jase check her out. She may have planned something for the wedding, but heard about the elopement."

"I have her cell phone number. Swiped it from Di's phone, just in case." Allison texted it to him.

"I have some calls to make." He went outside.

Judging from Rafe's tension when he returned, the news wasn't terrific.

"We were able to ping Lucy's cell phone to a tower in northern Georgia. She's close by as of a few hours ago."

Her heart sank as new fear rippled through her. The woman who hated Di the most, who had the most reason to do her harm was here.

And probably after Diana, who was still missing.

They needed to track down this bitch. Allison was certain wherever Lucy was, Di would be as well. She had to cling to hope her sister was still alive.

Rafe's cell rang. Blood drained from his face as he listened to the call. He hung up.

"Keith and Debbie need your nursing skills. It's an emergency."

Chapter 21

She and Rafe wove through traffic on his motorcycle. He parked in the back of the hotel and they ran for the elevators.

At room 505, Rafe pounded on the door. "It's me, Rafe, with Allison."

The door opened to a sobbing Debbie. Allison rushed inside. "Are you injured? Sick? What's going on?"

She dumped her pack on the floor. "I've got…"

"It's not me. It's Comet."

Then Rafe spotted Keith on the sofa by the window, their dog lying limp in his arms. Relief it wasn't his friends mingled with deep concern. He knew how much they loved their dog. Comet was more than just a pet. He was a family member.

"I don't know what happened!" Tears streamed down Debbie's face. "We went out for lunch and came back and found him like this."

True to her nature, Allison wasn't taken aback. She sat next to Keith and gently examined the dog.

"No vomiting or diarrhea?"

"No!"

"I'm not a vet. But…" Allison shook her head. Comet was panting rapidly and drooling. "Looks like some kind of poison. He needs an emergency vet."

Rafe scrolled through his phone. "I've got one. Texting it to you now."

As Keith dialed, Allison tried to think of what might help the dog. "He'll probably need oxygen and an IV. I don't know much about dogs, but he may have ingested something toxic. I'm sorry. I wish I could do more, but the vet should be able to help."

"We feed him only the best dog food and organic treats and a little people food once in a while," Debbie said as Keith talked to someone at the animal hospital. "What the hell could he have gotten into?"

Debbie looked around the room. "He was sniffing the teddy bears earlier. He loves playing with stuffed animals. I hid them away last night, but this morning I put them on the bed as a reminder to give them out when we met to ride into town for the photo opp with the bears."

Rafe had a bad feeling about this. "Which bear?"

Keith pointed to a tan bear near the foot of the bed. "That one. Okay, the vet is open and about fifteen minutes from here. We're taking him in. Rafe, lock up when you leave."

As the couple rushed out, Debbie carrying the little dog, his suspicions grew. "Stay back," he warned Allison.

He pulled on his black driving gloves stuffed into his jeans pocket and lifted the discarded bear, freed from its cellophane wrapping. He saw something peeking through a slight rip on the bear.

Immediately he set the bear down and covered it with the sheets. Peeling off his gloves, he dropped them onto the bed.

"Allison, leave the room. Now," he barked. "Get the hell out of here."

She sped out of the room. He swore in Spanish and walked to the door but didn't leave the room. His mind whirled. The bears were supposed to be left at several drop points after the photo opp. They'd received a text that anyone with a tan bear should drop them off either at The Dive Bar or a local store because the tan bears were designated for an orphanage.

Now he knew why the bears were separated.

Rafe dialed Jase.

Soon as his colleague answered, Rafe told him to contact Greg Whitlock with the Miami DEA.

"Tell him I need local DEA here within the hour. Have them dress like bikers to blend into the crowd here. I don't want to create attention. Call Keith and have him let the agents into his room. Use extreme caution. Pack test kits, respirators and gloves, hazmat gear. Tell them to get into the hazmat gear before entering Keith and Debbie's room. I need them to check out the tan bears on the bed inside that room."

Jase's voice lowered. "Copy that. Damn, Rafe, what did you find?"

"Fentanyl. I'm pretty damn sure of it."

A low whistle. "Copy that. You okay?"

"Yeah. I didn't touch it. I saw a clear package with pink and blue pills inside the bear. Keith and Debbie's dog Comet is at the animal hospital. When the cellophane was removed from the bears, he sniffed the bear and got sick. Dogs have extraordinary scent receptors. Tell Greg what happened."

"Copy that. What do I tell Lincoln?"

Rafe's mind raced over the potential bureaucratic pitfalls. As his supervisor, Lincoln had been hands-off the Hernandez investigation, letting Rafe lead his team until Rafe botched the undercover assignment at the Hernandez mansion.

Lincoln had been firm on Rafe staying out of the investigation while he was suspended. If he failed to follow protocol, Rafe knew he could ruin his career and get Jase into deep trouble.

"Tell him I found something and you're checking it out. If this turns out to be what I suspect, we'll bring the team in to investigate, but quietly. I can't risk letting Hernandez know we're on to him."

"Lincoln will want a team on this."

"He'll get a team."

"He'll be pissed you're involved."

"That's my prob," he shot back with impatience. "When Hernandez is finally arrested, Lincoln can get all the credit and the glory. And I'll finally sleep easier knowing that son of a bitch Hernandez is behind bars."

"Copy that. You think the local police will get wind of what's going on?"

"I don't want to alert them until we have something. Then we can work with the sheriff, if Greg vouches for him. Last thing we need is a corrupt local sheriff tipping off whoever did this."

"Copy that. Where are you headed to?"

"The Dive Bar. I saw more of those tan bears in a box and I need to check them out."

"Copy that. This sounds serious. Be careful, Rafe. I don't like you flying solo on this."

"I'm not solo. Thanks."

He hung up and thought of Allison and groaned. He had to find a way to ditch her until he checked out The Dive Bar. It was getting far too dangerous. But what the hell could he tell her?

Being left behind was not going to happen. She lingered near Rafe's bike, wondering what the hell he had found.

Somehow this had to be connected to her sister's disappearance.

Rafe laid a hand on her shoulder. Her startled shriek was cut off by his hand clapped on her mouth.

"It's me," Rafe whispered in her ear.

"You scared me." She turned. "What's going on?"

He peered over her shoulder. "I put the Do Not Disturb sign on the room so no maid enters."

"You have to tell me what's going on. Please. Is this related to Di's disappearance?"

"Not sure yet. Come on."

"I'm not leaving until you tell me what's going on."

"Get on." He didn't have time for this. "I'm taking you back to the cabin."

"No way. Tell me what's going on, Rafe. You're not leaving me out of this!"

"Allison, it's too dangerous."

"I don't care. I'll find out. If you found something, let me know unless you want me asking everyone in town what you're up to."

Eyes closing, he swore in Spanish. "All right. Get on, but you need to do everything I say. Otherwise, I'll drag you back to the cabin. Got it?"

Nodding meekly, she climbed back on.

They roared out the back entrance.

Allison was filled with worry. Rafe wasn't talking, and clearly he found something. For now she had to trust him.

As they headed on the main road, she clung to Rafe. She didn't know what happened. Didn't know where they were headed. Yet she trusted him. Rafe was single-minded and fierce in his dedication to bringing down the bad guys, and his protective streak extended to those under his care. For now, she had to rely on her instinct that he wouldn't turn Diana in, if her sister had fallen into trouble.

When he pulled into the entrance of The Dive Bar and parked, alarm filled her. Rafe cut the engine. Allison yanked off her helmet. Worry needled her.

"Why are we back here?"

Instead of answering her question, he pulled off his helmet and then the black driving gloves, his expression grim. Stubble on his face couldn't mask the tension in his jaw.

"Allison, you're sure you and Diana had the tan bears and you gave them to me? You didn't see any others?"

"No. Di gave me her bear at the start of the bike run because she didn't have any room. Then you took them."

"And I gave them to Keith and Debbie after we got into town because they wanted all the bears together on the bed for their photo album. We were supposed to ride into town with the bears at three o'clock. It'll be a media circus."

He blew out a breath and dragged a hand through his hair.

A sinking sensation filled her. Allison's pulse raced. "Oh damn, Rafe, what did you find in Keith and Debbie's room?"

His mouth compressed. "Can't say yet."

"Will you quit being so secretive? Does this have to do with Di's disappearance?"

"Don't know. Ally, did you touch those bears after the wrapping was removed?"

"No. I gave them to Keith still wrapped up." Suddenly she knew. "You found something inside of them?"

Rafe took a deep breath. "Fentanyl. I have agents coming here to test it, but damn it, Allison, we have to keep this quiet. Can't risk blowing the investigation into Hernandez or putting more lives at risk. Can I have your word?"

There was more to this than she realized. Much more. "I promise."

His tormented gaze met hers. He threw his helmet on the ground. "We've been operating a joint task force with the DEA and a few months ago succeeded in putting a man undercover close to Hernandez. We've spent years trying to nail that *hijo de puta* and put his ass in prison. He killed two of my best agents last year, and I took a bullet to the neck and one to my abdomen. If not for a Good Samaritan, I would have died."

I know. Her heart squeezed tight as she remembered that terrible night…

And had never told him. Never worked up the courage.

"Some of the task force is on their way here. That's why I have to return you to the cabin. You can't get involved in this."

"I'm already involved! Rafe, only two milligrams of fentanyl can kill. And you think the tan bears contain pills?"

"That's what I need to check out. Raine acted suspicious when you got near the bears in that box in the bar. Were all the bears the same color as yours and Diana's?"

She nodded.

Rafe looked grim. "That may be the reason why your room was broken into at the motel, Ally. Someone was looking for the bears they thought you had."

"I'm going with you." As he started to protest, she smiled sweetly. "I'm in this all the way, Rafe."

He gave her a level look. "Even if we find out your sister is involved?"

Allison swallowed past the fear rising in her throat. "As long as I find her and she's still alive. And safe."

His expression tightened. "Fine. Follow my lead and do exactly as I say, or I swear, for your own good, I'll drive you to the nearest gas station and make you wait there."

"I promise," she said.

As she dismounted, Allison had a bad feeling. Empty parking lot.

All the window shades were pulled down. The bar looked deserted. Yet they had been here earlier today and Raine said the place was open for lunch.

He caught her arm. "You're staying here. Raine may be armed."

She noticed the handgun at his waist. Allison bristled. "I'm going with you, Rafe. You're not doing this alone."

Another motorcycle pulled into the parking lot. The rider dismounted and pulled off his helmet. Sam.

"I'm with you," Sam said

She and Rafe exchanged glances. "How did you…?" Rafe began.

"Jase called me and thought you'd need backup until the

other agents could get here. He told me where you were going."

Sam gave her a level look. "Stay here, Allison."

They both looked menacing and serious, but she was in this all the way. "I'm going in. I'll be behind you, but you can't stop me."

Ever the cowboy, Sam muttered, "Yeehaw. Do you have any idea what fentanyl does, even a little dust?"

"You need to minimize skin contact if investigating a possible case of fentanyl."

"It doesn't get absorbed through the skin," Sam countered.

Allison rolled her eyes. "You're not likely to get sick from it touching your skin, but if you touch it, you need to wash your hands immediately. Don't rub your eyes or nose or mouth to avoid getting it into your mucus membranes. Dust can be dangerous as well. Even tiny amounts may become airborne. Always better as a first responder not to take chances."

She fished three N95 masks out of her backpack and handed two to each of them. "Here. I always travel with extras. They aren't as efficient as respirators but offer some protection at least."

Rafe studied the pack. "What else do you have in there, Mary Poppins? Got any Narcan?"

"Naloxone in my first aid kit."

When he and Sam exchanged puzzled looks, she bristled. "I'm a traveling trauma nurse. When you've seen as much crap as I have, you learn to pack drugs that can treat overdoses. Especially going to a large event like this, chances are it might be needed."

Rafe's gaze narrowed, but he nodded.

They took the masks, but put them into their pockets. Allison did the same. Maybe it wasn't fentanyl in those bears. Maybe it was a one-time deal.

She hoped. Surely her sister couldn't be involved in any of this, either.

"Stay behind us," Rafe told her again, this time his voice deep and stern.

Right. As if I'd listen to you. If this jerk is holding my sister prisoner for some reason, I'm headed inside.

They headed for the entrance. The door opened to a dimly-lit interior. It was quiet inside. Too quiet.

Allison's breath hitched. She had a bad feeling about this.

Silence greeted them as they advanced into the bar. Her nose wrinkled at the stench of sour beer and old food. And Di had eaten here?

Maybe she should check the hospitals again, see if Di was laid up with a virulent case of food poisoning.

Before she saw it, Allison knew. She'd dealt with enough death and blood to know exactly what they would find.

The bar's interior was dark, but enough sunshine poked through the slanted window blinds. Sam went to a dirt-riddled light switch on the wall and flipped it on.

Blood splattered the cardboard box where Allison had spotted the tan teddy bears. Lying next to it was Andrew Raine, the bar's proprietor. Blood pooled near his body, a round hole piercing his forehead. His eyes stared sightlessly at the worn ceiling tiles.

She licked her lips. "Guess we won't need that Narcan in my pack."

Automatically she crouched down to check for a pulse. Rafe grabbed her hand. "I'm wearing gloves. I'll do it."

When he straightened, he shook his head.

Sam was already speeding to the hallway. He returned with a frown. "Nothing. But the office is a mess as if someone went through it, looking for something, and the cash box is open, with nothing inside."

Rafe peered into the box. "The bears are missing as well.

The open cash box may be a decoy to convince the police that this was a robbery gone wrong."

"We have to call the cops," Allison insisted.

Sam and Rafe exchanged glances. "Yeah," Rafe said, holstering his gun. "But not here. And we can't risk getting involved, not right now. Let the local cops handle it."

"I don't understand. You can't tell them you found the body?"

He gave her an even look. "Ally, there's too much at stake here. Your sister is missing. We think some of the bears transported for the run contain drugs. Until we know we can trust the local police, we can't risk getting involved."

Outside, Sam made a call to 911, telling the dispatcher something was off about The Dive Bar and the police should check it out.

They left on the motorcycles. But instead of riding back to the cabin, Rafe and Sam pulled into the parking lot of a grocery store. They parked far from other vehicles.

Rafe palmed his cell phone. "Signal's strong here. I need to make a few calls."

He walked away. When he returned, the grim set of his jaw warned it hadn't gone well. She didn't ask.

"I have sandwiches and cold drinks at the cabin. Late lunch?" she asked them.

Sam nodded. Rafe seemed distracted.

Back at the cabin, Allison told the guys to sit while she rustled out three cold sodas and made ham sandwiches. They ate on the deck.

"I checked with a guy I know who knows the town well. Raine owed money. Could be a reason why someone killed him," Rafe told them.

"So we're no closer to finding my sister than we were before," she mused aloud.

"But you're in the clear to keep your investigation under wraps." She started to see the threads holding all this together.

"It's best not to involve the police until it's absolutely necessary. I don't know the locals. Right now the local LEOs could think it was a hit because the guy owed money, which is a good thing," Rafe said.

Allison's stomach churned. "And that's good how? Di is still missing."

Sam polished off his sandwich in four quick bites. "If the locals get involved, they could blow everything wide, even if they don't call the media. We'll bring them in when the time is right."

"Which is a matter that requires delicacy," Rafe muttered. "I'm good at diplomacy, but I've been ordered by my supervisor to stand down and let the task force investigate this new lead."

Sam and Allison stared at him. "Rafe, you're the lead agent on this," Sam protested.

"Tell me about it. If this case is linked to Hernandez, and I'm certain it is, I'm the one who needs to bring him down."

He was single-minded in his pursuit of Hernandez. Her temper began to rise. What about her sister? Diana was innocent and still missing.

She took a long pull of soda. "I don't care about your damn investigation, Rafael. I care about finding my sister. Every minute we're sitting here means she could be in horrible danger."

Rafe set his plate down on the side table and turned to her. "Ally, I still think Diana is involved in all this somehow. Either intentionally or unintentionally. There're too many coincidences."

"That's your answer? My sister is still under suspicion? Terrific. Paul is getting here tomorrow. Maybe he'll have answers since you can't provide any."

She expected anger, chastisement, not the guarded look on his face. He glanced at Sam.

"Can you give us a minute?"

The other man nodded. "Think I'll head into town, check on things. I plan to still ride in the Teddy Bear Run, unless you need me elsewhere. Thank you for the sandwich and soda, Ally."

Rafe glanced at his cell. "It's nearly one thirty. Sam, get your bear and ride into town for the photo op at three. When the bears are dropped off, I need you to see if any are tan or if all of them are dark brown. Coordinate with Chuck, who's arranging for the bears to be picked up at all the drop points. If any of the tan bears are still around…leave them, but put surveillance on how they're picking them up and who is transporting."

"Got it. I'll be in touch." He walked off, then roared off on his motorcycle.

Rafe turned to her. "Tell me exactly what Paul said and when he's arriving."

She debated telling him. Would it be another reason to deter him from helping to find her sister?

"Ally, you have to trust me on this. You're a professional and so am I. I trusted you with my tita to save her life, now I'm asking you to trust me. What did Paul say?"

She sighed. He was right.

"He's worried. Really worried. He planned to fly up Sunday and changed his flight to earlier. Tonight. He and Di were getting married Sunday. Eloping. Di still wanted a big party for the wedding.

"Paul said he never wanted the wedding at his uncle's house. Tried to talk Di out of it, but she wanted a huge, extravagant wedding." Allison blew out a breath. "Paul had been estranged from his uncle until the day Hector discovered he was marrying and insisted on paying for everything. Paul was going to refuse, but Di insisted."

Standing up, he began to pace. "I need to talk to Paul. Give me his number."

"I thought you were ordered to stay out of the investigation."

"I am staying out. I need to question Paul about where he thinks Diana may have fled."

Allison's heart fluttered. "So you're not going to abandon the search for my sister?"

His gaze remained steady. "No, Ally. I needed to alert the task force about what I found and I did."

Overwhelmed with emotion, she could only nod. Maybe bringing Hernandez to justice wasn't Rafe's sole purpose. Still, a lingering doubt pulsed.

"Are you doing this because you think the drugs and Di are connected?"

Rafe rocked back and forth. "Our first priority is finding her and making sure she's okay, Ally. I don't know how the two are connected, but we need to find her."

When he tried Paul's number, Rafe frowned. "Got a recording saying the number can't be reached."

"That's odd. It might be the signals out here."

"Maybe."

"Let me text him." She shot off a quick text, included the offer to pick him up at the airport.

No answer.

Rafe texted something on his phone. "I don't want to leave you here alone. Debbie and Keith are going to stay here with you."

"I'll go with you."

"No."

"I can take care of myself."

He gave her a scrutinizing look and gently touched her

head. "Oh? Maybe, *mi angel*, but I won't risk it. Comet is still at the animal hospital and Keith and Debbie need a break. They're worn-out and they can't return to their room yet."

She understood. Rafe was calling on her skills as a nurse and hostess, and at the same time, keeping her at the cabin.

"Okay."

She went into the kitchen to check on food and drinks. By the time she made more sandwiches, the couple arrived on their motorcycles. Debbie came into the cabin, eyes swollen from crying, her nose red. Allison hugged her.

When the couple finished eating lunch and drinking the lemonade she'd bought in town, they looked completely exhausted.

Allison changed the sheets on the king-size bed and hustled them into her room to rest.

She closed the door behind them and joined Rafe on the porch.

"Comet's going to be okay, but they're keeping him overnight just in case. I told them to spend the night here. I can run into town and get them fresh clothing, toiletries…"

"I don't want you leaving the cabin. You need to stay here, Ally."

His phone rang as she thought of a smart reply. He glanced at the number. "It's Sam."

He put the call on speaker.

"I'm here with Greg, from the DEA. He arrived with agents about an hour ago. We booked a hotel suite for a command center, and the field offices have deployed all available resources. Everything is on the DL. Tested the bears, and yeah, the substance in the tan bears in Keith and Debbie's room was fentanyl."

"Son of a…" Rafe's eyes closed for a minute. "I was transporting drugs over the state line."

"Yep. And if you got caught, well, try to wiggle your way out of that one."

"Hernandez isn't stupid. He wouldn't risk me finding out." Rafe frowned. "Actually the tan bears weren't mine. Ally and her sister originally got them, and I carried them as a favor."

Allison gulped as he turned to her. "Where did you pick up those bears for yourself and Diana?"

"It was…" Allison bit her lip and took a deep breath. Son of a biscuit, this was bad. But he needed to know the truth. "At the seamstress shop where Diana had her fitting. They had a pick-up spot there for bikers. I thought it was fine… I mean, they participate in a toy drive at Christmas."

His gaze remained steady. "Ally, did they know you took them?"

Flushing, she felt a stab of pure guilt and panic. "Diana insisted we do it to save time once we got to the rendezvous point with you and the others. When we got to the shop, the manager was there and told us those bears were already reserved, but Diana waved her off."

Rafe's jaw tensed. "This doesn't look good for her, Ally."

Didn't she know that? More and more it seemed Diana had gotten into the thick of it with smuggling drugs.

"I have to go into town. I'll pick up Keith and Debbie's overnight bags. Stay here." Rafe gave her a meaningful look. "I mean it, Ally. Call me if you need me. Or text. The signal sucks here."

One aspect of working for the FBI he admired was the Bureau's efficiency in setting up command posts. Several plainclothes intelligence analysts from the Atlanta field office worked on laptops on folding tables. A white board and large television screen was at one end, and the room curtains were drawn for privacy.

Jase had taken over the room's desk and was clearly in charge. He nodded at Rafe.

"Report," Rafe told him.

Jase swiveled on the chair to face him. "We set up a lab in the bathroom. Both bears belonging to Allison and Diana contained pills that tested positive for fentanyl."

Not surprising.

"Sam reported all the bears on the run today for the photo op were dark brown. The coordinator for picking up the bears said the tan bears were supposed to be picked up at seven by a private courier. Those bears are designated for a children's hospital in North Carolina. We have surveillance on the drop-off site now. It's inside a souvenir shop on Main."

His jaw tensed. If all those bears contained fentanyl, it meant possible exposure to innocent patrons.

"We contacted the owner, and he agreed to close early. He already contacted the man scheduled to pick up the bears and told him he'd return to the shop to let him get them, but he had to go home early because his kid is sick."

"Smart thinking."

Greg Whitlock came out of the bathroom, respirator mask covering his face, a white hazmat suit on his body. He stripped off the suit and mask, ditched it into a biohazard can and headed toward Rafe and Jase.

In his late thirties, with long brown hair and an intense look, Greg was an excellent DEA agent. He'd first met him on an op last year before the gun battle that killed two of his best agents.

"Need to show you something." The DEA agent showed him a photo on his phone.

As he recognized the baggie, Rafe's heart sank.

"We confiscated one of the tan bears at the souvenir shop to test it. Found a plastic bag. Tested it, and it contains one kilo of 4-Piperidone."

Rafe's heart raced. A kilo of the precursor drug necessary for making fentanyl was bad news, worse than he'd anticipated. Probably more was in the bears inside the shop.

"There's only one reason to smuggle that in the bears. Someone's setting up a lab," Greg told him.

One kilo of fentanyl was lethal. It could kill up to half a million people. His mind raced.

"What if they're testing out the water, so to speak? Cooking it in a remote lab in the woods, where no one would suspect, get the product faster into the hands of users."

"I agree. I'm sure this is Hernandez. He's expanding operations. We can't prove it now, but I feel like we're getting close. You have to stay on this, Rafe. I know you're supposed to be suspended, but…" Greg said.

"I have no plans to drop out." The hell with suspension. He needed to nail this son of a bitch.

Rafe shoved a hand through his hair, musing. "If the drugs are flowing north, and they're making fentanyl in a lab, it has to be someplace remote. Undetected. A warehouse, or a large home."

"I can get a list of warehouses in that general vicinity. It'll take time."

"No need. I want you to sew those bears back and return them to the store for pickup."

Jase and Greg exchanged glances. "Rafe, you sure? We have agents staking out the shop to tail whoever takes the bears."

"Can't risk them getting too close and tipping off the courier. Put tracking devices inside them first."

"What if they find them?" Jase asked.

"They won't, until they're opened. Whoever did this still doesn't know we're on to them, so let's keep it that way."

Rafe was certain it was Hernandez. He hoped Diana wasn't involved, because if she was, Allison would be devastated.

He couldn't think about that. He had a drug lord to capture.

Chapter 22

He returned to the cabin with Keith and Debbie's packs. Both had been swept clean by agents and were deemed safe, since the drug hadn't gone airborne.

Waiting for information proved tormenting. Rafe didn't seem any better at it than she did. He went outside, checked the property and his bike, then came back inside. Finally, around five o'clock, she suggested going into town for dinner. Neither of them had eaten much today. She remembered the breakfast she'd interrupted.

Utterly exhausted, she felt as if weeks had passed instead of hours.

Keith and Debbie had headed to the vet clinic to check on their dog. Rafe agreed on dinner in town. But today was the last day of the bike run. Most of the bars and restaurants were packed with bikers celebrating. Tomorrow, Sunday, they'd be leaving.

Sunday, Diana and Paul's wedding day.

They finally found a restaurant not overrun by locals or bikers. Nestled on the edge of a backroad about thirty minutes from town, and ringed by the peaks of the Blue Ridge Mountains, the Country Diner resembled a throwback to the days of jiving jukeboxes. Rebellious tufts of weeds sprang up in the cracked asphalt of the parking lot. Peeling, sun-bleached letters on the sign proudly announced today's special was honey fried chicken.

Suddenly hungry, Allison had a hankering for fried chicken. Or fried anything, as long as it didn't move on her plate.

They parked and went inside, a silver bell over the door announcing their arrival. Everyone looked up, looked at them and then returned to their meals. A vintage jukebox warbled out a country tune about a man missing his dog and his girl.

Rafe headed for a vinyl booth patched with duct tape at the window, far from the other four diners, and sat facing the door. Bacon, coffee and fried chicken smells all mingled together, accenting her hunger.

The waitress handed them grease-splattered menus and took their drink orders.

While waiting, Rafe drummed his fingers on the linoleum table. A lock of dark hair fell over his brow. Intense, brooding, he looked ready for action.

Restless herself, Allison called Paul again. Voicemail. Maybe he'd gotten a late flight and neglected to tell her. She left another message.

He set down the menu. "Who are you calling?"

"Paul. Still no answer, which is odd. Unless he flew into Raleigh and is driving south to Georgia."

"Why would he do that?"

"He owns a small factory for his furniture business in Randall. It's in western North Carolina."

To her surprise, the fried chicken was crisp and juicy, dripping with flavor, not grease. Allison focused on eating, not wanting to answer questions she knew he had for her. Certainly not here, where the other diners kept eyeballing them like aliens who'd landed in their midst.

Still, this silence bothered her. "I'm not one for artery-clogging chicken, but this is tasty. Usually I'll grab whatever

I can while I'm working. There's a cute Cuban place near my apartment. I bet you've eaten there."

He scowled. "I bet not. I seldom eat Cuban food."

Allison blinked and sipped her tea. "You're Cuban and you don't like Cuban food?"

"I like American food. Hamburgers and chicken."

"Next you'll tell me you don't like soccer."

"I'm into American football. Not soccer."

Another surprise. "Why? I mean, your family is Cuban."

Rafe toyed with his fork. "My dad was American. Jeff Jones. Thus my middle name."

"Was?"

He looked away. "You heard the story from my grandmother. Dad was a patrol officer in Miami. Got shot and killed when I was twelve. Drug bust gone wrong."

Suddenly she understood, perhaps because she'd felt the same kind of purpose and calling.

"And that's why you became an FBI agent. Your family must be proud of you."

He snorted. "They expected me to join the family business, not be a cop like my dad. My mama especially hated the fact I wanted to follow in my old man's footsteps. They kept nagging me to change professions, even though I've advanced through the ranks to become an SSA. I've thought about changing careers, but it felt all wrong."

Allison wiped her mouth, gambling on not triggering him. But she felt the need to point out the obvious, even if he couldn't see it himself.

"Because you want to go after the bad guys, the drug dealers who kill innocents. You want justice for his death. By following in his footsteps, you're making up for losing him, and you feel you can never measure up until you catch Hernandez."

Rafe glared at her, his dark brows drawn together. He

looked ready to leap across the table. Allison lifted her chin, waited for a response.

"Never, ever use Hernandez and my father in the same sentence. My dad was a hero. Hernandez is a spineless coward who took out two of my men. Two good agents with families who will never be the same again."

He shoved aside his plate of half-eaten chicken. Allison plucked a leg off the plate and gnawed at it.

"You're one to walk, Lexington. You're a nurse who's stuck to her sister's side out of misplaced obligation for her life for the rest of her damn life."

The chicken suddenly tasted like cardboard. She set down the leg carefully. "What did you say?"

"You're not her keeper. You keep defending her as if she's a saint. She's a grown woman, Allison."

She bristled. She didn't want to hear the truth. Hell, she didn't know what she wanted. "I saved my sister's life and…"

Suddenly the stress of the day kicked her in the gut as if she were reliving the past all over again. Allison scrubbed at her face, trying to hold the tears at bay.

"She's all I have."

He turned contrite, his expression softening. "We'll find her. But you have to let go at some point. You're not responsible for her actions."

"I am! It's because of me…"

"What?"

Now she did wipe away a stray tear. "I almost didn't do it. Didn't save her."

He didn't say anything.

"When the kayak flipped, she screamed for me to help her. I-I hesitated. My sister needed me and I froze. She was going under, her head bobbing up and down and I was treading water, thinking only of myself. How I didn't want to die. There was a tree branch that caught her and it held her for a minute, enough time for me to come to the realization that if I didn't try, I'd watch my only sister drown."

"Ally, you saved her," he said gently.

"But I almost didn't!"

"Cut yourself some slack."

"I can't! My parents would have died if Di drowned. They always loved her more than me, and if I let her die…"

Her voice dropped. "They wouldn't love me anymore. Not that they seemed to care much about me anyway compared to Di."

"Did they ever say they loved you?"

"Yes, but…"

Rafe shook his head. "Stop beating yourself up. You've spent your entire life trying to make up for the fact you had a human moment, Ally. You did save your sister. You can't save everyone."

She gave a smile filled with misery. "I can try. Isn't that why you do what you do? Because if we stop trying, and let the bad guys win, or the car accidents or the diseases or injuries, who's going to stop it? If good people like you don't care, then evil wins."

His mouth worked as if he struggled with something. Inner demons, perhaps, like she did. "Yeah, you're right."

"I saw that on a YouTube vid. Or maybe it was a commercial for beer."

Rafe smiled. "You're something else, Lexington."

"So are you, Rodriguez."

His cell phone pinged. Glancing at it, he groaned. "Sorry, have to take this."

A volley of Spanish ensued, too rapid for her to understand. Amused, she realized his family was checking up on him.

When he hung up and returned to her, she smirked. "Telling your family you're having a wonderful time isn't exactly the truth."

Rafe's gaze remained steady. "I'm with you. You make life wonderful, Ally."

Allison didn't know how to respond. She studied his face, his intent expression, and suddenly everything fell into place.

Rafe truly cared. Her heart thudded hard with unexpected joy.

"You're a smooth talker," she said lightly.

"I'm serious. I've never wanted to admit it all the time we've known each other. I've tried to separate my professional needs from my personal wants, but around you, they run together. It was more than having you as a confidential informant. You make me feel alive in a way I've never felt before. Sure as hell have never worried about a CI the way I worried about you or got jealous when you flirted with members of the Devil's Patrol."

"You…were jealous?" Her heart did a happy little flip-flop.

He nodded. "To the point where when Jase told me you kissed him, I wanted to yank you out of that assignment. If anyone was going to kiss you, I wanted it to be me."

"It meant nothing to me. I was playing a role. Jase and I both were." A tiny doubt filled her. "What about you? Was what we had in bed just…for fun and kicks?"

Please don't be like the other guys. Please.

"With me it's the real deal." Reaching for her hand, he held her gaze.

All her innermost longings broke to the surface. For years she'd run away from feelings, resolved to remain apart and never risk having her heart shattered again. Never daring to fully be herself and show men any vulnerability because they saw her as strong, and couldn't take advantage of her.

Rafe was different. He broke down her barriers, peeled back her prickly layers and wasn't afraid to tell her how he felt. With him, she could express her fears as well as her dreams.

They connected on a level more than sexual. It went deeper, despite the doubts she had about him regarding her sister.

"I feel the same, Rafe. What I feel for you is genuine," she said softly.

For a moment, they said nothing, simply held hands. This was sweet. Nice. She could be herself around Rafe.

"I always thought your family and the job were everything to you."

"I need more than the job and my family. I'm getting older, and my brush with death last year was a wake-up call I wanted to ignore, until now."

What would he say if he knew she had firsthand knowledge of that encounter with death? Allison sipped some tea. "At least your family cares what happens to you. My parents only care about Di. They hover over her. Never bother with me."

He looked thoughtful. "Have you ever considered maybe they worry more about her because she's not as independent?"

It had occurred to her, but the insight made her uneasy. Because it meant that all this time, she'd unjustly thought of her parents as cold and indifferent.

She pulled her hand away. "Have you ever considered your family worries about you because you have a job that exposes you to constant danger?"

He gave her a level look. "I don't want to discuss my family."

"And I don't want to discuss my parents. Okay? Leave my family out of it. I can handle my life."

The sweet intensity vanished. The moment was gone as if it never existed. "Let's finish and get out of here."

Yes, let's do that. But suddenly she wanted to cry, because she felt she was throwing out a chance for happiness.

I don't deserve to be happy. Not now. How could I be happy when Di could be lying in a ditch someplace?

Chapter 23

They returned to the cabin shortly before seven. Keith and Debbie were still at the animal hospital. Rafe kept glancing at his cell phone as they sat on the sofa. Allison wasn't going to like what he planned.

"I'm leaving soon, but I hate leaving you alone," Rafe told her.

"I'll go with you."

"No. This is Bureau business."

"You can't get rid of me that easily, Rodriguez. I want to help you catch that son of a bitch who's smuggling drugs and threatening my sister."

He considered. "You're swearing, Ally."

"Son of a biscuit is too nice to apply to whoever did this."

Gently he massaged her tensed neck muscles, enjoying the softness of her skin beneath his fingertips. "You need to stay here. I'll call Debbie, have her stay here while Keith is at the vet with Comet."

Moaning, she dropped her head. "If you keep doing that, Rodriguez, I just might listen to you."

"I can do other areas as well, much later when all this is resolved."

"I know what you're doing and it's not going to work. Not even the best massage in the world can convince me to abandon the search for Di."

His fingers worked the tired muscles in her neck even harder. Allison moaned.

"Though if you keep that up, I might promise you my firstborn child."

"Deal. As long as I'm the father."

His fingers stopped, and he stared at her. She stared back. The intensity of the moment made him wonder where they went from here. They both had baggage, hell, an entire train car of it. Yet he longed to change his life.

The idea of marriage, a family, Allison having his child. A boy? Or a girl? It didn't matter. The idea turned him on.

But if she didn't like children...

"I like kids," she whispered. "I've always wanted a family with the right partner."

Copy that. His breath hissed out between his teeth. This was not a good time to give in to his body's urges.

"Me, too." Then, because the moment was too heavy, he added, "Always thought a woman looked best barefoot and pregnant in the kitchen."

Damn, he adored it when her face scrunched up like that, ready to give him holy hell. Rafe laughed.

"I'm yanking your chain, Lexington."

"It's the wrong chain to yank, Rodriguez."

"Got it. I have another chain to yank. I want you to back off babying your sister and living your life for her."

Alison blinked. "I don't live my life for her."

"You've been doing it ever since you rescued her from the river, Ally. That Chinese proverb that you save a man's life and you're responsible for him for the rest of it is a proverb. Start living for yourself for a change."

"I..." She looked away. "If I don't live for Di, who the hell am I going to live for?"

Her mouth opened and closed. He cupped her cheek, lifted her woebegone gaze to his.

"Me."

Her lips parted. Oh yeah, an invitation.

Rafe pushed a lock of hair behind her ear. "You have beautiful hair and pretty eyes, Lexington. And your mouth, it drives me wild."

Rafe bent his head and kissed her, a gentle, sweet kiss full of passion and desire, but he held back.

When they finally parted, she put a hand to her heart. "I know what you're doing."

"I sure hope so," he muttered.

"You're not going to make me forget about following you into town. Not with a kiss or a promise of great sex."

He tilted his head. "Great sex?"

"Okay, spectacular sex. It was amazing."

"It takes two, Ally. It was amazing because of you."

"There's more to relationships than amazing sex, Rafe."

He played with a strand of her loose hair. "Of course there is, Ally. I think we have something dynamic between us."

"I know we do, it's just…"

She sighed as his cell phone rang. Rafe made an impatient sound. "Sorry."

Work always came first. As he pressed the button to answer the call, he wondered if it always would.

Jase sounded rattled. "Rafe, the bears were picked up an hour ago."

He frowned. "And you're just telling me now?"

"I was a little busy. Lincoln ordered me to keep you out of it."

Rafe swore. "Jase, I don't want you taking risks for me."

"The hell with that. You know I owe you a lot. But I have to warn you, Lincoln said if you get involved, your career is over. We traced the van's license plate. Stolen. We had a tail on it but lost it. Looked like it is headed north to North Carolina. We're going to move the op north to Randall in a grocery store parking lot. I've already informed the local sheriff here, and he'll coordinate with the county sheriff in North Carolina."

Torn between saving his career and being there to take down the bastard who cost his men their lives, Rafe hissed. "I'm coming with you."

"There's something else you need to know... Driver was a man, midforties, accompanied by a brunette woman. We got a clear photo of the woman as the van passed. Sending to your phone."

A chill raced through him as he studied the screenshot. Oh damn, this was bad. "*Madre Dios*. Is that...?"

"Yep. Diana Lexington. Allison's missing sister."

Chapter 24

Her worst nightmare turned into a hard reality as Rafe revealed the news. Allison couldn't believe it.

"I'm sorry. There's no denying it. Diana is helping to smuggle fentanyl."

"It's not possible. I refuse to believe it." She folded her arms. It couldn't be right. Had all his suspicions proved correct? Never.

"My sister wouldn't do this."

Rafe blew out a breath and muttered in Spanish as he paced, glancing at his cell phone. "The evidence is there, Ally. Diana is an accomplice. Agents tailed the van picking up bears stuffed with drugs to North Carolina. At least two of the bears contain fentanyl that we know of."

"Where?"

He shook his head. "They lost the van a short distance from the border." Jaw tensing, he studied his phone. "Ally, do you think Paul owns an iPhone?"

"Not sure, but probably. Di bragged he could get her a discount on a new one, so he probably is an Apple guy, not an Android. Why?"

"Apple phones make it easier to track AirTags." He looked distracted. "I have to go."

He kissed her swiftly and gave her a sympathetic look. "I'm sorry it came down to this. I'll do what I can, find out where she is, and exactly her involvement. We'll talk when I get back. Stay here."

And then he was gone, roaring off in the night on his Harley, leaving her behind with her misery.

Allison went inside and tried to think. Should she call her parents? Di would need a good lawyer. But where could they find one here? Maybe a lawyer in Miami could refer them to one…

She sank into the sofa and buried her head into her hands. Already assuming the worst: that Di was guilty. It made no sense. Yet, as Rafe pointed out, the evidence was against her.

Allison went to brew some coffee and tried to assemble her fractured thoughts. All this time she'd been thinking the best of her sister, shielding her as much as she could, and Diana had been fooling her all along.

Maybe the glitz and glamor of the drug lifestyle, and the luxury Hector Hernandez could give her, had gotten to her sister.

"But she's not that shallow," she said aloud to the dripping coffee maker.

Then there was Paul, who adored Diana and would do anything for her… Allison sighed and poured a cup of coffee, added sugar and cream and went outside. Insects hummed in the trees and brush. It seemed so calming, when all she wanted to do was scream.

Her cell phone rang. Allison glanced at the number and frowned. Didn't recognize it. "Hello?"

"Ally?"

Oh dear heavens. "Di! Where are you? You okay? What the hell is going on? Please tell me you're okay!"

The line crackled. She cursed the lousy reception and ran outside to get a better signal. Her sister's terrified voice crackled over the phone.

"I'm scared, Ally. Hector…warehouse…a gun…forced me."

"Where are you? Di!"

"Randall..." Diana rattled off the address. "Hurry please."

The line clicked off. "No, no, no," she screamed.

Allison called Rafe. No answer.

Coffee spilled over the deck, the mug crashing downward as she raced inside to grab her keys. Warehouse. Was Randall a man? A last name. Randall.

Randall. The name was familiar. Suddenly it clicked.

Paul's furniture factory was in Randall. She checked on her phone. The town was an hour north of here.

Diana had to be there.

Allison dialed Paul's phone. He finally picked up. "Allison, I've been trying to reach you."

"The signal here sucks. Listen, there's no time. Where are you?"

"Just landed in Raleigh an hour ago and I'm trying to get a car. Damn rental agency line is a mile long."

Her stomach clenched. By the time Paul drove to his factory, it would be too late. "Listen, Paul..."

"I heard from Diana."

Allison halted pacing. "You did."

"She's fine. Wedding jitters."

Wedding jitters? The panic in her sister's voice wasn't bridal nerves. "I don't know. She's not like this, Paul. Running away and not leaving any word of her whereabouts."

He laughed. "You don't know her like I do, Ally. Diana loves drama and attention. She's waiting for me at a hotel in Ashville. Look, I'll go there, we'll have a romantic evening and everything will be fine. I'll have her call you. I'm sorry she worried you so much."

Heart pounding, she tried to sound as casual as possible. "Sounds good. What a relief. Thanks. By the way, is your uncle in town?"

Silence for a minute. His voice came over the phone. Guarded. "Why would he be?"

"I don't know. I thought with the elopement, he'd want to be there for you."

"He's too busy." Paul sounded brusque. "The line's moving. Gotta run. I'll have Diana call you tomorrow."

The phone went dead.

Now all her suspicions flared. Paul couldn't be trusted. She knew her sister. No amount of drama or desire for attention would keep Diana from assuring her that all was well.

Allison changed into black clothing and soft-soled sneakers. She called Rafe again as she ran for her bike. Voicemail. Fine.

"I'm going after Diana. You're wrong, all of you are wrong. She isn't smuggling drugs. But check out Paul. He claims he's in Raleigh and Diana is at a hotel in Ashville. How the hell could she be there when you spotted her on camera less than an hour ago?

"And I heard from her. She managed to call me and tell me something about Hector, and holding her captive in Randall. She's at Paul's furniture warehouse, Rafe. I'm headed there. I have to save my sister."

Allison hung up.

As he headed for the arranged meeting location to join his team, Rafe's thoughts collided. All this time since the night he'd been shot and almost killed, he thirsted for revenge. Not justice for the men on his team who died. But revenge.

Revenge at the cost of everything else, including his family and worse…

His own damn code of honor and ethics. *When did I fall so far down the rabbit hole? What happened?* Using Allison to get close to Hernandez and then trying to coerce her sister into being a confidential informant.

Knowing the dangers involved, he'd still forged ahead with his plan.

His phone buzzed, but he ignored it.

Ten minutes later, it buzzed again. Glancing at it with impatience, he sighed. Allison again. Ally. Not now.

Allison was an honest and good woman, and, aw hell, he was in love with her. Not the idea of her, but her. All of Allison. Tough and gritty, with a spark for life and dedication to her family that exceeded his own. She made him look deep inside and acknowledge the guilt lingering there, and yanked off the cloak of the end justifying the means. Because it didn't. Not when everything, and everyone else, came at the expense of nailing Hernandez.

For every criminal like Hector Hernandez, ten more waited to take his place. He couldn't get them all. No matter how dedicated and determined he was, there would always be more bad guys out there to catch, more good men and women killed doing their job to keep the public safe from those scumbags.

Keep women like Allison safe. He couldn't stop thinking about her, worrying about her.

Caring about her.

He knew what this meant. He was deeply in love with her. He could compartmentalize his feelings, shove them deep inside and focus on the job. Stick with the job because the job was predictable and noble and honorable.

Or head to the abyss of a real relationship and see where he'd land after the fall. Soon as all this was over, he'd do it.

Rafe took a deep breath. Time to jump.

Less than an hour later, he pulled into the parking lot of the grocery store Jase had mentioned. Vans and an array of police cars with blinking lights greeted him. It looked like a goddamn carnival.

So much for discretion.

Jase, Greg and Sam milled around Jase's black SUV. Leaving his bike running, he walked over to join them. "Report."

"Sheriff told us there's only one warehouse in town that has been active. Town's economy tanked a few years ago and many businesses dried up or left. This one is a new business. Belongs to an LLC registered under Dynamic Arts. Dummy corp. Got the address, flew drones over the suspected warehouse and saw the van that had picked up the bears. A truck left about an hour ago, heading east for the interstate. We have surveillance on it now."

"Good. What are we waiting for?"

The trio exchanged grim glances.

"Permission," Jase finally said. "Sheriff wants part of the takedown."

Rafe snorted. "It's our op. My op."

Greg looked equally frustrated. "Your boss, Lincoln, and my director both agree they need the local cooperation for the raid. So we wait."

"For how goddamn long?"

"He's on his way. He wants to use infrared helos to see the amount of people inside the warehouse." Greg shook his head. "We wasted time arguing this is a covert op. No knock warrant. He finally relented."

"So we wait," Jase said. "He said he should be here soon."

By the time the sheriff arrived, everything could go to hell. Rafe chafed with impatience. Damn bureaucracy. The FBI always followed protocol, but this time, he knew it could cost them valuable time.

Sam checked his shotgun. "Wish we could leave now. Storm the place and get these scumbags once and for all. I hate jurisdictional chest beating."

Sounded good to him. Impatient to nail Hernandez and put the bastard behind bars, he itched to get going.

Suddenly he heard Allison in his head. "What's more important, Rafe? That Hernandez is finally arrested or that you do the arresting?"

Allison again. She was right. This wasn't his case, his show, his moment of glory. For the first time in more than three years, he didn't give a shit about Hernandez and the glory of taking him down. It was more important that the man was arrested.

Not who did the takedown. Rafe steeled his spine. "Lincoln's right. You need to wait."

"But Rafe," Jase started to say.

Holding up a hand, he shook his head. "Follow protocol. It's there for a reason. Without the sheriff's cooperation, we'd still be hunting for a warehouse to search. He pinned down the location. We need our local police partners. This isn't a contest to see who brings in the bad guys first."

Sam shuffled his boots. "Rafe's right. We need to chill. We can outfit you with tactical gear, mike and radio in the meantime, Rafe."

It killed him to say it, but he said it. "I'm not going with you."

Jase made a strangled sound. "Rafe, this is your takedown, your case. Hell, you've been running this task force since it started. You're backing out now?"

"Shut it, Jase," he told him.

The younger man went quiet.

"I'm suspended. I have no authority. I'm not going with you and risking the case. I'm following protocol." He jabbed a thumb at his friend and subordinate. "Either you follow as well or stay here with me."

Jase took a deep breath. "Deal. Have I told you lately how much I respect you?"

"Yeah, and I love you, too." Rafe chuffed his head.

With his gold shield dangling from a chain around his neck, Greg was getting updates on his phone. He frowned. "Son of a bitch Hernandez is home."

Rafe pulled out his phone. "Two of those bears they took

have AirTags in them. Let's make sure we know where they are before we chase our asses."

Rafe used an app to find the network to use an anonymous relay through other cell phones like his. Fortunately, the app showed the AirTag was active and located in a warehouse in Randall, North Carolina, the same warehouse they suspected the bears were being transported to.

The same town as Paul's warehouse. Suddenly everything fell into place. Rafe turned to Greg.

"You're sure Hernandez is home?"

"Dead certain. We have a tail on him now."

"Son of a…" Rafe squeezed his phone until his knuckles whitened.

His voicemail chimed again, reminding him of a message. Rafe listened to it and his heart dropped to his stomach. All the protocol, control and reason flew apart.

"Allison's going after her sister. She thinks Diana is being held captive in her fiancé's warehouse here in town. It's got to be the same one. I'll meet you there."

"Rafe, wait!"

But Greg's protest met with deaf ears as Rafe jumped on his Harley and sped off.

When she arrived on the outskirts of the town of Randall, Allison followed the GPS to the road leading to Paul's business.

After parking her bike a few hundred yards away from the building, she hid it in the brush.

Light from the lemon wedge of moon hanging low in the sky helped her see the way. Sticking to the shadows, she made her way on the road to the front gate. It was locked.

No matter. She tested the chain-link fence. Not electrified. Allison climbed it, dropped down and made her way in the shadows to the oblong building.

Sodium lights in the parking lot showed only three cars.

One she instantly recognized as the sedan Diana had taken. Next to it was the white panel van Rafe had mentioned.

Her sister was a victim in all this.

Aware of a building security camera pointed at the parking lot, she made her way toward the back. With so few cars here, she might be lucky enough no one would catch her.

A door was propped open near the loading dock. Two tractor trailer trucks sat at the dock. She walked inside.

Listening to the frantic beating of her heart, she allowed herself a minute to calm down and control her breathing. Furniture was stacked up in the warehouse near the loading dock. The warehouse seemed divided in half, with the storage for transport in the back half of the building. Light spilled into the room from the rest of the building.

Using the piles of furniture for cover, she slipped around them to the doorway of the next room. Stacks of wood near the door allowed her to hide while she studied the layout.

Near one of the work tables, Paul examined a tan teddy bear while a man she vaguely recognized stood guard with an automatic rifle.

It looked like an ordinary warehouse, with piles of lumber stacked to one side, metal shelving and work tables scattered with tools. A staged living room was near an office with large windows, far from the work tables.

A leather sectional sofa, which looked perfect for snuggling up to enjoy movies, had a lovely white oak coffee table before it. The sofa was flanked by two hand-carved white oak end tables, accented by the soft glow of table lamps. Lucy Martin, her sister's nemesis and Paul's ex, lay on the sofa asleep.

The cozy space was accented with an opulent high-backed sturdy armchair. On the buttery soft leather sat her sister, a dirty rag gagging her mouth, her feet and arms tied with frayed rope to the chair.

Allison bit back a gasp. Damn them. Damn them all for doing this.

A crash echoed through the building. Paul and the gunman looked up.

"Marty, check it out," Paul ordered. "It had better be the guys returning. They're running late. We have to get all these bears stripped, loaded and out of here by dawn."

As the gunman advanced toward the front of the warehouse, a dark figure crept toward her sister from the opposite direction. He dropped to his knees and began fiddling with her bonds.

Rafe. Allison clapped a hand over her mouth to stifle her gasp.

Diana frantically struggled. Rafe was trying to assure her.

But her struggles got noticed by Paul, who glanced over. Oh damn. Allison's heart leaped into her throat as Paul pulled out a gun.

She ran toward Rafe, her instinct urging her to keep him safe. "Rafe, watch out," she screamed.

Turning, Rafe saw Paul and ran. He was protecting her sister, she realized. Diverting Paul's attention so gunfire wouldn't harm her.

Rafe withdrew his pistol and ducked behind some crates as she raced toward her sister. Paul pulled the trigger as she ran. The bullet whizzed toward her, but Rafe jumped in front, grimacing as it grazed his arm.

Rafe pushed her behind him as they took cover behind a stack of crates. Bullets zinged through the air.

"Get out of here," he told her. "I've got this."

"I'm not abandoning you."

He pushed her downward. "Stay down. Backup will be here any minute." Rafe pulled out his cell phone and called, telling someone they were under fire and to proceed with caution.

As the men exchanged fire, she kept low and made her

way toward a terrified Diana, struggling to free herself. Allison crouched down and fiddled with the knots but didn't dare draw attention to what she was doing.

Gunfire rang out from the opposite direction. Rafe whirled, dropped to one knee and returned fire at Marty, taking cover behind a stack of crates. Now he had to defend himself from two positions.

Sirens sounded in the distance. "Get to the loading dock," Paul screamed. "Hold them off!"

As Marty ran to the loading dock, Rafe paused to insert another magazine into his firearm. Paul rushed him, knife in hand, gleaming in the harsh fluorescent light. He swiped at Rafe's arm. The gun fell from Rafe's grip. He kicked it away and struggled to keep the knife at bay.

The two men wrestled on the floor. Fretting, she wished she had a weapon. The knife in her back pocket—maybe she could stab Paul, but they were moving too much…

Suddenly she knew what to do. Allison unplugged one of the table lamps. Fishing out her switchblade, she cut the cord from the lamp and then stripped the covering to expose bare copper wires.

"Trust me and play along," she whispered to Di.

Allison plugged the cord back into the socket. Making sure to grab the protected part of the lamp cord, she screamed out. "Rafe, keep him busy! I almost have Di freed!"

Paul glanced up, and Rafe landed a solid punch to his jaw. Paul staggered and stabbed him in the chest.

Rafe dropped with a grunt of pain. Allison went still, panic rippling through her. Instinct urged her to rush forward, help him.

Don't panic. You can do this, and you can save him. You've got one shot at this, Allison.

For a wild minute the memory of her frozen in the river, her sister screaming for help, overcame her.

You can't save everyone, Rafe's voice echoed in her mind.

But you can try saving some, and live to fight the good fight another day.

She started on Diana's bonds, watching Paul as prey eyes an advancing carnivore.

Fury in his eyes, Paul came toward her, crimson coating the gleaming blade. Rafe's blood.

"You bitch. Diana's mine. We're going to marry and you'll be dead. No bridesmaid dress for you, stupid bitch. Everything would have been fine, except for you yammering at her to elope. Chew on this, Allison. I'll still have Diana, and nothing you can do will stop me."

Blood streamed from Rafe's chest. He crawled for his weapon. "Ally, hang on, I've got you!"

Even wounded, he had her back. Always. She kept her eyes on Paul, holding the live wire behind her.

Almost there. Almost.

As he lunged at her, Allison sidestepped Paul and touched the bare copper wire to his bare arm.

"Chew on this, asswipe."

Paul screamed, his body going into spasms as his grip on the knife automatically tightened. She wanted to cheer.

He fell downward, convulsing. Knowing he was paralyzed momentarily, she stomped on his hand and freed the knife, kicking it away.

Shouts of "Drop your weapon!" followed. Relieved, she glanced up and saw armed men wearing FBI and DEA flak jackets.

Ignoring them, she unplugged the wire to prevent anyone else getting hurt and then untied her sister. Diana tore out the gag and fell into her arms, sobbing.

"Hey, jellybean, it's okay. I need to take care of Rafe now. You're going to be fine."

Quickly, Allison checked on Lucy on the sofa. No pulse. Not sleeping.

Sniffling, Diana ran to Paul. Allison had a moment of fear, thinking Diana still loved the guy...

"You bastard! I hope you rot in prison." Diana kicked him between the legs.

Allison beamed. "Bull's-eye!"

She raced to Rafe lying on the floor. Blood streamed from the wound. His skin was pale and clammy. She checked his pulse. Weak and thready. He was losing too much blood.

Ripping open his shirt, she assessed the wound. Allison sliced his shirt into strips and bundled them up to apply pressure to the stab wound. She listened to see if air escaped. He moaned.

"Sorry, babe. I know it hurts like hell, but I'm not going to let you bleed out on me."

"Feels like he landed a hard punch to my chest," he wheezed.

"He stabbed you, sweetie. Adrenalin dump. The pain is setting in. Have to keep you from shock. Di, grab that blanket on the sofa and find something to elevate his feet."

While her sister did, Allison went into trauma mode. Didn't matter that this was Rafe, her heart, her love. He was a patient and she had to save him.

"What can we do? Damn, Rafe, you should have waited."

She glanced up at Sam's worried face as the US Marshal lowered his shotgun. "Tell me what you need, Ally."

"I need an ambulance, stat. Tell the EMTs Rafael has a penetrating chest trauma to the right upper quadrant. Checking him now for a pneumothorax."

Diana draped the blanket over Rafe and placed her shoes on the floor, putting his feet atop them.

"We'll need two ambulances." Sam spoke into a shoulder microphone.

"Rafe gets the first ambulance. That bastard Paul can have a slow ride to the hospital," she muttered.

Allison jerked her head toward the sofa. "And you'll need the coroner. Lucy Martin is dead. Possible drug overdose."

She stroked his sweat-dampened hair. "You're not going to die on me, Rodriguez."

Diana told the agents what happened. Allison listened as she treated Rafe.

"Paul came to the cabin that night you were gone, Ally. He wanted to elope that night. I was in my room, gathering my things when I overheard him in the living room talking in Spanish, so I snuck into the hallway to eavesdrop. He was talking with Lucy. They were still sleeping together. She was his mistress!" Diana sniffed. "He never realized I was eavesdropping.

"I was ready to tell him to go to hell when I heard him mention his uncle and I realized Paul was smuggling drugs. I knew if I went with him, I might never make it out okay. So when Paul came into the bedroom, I said I needed time to organize my things and I'd meet him at the hotel in Ashville.

"I left the veil for you, Ally, and the clues. I was hoping and praying you'd find me. I figured if you saw the blood on the veil and the ring, you'd know I was in serious danger.

"I hid in the old barn for a while, but he found me through my cell phone. Paul had placed a tracking app on my phone to know where I was at all times. He brought me here, and Lucy kept an eye on me. But she got stoned tonight and couldn't pick up the bears. They needed a woman to make it less suspicious, so Marty, Marty held me at gunpoint and forced me to do it."

As the EMTs rushed into the warehouse, pushing a stretcher loaded with equipment, Rafe opened his eyes. His breathing labored, his pain-wrenched gaze held hers.

She stroked his hair. "I'm here, Rodriguez. I'm not leaving you."

Ever.

Chapter 25

He woke up, dazed and confused. Everything looked clean and white and bright. Did he die?

Rafe shifted his weight and felt muscles in his chest pull painfully. Nope. Still alive. Unless he was in hell and this was his punishment.

Then he became aware of soft breathing next to him. Forget hell. This was heaven with an angel at his side, an angel he loved.

Allison was asleep in a chair next to his hospital bed, her head pillowed on the bed, her hand gripping his.

Not wanting to awaken her, he went to ring for the nurse. Allison woke up and rubbed her eyes.

Suddenly alert, she was all nurse, checking his vitals, smoothing his hair back. "How are you feeling?"

"Not too bad. No longer like a wrecking ball smashed into me."

Her beautiful mouth wobbled, but she smiled. "You're tough, Rodriguez. You'll live."

She helped him sip water. "You had visitors. I got Keith and Debbie in to see you. They snuck in Comet."

"He's okay now?"

"Yes. Back to normal. He licked your nose."

"No wonder it itches." He rubbed it.

Allison laughed. Damn, he loved the sound of her laughter.

She glanced at the door. "Sam and Jase are waiting outside. The nurse wouldn't allow them in, but I'll get them."

The two men came into the room, looking relieved to see him. "I need an update." Rafe struggled to sit up.

"You relax," Allison scolded. "You're fresh out of surgery."

"Bossy."

"Get used to it, Rodriguez. I'm not going anywhere."

They both listened as Jase reported what had happened. Agents and police arrived at the warehouse to secure the scene. In a barrel marked Furniture Polish they found the raw ingredients used to make fentanyl. False bottoms in the dressers contained fentanyl pills. Paul used the furniture business as cover and started setting up a lab for mass production to make the stuff and distribute it across the country.

"The local cops did a presser and got credit for the bust. Lincoln was more than happy to let them. He nailed Hernandez. We finally got him, Rafe." Jase grinned.

Sam smiled. "He was sailing to Bermuda. Along with fentanyl hidden in the yacht freshly picked up from Mexico. Coast Guard did a thorough search."

"We never could pin anything on Hernandez because he wasn't actually running the operation. Paul with his clean rep was. But then Hernandez began using his luxury yacht to smuggle drugs when their regular pipeline got shut down because of a raid. It was Paul who shot you last year, Rafe, and killed our guys." Jase scowled. "Bastard."

They filled him in on the rest. The list found on Marty's phone was for Marty to keep an eye on Diana and Allison and check out Rafe. It was Marty who broke into Allison and Diana's motel room to search for the tan bears that contained fentanyl. Paul had instructed Marty to leave a threatening message in hopes of getting Diana and Allison to return home. Ten bikers who worked for Paul dealing in dope had volunteered to transport the tan bears on the run to bring them to the factory.

"How did you figure out it was Paul and not Hernandez?" Sam asked.

Rafe felt the warmth of Allison's hand in his.

"Paul seemed too eager to have the wedding at his uncle's house and have Hernandez pay for everything. It seemed off for a man who was supposed to be estranged from his uncle. That and the fact Paul had a warehouse in a remote area, a perfect location for setting up a lab."

Jase frowned. "We raided Hernandez's house and found candy labeled for the wedding. Half of it was fentanyl. He was using the wedding as cover to smuggle drugs out. Paul seemed squeaky clean and never fell under suspicion. We were so sure Hernandez was the ring leader that we never paid enough attention to Paul."

Rafe grimaced as Allison held up a machine for him to blow into. "Must I?"

"Don't knock the incentive spirometer. It helps your lungs recover after surgery." She gave the two agents a pointed look. "Visiting time is over, gentlemen. You can check on him later."

When they left, he struggled to blow a breath into the machine. Hurt like a bastard, but finally Allison nodded. "Enough for now. I want you to rest, and in a while we'll try again."

Rafe fell back against the pillows and eyeballed her, marveling at what a miracle she was. "One question. How did you nail that son of a bitch when he was coming at you?"

"I told you, knives come in handy." Allison studied the IV dripping fluid into his arm. "I stripped the lamp wiring and shocked him. Makeshift Taser."

"They teach that at nursing school?"

"Nah. Saw it on television once."

Her hand rested on his. "I wasn't going to let them get you again, Rodriguez." Allison's expression turned haunted. "Not like the last time I treated your gunshot wounds."

Stunned, he realized she was ready to cry. "When was that?"

"Last year." Allison took a deep breath. "Now you finally know. When you got shot, you could have died. That one bullet nearly nicked your carotid artery. I applied pressure and…"

His eyes widened. "Allison? That was you? *Mi angel*, the one who saved me? Who told me, 'Don't you die, you bastard'?"

Heat crept up her neck to her cheeks. "Yeah. I was leaving a small convenience store a few blocks away after a night shift, heard the gunfire and called 911 and ran there."

"Ran to the danger instead of away from it." Rafe marveled at her dauntless courage. "I tried to find out who saved me that night, but police said the woman left before they arrived. They only saw the paramedics. Why didn't you ever tell me?"

Her blush increased. "I wasn't even sure it was you until I checked the hospitals later."

"And then I roped you into being my CI for the Devil's Patrol. I never knew."

She met his gaze directly. "Your threats about jail time weren't the reason I agreed to work for you, Rafe. I wanted to do it, get to know you better. That night on the street when you got shot doing your job, trying to keep the streets safe against drug dealers, told me exactly what kind of man you are."

"And what kind of man am I?"

"The kind I wanted in my life because you made me believe I could love again. I love you, Rafael Jones Rodriguez. Took me a long time to admit it to myself, but I do."

He wanted to kiss her. Later. When he could do it properly, and long into the night.

He would keep kissing her for a long, long time, if she had him as her partner for life.

Chapter 26

Two months later

The time had come to finally introduce Allison to his family. Rafe glanced backward at her parents and Diana.

"Ready?" he asked. "My family can be a little…overwhelming."

"Ready." Diana grinned. "You're forgetting I'm used to overwhelming, Rafe."

"That's an understatement," Allison agreed.

Diana looked sad for a minute, and then smiled. In the weeks since Paul's arrest, she had started to smile a little more each day. Her testimony would help put her ex-fiancé behind bars for a long time.

"You sure I look okay?" Allison asked.

Glancing down at her pink sheath dress, with her silky hair spilling partly down her back, the black stockings and the Dr. Martens on her feet, he nodded. "You look fabulous and utterly yourself, Ally. I wouldn't want it any other way."

Her mother sighed. "The dress is divine, but the boots…"

"They're fine as well," her father interrupted.

"Mom, they're stylish. Ally looks great. It's fashion," Diana added.

"As long as you don't wear them with your wedding gown,

Allison." Her mother looked worried for a minute. "You are having a wedding?"

"Probably a big one, and don't worry, Mom. I won't wear them at the wedding," Allison told her.

Sadness reflected in her mother's brief smile. "I never worry about you, Allison. You have a good head on your shoulders."

Rafe exchanged knowing glances with Allison and squeezed her hand in reassurance. "Let's go."

They went inside the ballroom, where everyone in his family had gathered to welcome them. Balloons and streamers adorned the room, and long tables filled with food were set against the windows, along with a big banner announcing CONGRATULATIONS ALLISON AND RAFAEL.

"They're here," Ronnie shrieked, nearly dropping a bowl of potato salad.

She ran forward and hugged Allison, who laughed and hugged her back. Then everyone was surrounding them, as he struggled to make introductions that suddenly weren't necessary.

His mother's eyes filled with tears. "I couldn't be happier, Rafey. You finally fell in love."

"When's the wedding?" Sofia demanded. "Can I be a bridesmaid? Can I help you pick out a dress? Oh, this will be so much fun!"

"Hush, Sofie, let the poor girl speak." Elena took Allison's hands. "Thank you for saving our Rafey. I knew you were perfect for him."

Rafe drew Allison forward. His family swarmed around her, exclaiming in Spanish and English. How pretty she was. How thankful they were she was joining their family. He watched Allison's parents and Diana chat with his mother and grandmother.

They moved over to the buffet. In addition to the *croquetas de jamón* and *mariquitas de plátano, lechón asado, frijo-*

les negros and boiled yucca, there were platters of American hamburgers and fried chicken.

He selected two plates and filled them with Cuban food and brought them over to their table. His bride should get to know the cuisine his family enjoyed.

Hell, the food he enjoyed as well, he realized.

Feeling a tap on his shoulder, he turned to see his cousin Luis with an ear-splitting grin. "Congratulations. The way your face lit up when you talked about her, I knew she was the one. Look how much everyone adores her, Rafe. The fam only wanted you to be happy."

He had to agree.

Luis sipped his drink. "Heard through the grapevine you were offered a promotion after the big drug bust. Moving up to DC. Career advancing move."

Hearing the uncertainty in his cousin's voice, Rafe shrugged. "I turned it down."

Luis nearly spit out his soda. "Wow. You, career FBI agent, turning down a promotion?"

Funny how Lincoln, Rafe's supervisor and the assistant agent in charge of the Miami office, had said the same thing. Lincoln had been instrumental in securing the promotion for Rafe.

Gazing at Allison and his family, he shook his head. "Some things are more important than career, Luis."

Never had he felt such pride, nor such joy. He was home at last, and with a woman at his side whose passion for life and love equaled his own.

When his family finally gave her space, he escorted her to the bar and asked for champagne for them both.

"To my beautiful bride-to-be." Rafe smiled.

"To my big, handsome sex stud." She winked.

He laughed as they clinked glasses.

Allison's eyes sparkled as she gazed at him. "So this is your fam, huh? They're terrific. Big, noisy, loving. You're blessed, you know, Rodriguez? And you don't identify with them?"

Rafe studied his beaming family as they chattered and settled around the platters of good food. He slid his arms around his partner for life, his love. The woman in the world he loved the most and would die to protect and cherish.

It was a good day to be alive and live simply for the joy of the moment. The joy of love and family.

"But I do, *mi angel*. I am an American and *soy Cubano*." *I am Cuban*.

* * * * *

Get up to 4 Free Books!

We'll send you 2 free books from each series you try PLUS a free Mystery Gift.

FREE Value Over **$25**

Both the **Harlequin Intrigue®** and **Harlequin® Romantic Suspense** series feature compelling novels filled with heart-racing action-packed romance that will keep you on the edge of your seat.